PROLOGUE

A sher's truck sped past, chasing after the van. I faintly heard the squealing of his tires over the sound of my heart booming in my ears. They'd gotten Maura in the van.

"Louie's been shot," Jameson said into his mic.

Through the earpiece, Brenna responded, "We'll get help."

"Don't worry about me. Go back up Asher and Dean," I grunted and tried to sit up. Jameson shoved me back to the ground by my shoulder, pinning me there. He placed his other hand where I'd been shot, just under my ribs, to slow the bleeding. The pain made my breath hitch.

With a clenched jaw, his gaze flicked from me to the two vehicles disappearing in the distance. His hand at my shoulder fisted my shirt before his head turned downcast and he squeezed his eyes shut.

"They won't catch them," I gritted what we were both thinking. Dean and Asher were chasing after them, but the van had a distinct lead. We needed to do something. We needed to get her back. "Jameson." I sounded desperate and panicked but I didn't fucking care.

"I know," he snapped, his eyes shooting open to glare down at me. His regret was easy to see.

I stopped fighting to sit up and rested my head on the asphalt. I regretted him saving me too. "You should have kept going for her instead of protecting me."

His glare lessened. "If I had, I'd be bleeding out or dead on the ground a few feet away." He clenched his jaw again. "I just don't want her to think I didn't choose her."

I knew he wasn't talking about dying recklessly trying to save her. Maura had asked us to fight for her—to prove to her that she was enough.

I grabbed his arm. "They're going to torture her."

He nodded slightly.

A growl overtook my voice as I said, "They're going to rape her."

He put more pressure on my wound. It hurt like hell but that was alright. I could take it.

"Once they see that they've broken her, then they'll kill her," I said as evenly as I could.

"She's too stubborn to give them the satisfaction." His tone was confident, and he was right. Our girl was indeed stubborn. As much as it pissed me off, right now, I was glad.

"Besides, she already thinks she's broken." He shook his head, more apparent regret furrowing his brow. "So she'll fight them like she has nothing left to lose."

My strength was fading fast, and the cold had long since seeped in. I didn't have much time left.

Unable to hold onto him any longer, my hand fell from his arm. "You have to prove it to her, Jameson." He gave me a puzzled look. I took in a shallow and shaky breath before continuing. "That she's enough. Don't just say she is but show her. She won't believe you otherwise."

Understanding, he frowned. "Don't talk like you aren't going to be right there with me proving it to her."

The next breath was even shallower than the last. "Promise me?"

His lips moved but I couldn't hear him. Then my vision turned blurry before everything faded to nothing.

CHAPTER ONE

MAURA

I awoke on a dirty floor in a strange room. Panic surged through me, making my heart gallop. Memories of a hospital, gunfire, and sapphire eyes riddled with pain flashed in my mind.

Louie!

I jerked to sit up, only to fall back to the floor. My head spun and my hands felt like they were restrained around something behind me. I blinked rapidly to clear away the dizziness. The Aryans had drugged me. *Bastards.*

The more things came back to me, the more clearheaded I became. That helped slow my racing heart. I went to sit up again. This time, after some wiggling and shifting, I was successful. Metal bit into my wrists, evidence that I was hand-cuffed. I leaned back against something cold and hard. With a quick glance up, I saw that I was bound to a steel structural post.

I scanned my surroundings. I was in a small living room. By the size and feel of the space, I'd say I was in an apartment. A fucking junkie's run-down apartment, by the looks of it. The carpet was dirty and stained. The air was stale and faintly smelled of piss. Directly across from me was a mustard-colored couch that I assumed used to be tan. The upholstery was ripped in many places and the cushions were as flat as a pizza box. To my left was a window with newspaper taped over it. Spots of light dotted the carpet where pieces of the newspaper had peeled. Right under the window was an old metal radiator. By how cold the room was, I doubted it worked. To my left, within touching distance if I'd had access to my hands, was a round wooden dining table that only had one chair. I craned my neck to look behind me and saw that the other side of the room was taken up by a filthy, tiny kitchen. A beaten-up refrigerator, a stove, and a sink filled with dirty dishes lined the far wall. I tried not to shiver with disgust as a giant cockroach scurried across the countertop toward the sink. I knew cockroaches weren't my biggest problem at the moment, but my entire body itched to get off the fucking floor.

Said floor creaked on the opposite side of the room from where I was. My gaze darted in that direction just in time to see a haggard-looking Amelia, Buck's child bride, with her baby clutched to her chest, shuffle in from a hallway that led to the rest of the apartment. She was wearing a long tan peacoat over her hospital gown. My tan peacoat that I'd had on before they'd chloroformed me. There were dark bags under her eyes, sweat beaded her forehead, and each step she took into the living room seemed to cause her to wince. She was clearly headed for the disgusting couch. As if sensing me staring, her pain-filled eyes slid to me and she froze.

I found it ridiculous how easy it was to read the thoughts and emotions that passed through her. The panic, the pity, the discomfort, and the debate of turning around and going back from where she'd come from. I read it all with a blank face.

As if unable to hold my gaze any longer, she looked down.

"Pathetic." The word tumbled from my mouth before I could think to stop it.

With a frown, she forced herself to look at me again. I didn't let my blank expression waver.

She didn't say anything as her eyes bounced all over my face, but her frown hardened into a glare. With irritation buzzing off her, she finished making her way to the couch.

Easily manipulated as well, I thought, but managed to keep to myself.

Pain quickly replaced the glare on her face as she lowered herself to sit on the couch. She released a shaky breath once she found a comfortable position on the flat cushions.

I should have felt empathy for her, or at least pity, but I didn't. I wasn't capable. Not when the memory of Louie being shot was playing in the back of my mind on repeat. "I guess your husband forgot to lift you pain meds when he picked us up from the hospital. Such a thoughtful and caring man you've chosen to spend your life with." My words were venomous and each one faintly tasted bitter—easy to ignore, but nasty enough to serve as a warning that I might regret them later if I lived long enough.

Her glare returned, replacing the pain.

"I know from personal experience how painful it is to have surgery on your lower abdomen," I continued my verbal assault. "Every move you make seems to tug on your incision. At the time, my baby wasn't as big as yours when the doctors pulled her out of me. So I'm sure your cesarean incision is hurting like a bitch."

The guilt that overcame her face made me scoff.

"Does it make you feel better to know that I'm in pain?" she finally said. Her voice held a hint of a tremble.

I stared at her for a breath, then another, knowing what I

was doing. I was chasing the rabbit. "It doesn't matter what I feel. I am your captive and you're going to kill me."

"I'm not going to—"

"You'd be a fool not to," I cut her off.

Her throat bobbed as she swallowed. "So what you said in the hospital was a lie?"

"You mean when I offered to send you and your son somewhere safe?" I glanced around and shrugged. "I can't do anything for you tied up in this shithole, now can I?"

It was apparently her turn to stare at me for a breath or two. "Is this your way of trying to convince me to help you escape?"

I held her gaze as I dropped my schooled expression and let show what her husband had unleashed. Memories of blood-soaked hands pulling away from my belly, screaming as I dragged my bleeding body across the floor, the fear in Stefan's eyes when he'd found me, the rage that could rival mine in Jamie's, and Louie collapsing to the ground as more bullets rained down around him overwhelmed my mind. "No," I answered in a calm, dark voice. "I have no intention of escaping."

Her hand fisted a little bit of the pale blue blanket she had wrapped around her baby.

Good. She should be afraid.

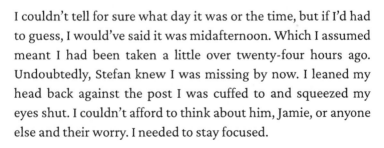

I couldn't tell for sure what day it was or the time, but if I'd had to guess, I would've said it was midafternoon. Which I assumed meant I had been taken a little over twenty-four hours ago. Undoubtedly, Stefan knew I was missing by now. I leaned my head back against the post I was cuffed to and squeezed my eyes shut. I couldn't afford to think about him, Jamie, or anyone else and their worry. I needed to stay focused.

With how numb my ass was from sitting, it had been hours since I had woken. Within that time, it had become obvious that Amelia, her baby, and I were the only ones in the apartment. Buck and his remaining Aryans had yet to make an appearance.

Since I had woken and had that brief chat with Amelia, we hadn't said another word to each other. In fact, she was doing her best to pretend I wasn't restrained to a metal post no more than six feet from her as she tended to her baby on the couch or the few times she dragged herself into the kitchen. Her first venture in there, she had discovered that there wasn't any food in the fridge besides beer and old takeout containers. After searching all the cabinets and yelping when a cockroach had leaped out of one of them, Amelia had been able to find some crackers. She ate them slowly with one hand and held her sleeping baby with the other.

Her baby's cries made my molars hurt. My whole body seemed to clench up at the sound. I hated that I had a front-row seat as she changed her baby's diaper with a small amount of supplies she kept in a plastic grocery bag, or when she opened her gown and brought him to her chest. The breastfeeding never lasted, though. For some reason the baby wasn't having it. He fussed and cried against her chest each time. Then Amelia would eventually curse and reach into her grocery bag of supplies and pull out a small premade bottle of formula. The baby had taken to it each time as if he had been starved. Either Amelia's milk hadn't come in or her baby had difficulty latching. That knowledge ripped me apart on the inside. I wouldn't have known that had I not read baby books when I'd been pregnant.

I hated her. I hated her baby, and as the time ticked by, that hate made it harder and harder to remember how important it was to stay calm—to stay clearheaded.

"Did your husband tell you to babysit me?" I snapped when I couldn't take it anymore. For someone who had been doing their best to ignore my presence and clearly didn't want to be around me, I didn't understand why she stayed in the living room. Surely she'd be more comfortable in bed if there was one. From what I'd seen of this apartment so far, I wouldn't be surprised if there wasn't.

Amelia finally looked over at me with pity molding her face. "He wants the baby and me to stay in the living room."

I pulled my cuffed wrists apart with all my strength. The biting pain of the metal digging into my skin was the only thing keeping me from exploding. That bastard wanted me to see what he had taken from me.

I tried to not let anything show on my face, but I must have revealed something. Amelia stiffened and fear filled her pretty ice-blue eyes.

I had to look away from them. I was going to lose it if I didn't. I made myself stare at a stain in the carpet by my knee and I screamed on the inside. For I didn't know how long, all I could hear was screaming in my head and all I could feel was the pain I was inflicting on my wrists.

It took many deep breaths to battle for control. If I didn't regain it, he'd win.

With one last, long, calming exhale, I turned my attention back on Amelia. "Do you love your baby?"

She didn't respond, but she did bring him to her chest, hugging him close. That was answer enough for me.

"Then you need to take him and walk out that door right now," I said. "Buck isn't here, and I doubt any of his remaining gang are around either. You won't get a better opportunity." This was my last effort of mercy or kindness or whatever the hell it was.

She glanced at the door, biting her lip. I could see the

wheels spinning in her eyes and it was obvious that fear was shutting everything down quickly.

"You see, Buck thinks he has you so well-trained or broken that you won't leave him. He knows he has you too scared to disobey. But what he doesn't understand is that love can be just as strong as fear." I glanced at the baby in her arms for a heartbeat before I had to look away. "Right now, you need to love your son more than you fear his father and get the two of you out of here."

My words didn't seem to reach her. She went back to pretending that I wasn't there.

"You stupid, weak bitch," I seethed, my control and patience with her completely dissolving.

My words made her wince, and I relished the reaction.

"You will be the reason why your son suffers. You'll both most likely die because you're too much of a coward to do—"

"Because you're going to kill us?" she snapped.

I couldn't deny it. I wanted Buck to suffer. I wanted him to suffer worse than I had, and I didn't know what that made me capable of. So instead, I snarled, "You don't deserve to be a mother. You don't deserve to know what it's like to hold that baby in your arms!" As the words left my mouth, evidence of my pain left with them. *Damnit!* This was what Buck wanted.

Tears filled her eyes and she stood with a wince. She walked away without a word. For a moment I thought she was actually heading for the door, but she veered to the right and disappeared down the hall.

CHAPTER TWO

Amelia didn't stay away long. I barely had time to relax —well, as much as I could in my predicament— before she rushed back into the living room. This time, carrying a laundry basket instead of the baby. For a moment, I was relieved she didn't have him, but that relief was snuffed out as she set the basket on the floor carefully before taking a seat on the couch. Through the open slits along the side of the flimsy, white basket, I saw the baby was swaddled inside on a bed of crumpled linen.

The front door to the apartment opened not even a minute later. One of the last three of Buck's Aryan lackeys walked in. He was a short man. Maybe just an inch or two taller than me. He had a beer belly and greasy dishwater hair. His gaze traveled to Amelia first before it landed on me. He smirked and moved further into the room, heading in my direction. "Buck will be happy to see that you're awake when he gets back." His eyes lit up with what looked like excitement and hunger as they dropped down to my chest. "He has special plans for you, bitch."

I blinked slowly and let out a bored sigh. "I have to pee."

The Aryan's smirk slipped a little.

"Unless Buck has a thing for golden showers, you might want to take me to a bathroom before these special plans begin," I added.

The excited light in his eyes went out and was replaced with irritation.

Ah, shucks. Poor little Aryan is upset that I'm ruining his fun.

I had to bite my tongue to keep myself from smiling as he made his way behind me with a scowl. Shoving his hand in the back pocket of his jeans, he pulled out a little key. He squatted behind me and out of my view. I held back the relief-filled moan that tried to barrel its way up my throat as one of my wrists was uncuffed and I was able to relax my arms forward.

Not even bothering to uncuff my other wrist, the Aryan stood. "Get up."

I took my time climbing to my feet just to piss him off. It worked. I was halfway up to standing when he grabbed my arm, yanked me up the rest of the way, and forced me to get walking. With a bruising grip on my arm, he steered me toward the hall, which held three doors. The Aryan pushed me through the closest.

The state of the small bathroom was horrific. The smell of urine that filled my nose was potent enough to gag on. The Aryan flipped on the light and three cockroaches that had been hanging out in the sink dashed for the drain. Brown stains covered the walls and the inside of the toilet was black. At this stage of disgusting, it wasn't worth cleaning. Just burn it down and start over.

The Aryan shoved me further into the tiny room until he could shut the door behind him. He released me to fold his arms over his chest and watched me expectantly.

I kept my expression unfazed as I unbuttoned my jeans and shoved them down to hover over the toilet. There was no way in hell I'd sit on it. As I relieved myself, I planned, I prepared. After I was finished, I stood, and as I pulled up my pants, I gave my back to the Aryan as if wanting privacy. What I was really doing was hiding my hand that was still cuffed. I quickly buttoned my jeans and then wrapped the unlocked side of the cuffs around my knuckles and fisted my hand.

"Are you finished?" he snarled.

I let out a little sniffle and hunched my shoulders.

"Tears won't get you anywhere." His hand came down on my shoulder and yanked to turn me around.

As I spun, I threw my fist out. The metal of the cuff curved over my fingers collided with his eye. He let out a grunt as his head jerked backward. I swung at him again, hitting him in his jaw. He fell back against the door and began sliding to the floor. He landed on one knee and reached behind his back, leaving his middle exposed. I kicked him in the stomach as he pulled a Glock from behind him. He hunched forward with his gun pointed aimlessly. Moving quickly, I grabbed the wrist of his gun hand and slammed it down on the rim of the sink repeatedly. I felt something crunch beneath his skin and he let out a scream. The gun flew from his hand and almost landed in the toilet. I barely heard it thud on the floor over my own heart pounding in my ears.

I released his wrist to punch him over and over again in the face, cutting open his skin with the metal cuff each time. I couldn't stop. Not for a moment. Not even when my own skin on my knuckles began to break open more and more after each blow. I couldn't risk letting him get the upper hand. I was rabid with the need to kill.

He tried to put his arms up to stop me, so I kneed him in the sternum. He dropped his arms and I grabbed the back of his head. Using all my strength, I slammed his head down onto the sink once. As I tried to bring his head down again, he twisted his body and jabbed out his fist.

The blow met my stomach. All the air seemed to leave my lungs with that hit, but I didn't let him go. I fisted his hair and yanked his head to the side before punching him in the ear.

He let out a roar, but it was cut off as I shoved his head down onto the top of my knee.

Three months.

For three fucking months I had trained for this. As soon as I'd felt healed enough, I'd had my goons help me brush up on the self-defense skills I had learned as a teenager. I hadn't just sat on my ass waiting to take out the Aryans. No. I'd trained right alongside Brenna for this moment.

The Aryan fell face-down on the ground. I straddled his back and slid my arm around his neck. With a secure hold, I squeezed. Like Tina had when I had cut off her air with Tom's tie, the Aryan came to and began to struggle under me. He tried to buck me off. When that didn't work, he did a push-up and got his knee under him. Then he flung himself and me backward. My back hit the door. If there was pain, I didn't feel it. All that mattered was that I didn't let him go or loosen the pressure around his neck.

He thrashed and dug his nails into my arm. "You're going to die," I forced out. "All of you are."

He eventually went limp, but that *eventually* felt like forever. The entire time, my heart pounded in my chest painfully, I'd had to suck in air between clenched teeth, and I prayed the strength in my arms held out for another moment, then another, and another.

I shoved his body off me with weak, spaghetti-feeling arms.

All of me shook as I panted, the sound echoing in the small room. I only gave myself a minute to catch my breath before I reached around the side of the toilet where the gun had dropped. I ejected the magazine and was relieved to find it full. I reloaded the Glock and began patting down the dead Aryan. I found his phone in his back pocket. I stared down at it. It was my chance at escape. All it would take was one phone call. However, with that one phone call I'd find out if Louie was alive or dead.

I squeezed the phone in my hand. *Not yet.*

Outside of the bathroom, the sound of a door slamming followed by a male voice drew my focus. I stuffed the phone in my pocket. Gun held out in front of me, I opened the door and slowly stepped out of the bathroom. No one was in sight.

Bedrooms or living room? I debated on which to check first. Because the male voice I had heard from before had sounded like it had come from the living room, I headed in that direction. I crept down the hall, my heart booming a handful of times between each step I took.

As I was about to enter the living room, the front door opened. Another one of Buck's lackeys walked in. I aimed for his head and pulled the trigger. The sound of the gun rang loudly as the bullet hit its mark. Blood sprayed from the opposite side of his head, splattering on the apartment wall. Amelia let out a scream, and as the Aryan began to fall, another stepped into the apartment behind him. I aimed at him next, but as I pulled the trigger, I was tackled from behind. My shot went wide, missing its target.

Shit!

I was barely on the ground for a breath before I was rolled over and came face-to-face with Buck. His brown eyes were filled with violent rage. "You stupid bitch," he seethed as his hand rose.

I caught his forearm before he could strike me and went to point the gun at him. He caught my wrist before I could.

Thinking quickly, because I knew he had the ability to overpower me, I brought my knee up between his legs, nailing him in the balls. He grunted, falling forward a little. With him closer, I jerked my head up and bashed it into his nose. I heard a satisfying crunch followed by his roar. Blood dripped onto my face and neck. I didn't have time to care. I let go of his forearm to punch him in his already-broken nose.

He fell off me with a groan. Rolling over, I climbed as far as my knees before fingers fisted my hair and I was pulled the rest of the way to my feet. The moment I was standing, I got a glimpse of the other Aryan and his fist before it slammed into my cheek.

Pain took over one side of my face as I fell back against the hall wall. The world was spinning too much for me to catch my bearings fast enough. I heard the floor creak. It was the only warning I got that the Aryan was about to attack.

A large, calloused hand wrapped around my throat. The Aryan shoved me by my neck against the wall hard enough to cut off my breath. I lifted the gun to point it at him, but he caught me by my wrist. Like I'd done to his fellow Aryan, he slammed my hand against the wall, trying to knock the gun out of my grasp. Unless I wanted a shattered hand, I had to let go of it. I dropped it and he released my wrist to squeeze my neck with both hands.

I felt a tiny flutter of panic in my chest at my lack of air. Not because I feared dying, but because I didn't want to die before I killed them first.

Focus, Maura!

I slammed my elbow down on his forearms, making his arms bend at his elbows, and his hold loosened enough for me to twist sideways. Holding onto one of his forearms to keep him close, I rammed my elbow into his face. I got him in the mouth, making his head jerk back.

I got the open cuff around my knuckles again and punched him in the ribs. He released me. I sucked in delicious air as my legs gave out and I slid down the wall to the floor. Knowing I didn't have a moment to lose, I reached for the gun I had dropped.

My fingers barely brushed the cool metal when I was yanked back by my hair again. This time it was Buck. He pulled me to my feet and punched me in my stomach. He didn't release his hold on me as I tried to hunch over, gasping. Next thing I knew, I was being dragged into the living room. I lost my footing. His death grip on my hair kept me from falling. I yelled out at the fiery pain that seared my scalp.

With what seemed like all his strength, he tossed me forward. I collided with the dining table and rolled on top of its flat surface. I thought I might fall off the other side, but Buck grasped my right calf just in time.

He pulled me toward him, sliding my body across the table until my butt reached the edge. He stepped between my legs as I sat up. I shoved at him, smacked him, all while trying to scoot away. He was able to capture my wrists in one of his hands before he backhanded me with his other. I fell back on the table. Despite the dizziness and pain, I tried to sit up again. Hands clamped onto my shoulder and throat, pinning me down. I looked up to see that it was the other Aryan. I thrashed, trying to get free to no avail as the two of them held me down, the table wobbling and creaking beneath us.

"Fuck!" Buck roared as blood dripped out of his nose and off his chin. "I'm gonna kill you!" He slammed his fist into my ribs, forcing from me a strangled, choppy sound.

"I'm going to *fucking* kill you!" He was so livid every part of him was shaking, even his voice. He grabbed at the top of my jeans frantically. "I'm gonna make you pay first. You'll see." The button on my jeans went flying off as he tore them open. "I'm gonna break you. I'm gonna make you beg me to kill you."

I stopped struggling as he tried to strip me from the waist down. He let out a frustrated growl when my pants got stuck at my shoes.

I chuckled. "You think you raping me will break me?" My chuckling turned into full-on laughter and I found that I couldn't stop. I felt downright manic, maybe even crazed.

"Shut up!" Buck yanked one of my shoes off with more effort than it should have taken and tossed it across the room, almost hitting Amelia, who I had just noticed was sitting on the farthest corner of the couch. She clutched her baby as she watched us with wide eyes.

Buck pulled my jeans and underwear completely off one of my legs before grabbing my hips and flipping me onto my stomach. The other Aryan had to let me go, but didn't move from where he was standing.

Still laughing, I pushed up on my hands.

Buck grabbed me by my hair yet again, jerking my head back, and my eyes met hazel depths that were nowhere near as beautiful as Jamie's. I saw nothing but loathing and rage in them as the lackey stared back at me. *Good.* I hoped they still showed those feelings when I plucked them from his head later.

"Stop laughing!" Buck snarled.

"Why?!" I roared back at him as I continued to stare at the other Aryan. My seriousness only lasted a few seconds before my shoulders started bouncing with laughter again. I wiggled my ass. "Come on, Buck. Show me what that tiny dick can do!" My mouth stretched into a crazed smile. "Show me how much of a man you are."

"I said shut the fuck up!" Buck shoved my head down,

laying me flat on the table again. His boot tried to kick my feet apart. "Spread your legs!"

I snorted. "Don't you want me to feel it?"

He yanked me up again until my back was flush with his chest. The cold barrel of a gun pressed to my cheek before Buck said, "I'm gonna kill you."

"What are you waiting for?" I snarled. When he didn't answer, I thrashed against him, "Pull the trigger!" The hollow, cavernous part of my soul ached for him to do it, to finish what he'd started, to put me out of my fucking misery. "Pull it!"

He jammed the gun bruisingly against my cheek, but it was all for show.

I gritted out, "Just fucking do it! Because I won't break." Because he couldn't break what was already broken.

For a moment, the only sound Buck made was panting. He pressed his lips to my ear. "We'll see about that." He shoved me back on the table. "Lift her shirt and hold her down," I heard him order.

The other Aryan pulled my shirt up to my neck, then ripped the band of my bra open, exposing my back completely. He pinned me face-down on the table by the back of my neck. Buck pinned my lower half by leaning his pelvis against my bare ass. I heard the rattle of a belt being unbuckled and the whoosh of it being pulled from belt loops. "I can't wait to hear you scream," Buck said.

Whack!

I wasn't prepared for what felt like lightning lashing across my back, or the second time or the third. My whole body jerked each time beneath the Aryans who held me down. But I didn't scream.

Buck paused and snapped his belt by my ear, making me jump a little. "That was just a taste, bitch. You'll be screaming for me soon."

Did he really think I'd give him the satisfaction?

He had already taken so much from me. So no. I would not give him my screams. I would gladly take on this pain—this torture—rather than give him anything. I reached out with both hands and grasped the edges of the table, bracing myself for what was to come. "Do your worst."

CHAPTER THREE

I didn't know when I had separated myself from what was happening. One moment I was gripping the edges of the table to the point I thought the bones in my fingers would snap, and the next, I saw Stefan staring down at me. Even as the belt continued to lash at my back, bruising and tearing open my skin, everything in me relaxed. The pain became nothing more than a shadow in the back of my mind. It was still there, but it was as if Stefan was a light holding the shadow back.

My father stared down at me, hands stuffed in his pockets with an unreadable expression. "Maura."

The comfort of hearing his voice pulled at me and the sight of dirty carpet and stained walls faded. I found myself sitting in the chamber with Stefan in his seat and me in mine.

I glanced around the room and found buzzing darkness surrounding us like a veil—blocking out the rest of the world. Somehow, I knew if I stared too long, the veil would fade and show me what I didn't want to see. I stared back at Stefan.

I knew what I was seeing wasn't real. Just a trick of the mind to protect myself.

I took in the features of Stefan's face, committing it to

memory, which was silly because who I was seeing was a memory. I ran my hand over the surface of the table. It felt as I remembered, smooth but with small, thin crevices here and there. So many things changed in a home as years passed by. Paint, furniture, carpet. I picked at a crevice with my nail. This table never changed. It had been a constant. It was a symbol of my home.

The sound of a crying baby echoed through the veil.

"Shut that baby up!" Buck yelled, his voice sounding far away.

Then I felt pain and it was pulling me back to reality. I ground my teeth so hard I thought they'd crack to keep from screaming.

"Buck, please!" Amelia wailed.

Another lash struck my back. I squeezed my chair's armrests. The buzzing darkness closed in around us until Stefan was swallowed up by an abyss of ebony.

"You want to be next, Amelia?" Buck snapped.

It felt like I was coming out of a daydream as my vision focused back on reality. Not even a breath later, I was yanked off the table. Buck tossed me to the ground. I barely hit the floor when his boot rammed into my ribs. I grunted out all the air in my lungs and I curled into a ball, protecting my middle from him doing it again.

"Lock her up," Buck barked at the other Aryan before he turned to Amelia. She was backing away from him toward the hall, with her baby crying in her arms. She didn't get far before Buck took two large steps to get to her and grabbed her by the back of her neck. She let out a pain-filled yelp.

"Put the baby down," he ordered as he shoved her head toward the laundry basket on the floor by the couch. He didn't release his hold on her as she gently placed the baby in the basket, tears spilling down her cheeks.

Once the baby was out of her arms, Buck yanked her to stand straight and smacked her across her face. "Dumb junkie whore! You don't ever interrupt me!"

Amelia cried that she was sorry and pleaded that she wouldn't do it again. What Amelia didn't know was that she was giving Buck what he wanted most—what I refused to give him.

Fear.

That fear made him feel powerful and he would wring every ounce of it out of her until she broke. It was evident from the bulge growing in his pants.

Fool, I thought as the other Aryan grabbed my hands and cuffed them around the structural post again. I didn't fight. I didn't have the energy. Instead, I lay there on my side awkwardly with my hands cuffed above my head, naked legs curled up to my chest. My shirt was at least back in place, but my pants were still hanging off me by one ankle.

The Aryan stood behind me and we both watched as Buck shoved Amelia toward the table, bending her over it. He held her down by the back of her neck as he ripped my peacoat off her. He dropped it to the floor and spread open the back of her hospital gown. Amelia repeatedly begged him to stop. She tried to remind him of her C-section. He didn't care. It was obvious the thought of causing her pain excited him more.

I had to look away after he ripped off her underwear. Amelia's screams filled the apartment along with Buck's grunts and the table rocking.

I tried to focus on my own pain to help me drown out the noise, but it didn't work. The agony in Amelia's screams was stronger.

The baby woke me with its crying. It was the middle of the night and freezing. The only light was coming from the kitchen, and it wasn't the brightest light either. It gave off a dim tan hue, which told me it might go out before the sun rose.

When I went to sit up off the floor, pain roared down my back and I almost cried out. I reached a shaking hand behind me and touched a really sore spot I could reach through my shirt. I winced at the slight touch. My shirt felt cold and my fingers became wet. I brought my hand back in front of me. With what little light there was, I could see blood coated the tips of my fingers. It was then that I realized that my hands weren't handcuffed anymore and there was a chain around my waist. Sweat beaded at my brow as I pushed through the pain to sit up. Once I was upright, I saw the large five-gallon painter's bucket on the floor to my right. I had a feeling they didn't want to risk taking me to the bathroom again.

The cries coming from the baby pulled my focus toward the couch. The laundry basket was on the floor. Through the slits on the side of it, I could see his tiny hands flailing as he wailed. I looked at his mother, passed out on the couch. Her arm was hanging off the edge, her fingers barely touching the carpet. On the floor next her hand lay a hypodermic syringe with a needle, a spoon, and a lighter.

Heroin.

From what I could remember from all the research we'd done on the Aryans, Amelia had used to be a junkie until Buck had knocked her up, and it was her addiction that had made her cross paths with Buck when she'd been seventeen. Events from the previous day had obviously caused her to relapse. I couldn't blame her. I'd probably never get the sound of her screams out of my head.

Because she wasn't waking at her baby's cries, I thought for a moment she had overdosed. Then I saw her fingers twitch. A very small part of me was relieved. It was the tiny part that was grateful she had interrupted Buck and, unfortunately, pulled his wrath toward her instead of my back.

Why did she help me?

The baby continued to cry, pushing that question to the back of my mind. If he kept crying like that, he'd probably wake Buck. I wasn't ready to take him on again and I didn't care to see what he'd do to Amelia for not tending to his spawn.

"Hey," I whispered and got no response. I spotted my shoe, the one Buck had ripped off, near the radiator. Hissing and grunting through the pain, I crawled as far as the chains would let me, which was about three feet at most but was enough to easily reach my shoe. I scooped it up and tossed it at her. It landed on her chest. She twitched a little but didn't wake up.

I glanced at the basket and noticed a plastic grocery bag of supplies next to it. I let out an irritated sigh through flared nostrils. *I have no fucking choice!*

I reached and I was able to grab the lip of the flimsy basket and pull it closer. I stared down at the crying baby. The very sight of him made me want to roar down at him.

I can't do this.

You have no choice.

It took more strength to reach into the basket and scoop him up than it had to not scream as Buck had whipped me repeatedly.

I was surprised for a moment at how light he felt. I bounced my arms a little to soothe him, all while ignoring the barking pain from my back. His cries lessened but didn't stop. He kept turning his face toward my chest or sucking on his little fist. He was clearly hungry.

I eyed Amelia with disdain. I was grateful for what she had done, but at that moment I would have strangled her if I'd been able to reach her.

I reached for the grocery bag. Inside, I found five diapers, a package of wipes, and four premade formula bottles. I grabbed one of the tiny bottles. I ripped off the plastic seal, then the lid covering the bottle's nipple. The moment I put the nipple to the baby's lips, he latched on and began sucking like he was starved.

I sighed, relieved to finally get him to shut up. I didn't want to look down at him as he fed, but the tiny noises he made tempted me. Biting my lip, I gave in and glanced down. He was staring up at me, fixated, as if he found me fascinating. Even in the darkened room, I could see his eyes were an icy blue like his mother's.

I released my lip and the taste of copper leaked into my mouth. "I've debated killing you," I whispered to him and licked my lip clean. "So this means nothing. Doing this is beneficial to me. Nothing more."

Once the baby was done feeding, I changed his diaper and wrapped him up in his pale blue blanket like a burrito. With his needs met, I didn't have to rock him in my arms for long. He fell asleep quickly. After placing him back in his basket, I returned him to his mother's side as if nothing had ever happened.

Scooting back, I made the mistake of leaning against the post. Hissing, I screamed every curse word I knew in my head. For a good minute, I had to just focus on breathing. As I did, I stared down at my bare thighs. My pants and underwear were still hanging on by one ankle. Moving stiffly, I began to put them back on. Once I got my pants up, I noticed the phone I'd lifted off the Aryan I'd killed in the bathroom was still in the back pocket.

I pulled it out, shaking my head. *What fucking idiots.* Intelligence apparently was not a requirement to join the Aryans. Staring at the phone, I was looking at my second opportunity to escape. Only a fool wouldn't use it.

I began dialing a phone number and my finger hesitated over the call button. I was as terrified as I was desperate to push it. With the release of a breath, I hit it and brought the phone to my ear. It rang and rang until the voicemail picked up.

"Hey, you've reached Louie..."

The sound of his carefree and joyful voice made my eyes burn. I hung up quickly and squeezed the phone in my hand to help me keep it together. I grabbed hold of my rage like a lifeline and used it to push back the need to fall apart. Only one tear escaped, and I quickly wiped away the evidence. I dialed another number and brought it back to my ear.

It rang three times before a tired voice answered. "Hello."

"Stefan," I said in a low voice.

The exhaustion in my father's voice evaporated instantly. "Maura?"

"I've killed two of them. I have two left."

"Do you know where you are?" he asked.

"No."

"Stay on the phone," he ordered, and I could hear him moving. By his breathing, he was moving fast.

"I can't let you trace the call." I sounded worn out even to my own ears.

"Why?" he demanded before I heard him tell someone in the background that I was on the phone.

"Because there's two left," I answered.

"Maura." His voice was pleading, and I found that shocking.

"I need to do this."

"There aren't just two left." His voice was frantic. "There's still whoever betrayed us to the Aryans. If you die there, you won't be able to finish what you set out to do. You have to come home."

"She's in New York," someone said in the background, and I could have sworn it sounded like Vincent.

"Manipulative bastard," I said with affection instead of anger.

"You're my daughter."

I nodded because I understood. But it didn't change anything. "I love you, Daddy."

"Maura, wait—"

I hung up the phone.

Apparently, I was a fool.

CHAPTER FOUR

The baby woke one more time before the sun rose and Amelia still didn't even stir at his cries, nor when I toed off my other shoe and threw it at her. That meant I was left to attend to him *again*.

Annoyingly, he didn't go right to sleep like he had the previous time. Nope. I was currently holding him as he stared up at me. His little hand found his cheek and began to claw at it. I took hold of it to stop him from hurting himself. His tiny fingers wrapped around my thumb and didn't let go.

The curiosity and wonder in his big blue eyes absorbed my full attention. Being a few days old, everything was a new discovery to him. I didn't realize at first the way his innocence had sucked me in or how easily it had happened, but when I did, I was completely rattled.

I quickly grabbed his blanket and wrapped him up. As I began rocking him, I tried to deny the brief moment of ease he had granted me from the weight of reality and the realization of what I was truly capable of. But no matter how much you deny something, you can never escape the truth.

I didn't hate this baby. I hated the idea of him and what he reminded me of. Out of desperation, I needed him to just be a *thing* to me, a weakness to use against his father. But the first time I'd held him, he had stopped being a *thing*. Or maybe I had found my limit of what I was willing to do, even to get revenge.

Every part of me felt heavy by the time he finally fell asleep. My body. My soul. I sat there battling with myself for a little bit. Should I just throw in the towel and call Stefan back? He'd send Jamie and the cavalry in and Jamie would end this. Just envisioning that pissed me off and my anger fueled me more than my exhaustion dragged me down.

I lay on my side and tried to sleep after I returned the baby to his mother's side. Just as I was about to doze off, I heard voices coming from the hall. I took in a quiet, calming breath to keep myself relaxed and kept my eyes closed, pretending to be asleep. With my ear close to the floor, I could hear every step Buck and his one remaining fellow Aryan took as they made their way into the living room.

"Want me to wake the bitch?" the Aryan lackey whispered.

From the sound of the steps, one of them moved closer until I could feel them standing over me. "Nah." Buck's voice sounded like he was hovering right over me. Then came the snap of a camera phone taking a picture and a flash of light that I could see through my eyelids.

"She looks dead. Are you sure that's enough proof for that Irish prick?" the lackey asked.

"It's all the proof he's going to get," Buck said as he moved away.

"I don't understand why you're even considering handing her over to him. We should just kill her." The lackey's voice was laced with equal parts trepidation and frustration.

"We can't kill her until we get the money," Buck said, his own irritation evident in his tone.

The lackey sighed. "I don't know, Buck."

"We have nothing left, nowhere to go, and our allies have turned their backs on us because they're too scared of Quinns," Buck argued.

"Yeah, because it only took one of them to wipe us out," the lackey snapped. "And now you're making deals with another, who happens to be the same fuck who put us in this situation in the first place. You should have never taken that deal with him. The guns weren't worth it. Everyone is dead—"

The lackey's words cut off with a grunt and a thump.

I cracked my eyes open just enough to see that Buck had the lackey pinned to the wall by the apartment door with his arm pushing against his throat. "We all voted on that deal for the guns," Buck snarled at him. "So don't put that shit on just me."

The lackey thrashed a little. Buck shoved his arm harder into the lackey's neck and leaned closer until their faces were inches apart. "We need the money. We're dead without it." Buck's voice had gone low and authoritative. "You standing here bitching about shoulda-coulda ain't fucking helping. Get your shit together."

Straining to breathe, the lackey nodded slightly. Buck released him and took a step back.

Glaring at Buck as he rubbed at his throat, the lackey forced out, "She needs to die."

Buck nodded. "She will, along with that bastard Quinn. We'll kill them both during the exchange. Now let's get going."

I closed my eyes just in case they happened to glance over at me as they went to leave the apartment. Even after I heard the door shut behind them, I kept them closed and processed everything they had said.

At some point I eventually fell asleep. It didn't feel like long before the baby started crying again. I refused to take care of him this time. Buck was gone. So he'd cry until his mother woke her ass up.

I sat up and slowly rested my shoulder against the post. Every inch of me ached. Trying my best to ignore the baby's cries and the unsettling urge to reach for him, I glanced at the window, trying to gauge the time. Bright, pale light was shining through the rips in the newspaper. Morning was all I could guess. The desire to know wasn't strong enough to risk pulling out and powering on the phone I had in my pocket to check.

Movement in the corner of my eye pulled my attention from the window. Amelia was sitting up, staring down at her now-wailing baby in the basket as if in a daze. She sat like that for the longest time with emptiness in her eyes. Unable to take his cries any longer, I was about to say something. Then she reached for him. The way she moved as she changed his diaper was as if she was on autopilot.

I couldn't stay quiet any longer as she began to pull the top of her dirty hospital gown down to expose one of her breasts. "What you put in your body you feed to your baby." My voice was sharp and angry. Angry because of her carelessness. Angry because I cared.

Her eyes traveled to me. It seemed as if my words took a minute to process, but she eventually fixed her gown and dug around in the grocery bag for a premade bottle. As she fed the baby, she stared down at him with that emptiness until tears filled her eyes. "I can't do this," she whispered, her face crumpling.

With how tired and hurt I was, it took effort not to show my annoyance. I preferred the emptiness over the crying.

Tears poured down her cheeks. "I can't do this anymore," she repeated.

"Being a mother or life?" I asked.

Her eyes met mine and I could see in them the desperation for peace she thought only death would provide.

I owe her, I reminded myself. "I doubt anyone will stop you from killing yourself, or care, for that matter," I said coldly. "Except for that baby in your arms. I think he'd care a great deal."

She looked back down at him and sadly, nothing changed in her eyes.

The urge to smack the shit out of her had me fisting my hands. I knew everyone handled trauma differently. I knew some could step up when it was needed despite what was killing them on the inside and others couldn't. If her husband hadn't taken from me what he had, I might have been able to apply that understanding toward her. But he had. And right now, all I could see when I looked at her was that she was about to abandon the one thing I'd give anything to have.

My gaze dropped to the baby in her arms, who was staring up at his mother like she was his whole world.

"He needs you, Amelia," I said. Not for her, but for him.

She ignored me as she continued to cry.

One more push, I urged myself. "He won't have anyone to care for him and protect him. He needs—"

"I can't even protect myself!" she screamed.

I waved a hand at the door. "Go! Take him and go. Right now. That's how you can protect you and him."

She shook her head, crying harder. "I—I can't." She began rocking back and forth and lowered her forehead to her son's, whispering, "I'm sorry. I'm so sorry." The agony in her voice made my chest feel heavy.

As she sat up straight, she held a look of acceptance that made my heart speed up. She pulled the bottle from his mouth and laid him back in the laundry basket. Right away, he began to fuss. Amelia stood on shaky legs and headed for the kitchen.

"Amelia," I begged, knowing in my gut what she was going to do.

She kept walking as if she hadn't heard me.

"Don't do it. Don't do this to your son," I pleaded and tried to turn to still see her. The movement forced me to hunch forward, whimpering.

Amelia still kept walking.

Ignoring the pain, I started to climb to my feet. "If you do this, he'll have no one."

She grabbed a dirty steak knife from the sink. She stared at it for a good minute, which gave me the slightest hope she was trying to talk herself out of it. That hope was snuffed out as she brought the knife up to her wrist and cut. I grabbed the post, needing something—anything—to do what, I didn't know. I just needed something to hold onto as she put the knife to her other wrist, slicing that one as well.

She slowly glanced over her shoulder at me. The look she held was unsettling. Not peace, but overwhelming sorrow etched her face. I recognized that sorrow. I had seen it before in the mirror. I wanted to look away. Not that it would do any good. The image of her face was already seared into my brain, and I knew it would haunt me until I took my last breath.

With a weak sway of her arm, she tossed the knife to the ground. It clattered and slid across the floor toward me. She looked forward and just stood there, staring at the wall above the sink as blood spilled from her fingertips. It wasn't long before her breathing picked up and she staggered.

I finally made myself look away as she fell to the floor. The weight in my chest made it hard to breathe to the point I had to rest my forehead on the post.

I don't care.

I. Do. Not. Care.

Then why did the backs of my eyes burn? I closed them, focusing on just trying to breathe. The need to fall apart felt like it was being held back by a thin dark thread.

"Damnit!" I growled as I pushed my forehead against the metal post until it hurt.

Everything was fucked.

A broken, guttural noise escaped me as I sank back to the floor to my knees, my forehead sliding down the post as I did. My eyelashes turned wet from the tears I wouldn't let fall.

"Pull yourself together, Maura," I said out loud. I couldn't feel this right now.

I took in deep breaths through my nose and exhaled them loudly through pursed lips as I tried to regain myself. When I had a little bit of control back, I used my sleeve to wipe my wet eyes before I opened them. I didn't want to look at her, yet my gaze drifted in that direction. Before I could look at her, I saw the knife. Its blade was dirty with old food and fresh blood.

I could reach it.

Did Amelia do that on purpose? I crawled for it until my chain went taut and scooped it up.

The baby chose to start crying loudly at that moment. He was probably still hungry. Amelia hadn't finished feeding him.

Fisting the knife's grip in my hand, I let myself look at her. Blood was spreading around her on the floor, her skin was pale, and her ice-blue eyes were empty. A part of me wanted to roar at her for her selfishness, for what she'd left behind. The other part, the one that understood pain that was too much to bear, hoped she found peace.

I didn't know how long I'd stared at Amelia's body, but in that time, this calm determination had slithered inside me, coiling around the emotions that threatened to cripple me, making it easier for my darker half to fully take over. I'd forgotten how good it felt to be fully relinquished to my darkness. Months ago, when I had been lying in a hospital bed completely consumed by despair, it had been my darkness that had pulled me to my feet. But, unlike all the times before, the darkness in me hadn't been able to shield me from everything that I had been feeling. Instead, it had helped me harness my rage and done its best to push back some of my pain to keep me moving. Since then, I hadn't let my darkness go, and I wasn't sure I'd ever be able to.

It was time to end this—to bring an end to Buck and the Aryans. And I was ready.

When I heard the front door unlocking, I quickly lay my head to the side and pulled some of my hair over my face. I was already lying on my back, which at first had been agonizing. Putting any pressure on it plus the rough carpet rubbing sightly against me had been enough to make my shirt, which had been somewhat dry, feel wet again. Not that any of that mattered— the pain or the bleeding. What mattered was what was about to happen, right now.

As the door opened, I held my breath. I only heard one set of footsteps vibrate through the floor. At the same time the door closed behind whoever was back, they let out a curse. I listened as they rushed toward the kitchen, then stopped.

"Fuck!" they said in a panic, and I knew then that it was the lackey and not Buck. I was slightly surprised by the emotion in his voice. To be honest, I expected indifference, especially the way he'd just stood to the side and watched Buck rape her yesterday.

He let out a strangled growl before I heard him move again. This time toward me. His steps had turned into heavy stomps.

"Wake up, bitch!" he snarled.

I kept myself relaxed. I knew he was going to kick me. I was prepared to take it.

"Hey!" he said before the toe of his boot rammed into my hip.

I didn't react and let my body move naturally at being kicked. The only thing I didn't let move much was my arm that was draped over my stomach. Hidden beneath my hand and inner arm was the knife.

The Aryan let out another curse and I felt him get closer. His fingers went to my neck, searching for a pulse. The moment he found it, my hand wrapped around the knife and my eyes snapped open. He was down on one knee, leaning over me.

Surprised that I was alive, his eyes darted to the one I had visible through my hair. It was the perfect moment of distraction. With my free hand I grabbed the hand he had at my neck and struck fast with my other. Before he knew what was happening, the knife sank deep into the side of his neck.

He started to let out a choking noise. I twisted the blade to cut it off. He didn't fight back. Instead, he went still and stared down at me with wide eyes.

I gave him a quick once-over for a weapon and found a pistol holstered at his belt. To distract him, I yanked the knife from his neck as I pulled the gun from his holster. Blood splattered down on my face, neck, chest.

Removing the knife knocked him out of his shock and he quickly reached up to his neck to try and stop the bleeding. He watched me in horror as I brought up his gun, aiming it at his head. He flew backward, scurrying to get away from me.

I sat up and watched as he tried to army-crawl, heading for the door. With how fast he was losing blood, I knew he wouldn't get far.

I ejected the magazine and found it full. After reloading, I got to my feet. The second I was up, the door began to open. I aimed the gun in that direction just as Buck had the door all the way open and took a step inside.

He froze when he saw me and the gun I had pointed at him. In one of his hands, he was carrying a couple of plastic bags from a store.

"Shut the door," I ordered.

Slowly, without taking his venomous eyes off me, he used his foot to kick the door closed behind him. His fellow Aryan made a gurgling noise, drawing Buck's attention to the floor. The lackey reached a bloody hand up to him out of desperation. Buck didn't take it. He only spared him a brief, indifferent glance before looking around the rest of the room.

Losing strength and life, the lackey's hand dropped to the ground. He didn't move again after that.

Buck spotted Amelia in the kitchen. When he took her in, annoyance graced his face. "Did you kill her?"

Such a dumb question, since I was still chained up. I studied him, trying to see what his words wouldn't tell me.

His annoyance deepened. "Is my kid dead, too?" he asked as he moved farther into the room. The bold move was to show off how big his balls were and to test if I'd get nervous. Unfortunately for him, I enjoyed such games.

When he didn't get a reaction from me, he practically tossed the bags he was holding onto the table. Whatever he had bought clanked and plopped against the wood surface.

I tilted my head toward the basket where his baby lay sleeping on the floor next to the couch.

He stared in that direction for one whole second, and in that short period of time, nothing changed in his face. No worry for his son or relief that he was still alive, now that he'd gotten a good enough look to know for sure.

"So is this how you're going to end it, bitch?" he asked. "You're just going to shoot me?"

He's stalling.

Even though I knew what he was doing, I itched to play his little game. "After months of envisioning how I'd torture and gut you a million different ways, it is a little anticlimactic."

An evil, pleased grin pulled at the corners of his mouth. He was blatantly happy that I wasn't getting the revenge I wanted. Or at least that was what he wanted me to think.

I found the latter to be true after I asked, "Would you like to say goodbye to your son?"

His grin dropped and his rage grew. I could feel it come off of him and thicken the air. A pleased grin of my own threatened to show as I saw the scheming and plotting brewing in his eyes.

"*Tick tock*, Mr. Werner, or I might change my mind," I said.

His hands fisted at his sides. Not out of anger or frustration, but to steady them. He straightened his shoulders next before he began making his way toward his son. I knew what determination looked like when I saw it. And if he was determined, he had a plan. And if he had a plan, he had hope of getting out of this. That was what I'd been waiting for.

"Time's up," I said just as he'd stepped over the dead Aryan. He barely had enough time to register my words before I pulled the trigger twice. The first bullet to the chest made him jerk backward. The second put him on his ass.

Down he went. I savored the sight as he went almost completely prone and struggled to sit up. He put a hand over one of the places on his chest I'd shot before pulling it away to look at it. His palm was covered in blood. The action reminded me of Louie and how he had done the same.

The baby began to cry. Buck didn't even seem to hear him, or he just didn't care. With a pain-contorted face he stared up at me. "What are you waiting for?" he struggled to get out between coughing and choppy, wet breathing. By the time he was done speaking, blood was dribbling from his mouth.

"I'm debating whether or not I want to watch you drown in your own blood," I replied in a low voice, which I doubt he heard over the baby's cries. I really was tempted to watch him die slowly, but I was sure he had a weapon on him. I couldn't risk him taking any opportunity he could to reach for it. With a sigh, I aimed the gun between his legs and pulled the trigger again.

The shot rang out, terrifying the baby even more.

Buck yelled, rolling onto his side with his hand covering his groin. "You fucking cunt!" Despite the blood spraying from his mouth, he sure got that out clearly.

"That was for your wife," I said loud enough for him to hear me over the baby.

Buck moved his hand from his now bleeding member and reached into his jacket. I adjusted my aim one last time. Just as he pulled a gun from his jacket, I fired. The bullet hit its mark right below his left eye. His head whipped backward and then he went completely limp on the floor.

I stood there for a good minute or two letting what had just happened sink in.

I had done it.

I should have felt relieved.

I supposed I did to a point, at least enough for my adrenaline to crash and all my pain to resurface. It hit quicker than I was prepared for, and my strength left my legs. I dropped to the floor on my hands and knees.

Something that tickled slid from my back down and around my side. I reached into my shirt to feel whatever it was. My fingers slid through liquid. I had an idea of what it was, but was still unsettled to see my hand covered in blood when I pulled it from my shirt.

Up until now, I really hadn't let myself process how badly I had been hurt.

The baby's cries were turning hoarse.

Now isn't the time either. I wiped my hand on my jeans before reaching for the basket and scooting back to the post. I felt weak all over and I was shaking uncontrollably. Leaning the edge of my shoulder against the post for a little support, I scooped the baby out of the basket.

"It's okay," I said softly as I brought him to my chest and did my best to soothe him. Blood that had spilled on me when I had stabbed the Aryan got on his blanket and his little cheek. Once I calmed him and he fell right back to sleep, I used a wipe to clean the blood from his face. There wasn't much I could do about the blanket.

I didn't put him back in his basket right away. For a while, I stared down at him, wondering what was going to happen to him when we got out of here.

I pulled the cell phone from my pocket and powered it on. I began dialing Stefan's number, then stopped.

Was I even ready to return home?

I was, but on my terms.

I typed in a new number and brought the phone to my ear. It rang a few times before a young voice picked up. "Hello?"

"Brenna, it's Maura."

CHAPTER FIVE

I had an informative conversation with Brenna on what had been happening at Quinn Manor. Stefan was desperate to find me and get me home, as most fathers would be if their child were taken. He was currently negotiating with Nicoli De Luca to allow our people into New York, AKA De Luca territory, to search for me without causing problems.

Since I'd been taken, my inner circle, which consisted of Dean, Asher, Brenna, Finn, and Vincent, had been watched very closely. Especially Vincent and my goons. I'd had a feeling Stefan would do that. He didn't want to risk me extending the *vacation* I'd been on for the past three—no, almost four months now, and assumed if I managed to escape from Buck, one of my goons or Vincent would be who I'd call to help me. Which was why I'd called Brenna instead. Stefan had made the mistake of overlooking her. Most would until they realized how strong she had become.

"Do you think you can slip out?" I asked her.

"Undetected?" she said. "No. But that won't stop me from getting out of here."

"Good enough. I'll let you know where I am as soon as I can."

"Are you sure you don't want to call Vincent?" Worry was apparent in her voice. "I don't have complete confidence in the De Lucas and it makes me nervous that they will know where you are before we do."

I understood her worry, but it had to be done this way. "I can't have Stefan come save me. I need to walk back in that house on my own or else it'll taint everything we've accomplished since we've been gone."

"Why?" she asked.

"It's so I don't have to relinquish control to Stefan. It's to prevent people from twisting the story and saying that I ran off, bit off more than I could chew, and Daddy had to come save the day. It's a show of strength." Those were just a few of the many reasons why, but they were the biggest. "This world is not easy, Brenna. To survive it, we must play dangerous games, even with those we call family. Respect isn't given, it's earned."

"Hard to win, easy to lose," she mumbled.

"Especially for a woman," I added. "The risk of asking Nicoli for a tiny favor is what I'm willing to take."

She sighed. "Be careful."

As soon as I hung up with her, I called Nicoli next. He didn't answer. I waited an hour and tried again.

"Hello?" Nicoli answered.

"Hello, Nicky."

"Maura?" He didn't hide his surprise.

"I need a tiny favor," I said with forced lightness.

The other end of the line was silent.

"Have I rendered you speechless?" I asked and pulled the phone away from my ear to make sure the call was still connected.

"You've just surprised me, yet again," he finally said.

"Why? Because I was kidnapped by Aryans a few days ago?"

He chuckled. "Two nights ago, I received a call from Jameson Coleman of all people. He told me what happened and about the large amount of money the king of the Irish is offering for his princess's safe return."

"Is the money the reason you haven't allowed Stefan's people into your territory?" I asked.

I could hear his smile through the phone as he spoke. "If I didn't like you, I would answer yes."

"So why'd you say no?"

"My territory is big, and I have a lot of people within it. The last thing we need are a bunch of Quinns searching aimlessly on De Luca soil and accidentally running into one of my people, who may or may not be holding onto a grudge against the Irish. If someone dies on either side and the other is responsible, it won't matter anymore how much I like you."

That made sense. "Just so you know, that money is no longer on the table."

"Is that so?"

"It's no longer on the table, Nicky," I repeated, my voice turning serious.

He huffed a laugh. "Alright, Maura. What's this favor?"

I took a leap of faith because what choice did I have? "Can you trace this call and tell me where I am?"

"You don't know where you are?"

I pinched the bridge of my nose. "I just need an address, Nicky. Can you trace the call or not?"

"I can do that," he said. "What do I get for this favor?"

I held back my sigh. "Why ask, Nicky? You already know what you want."

"Let's have dinner again."

"As a friend?"

"As a friend," he agreed.

"Fine."

"Give me a moment." I could hear him moving around. Then he began speaking to someone in Italian. A few minutes passed until he said, "You're definitely in New York."

"Address, please?"

Whoever was helping Nicoli trace the call said the address loud enough for me to hear.

"Great. Don't tell Stefan." I hung up and immediately called Brenna.

She answered on the first ring. "I'm almost to New York."

I told her the address.

"I'll be there soon," she said before hanging up.

Now all there was to do was wait.

I was starting to doze off when I heard the sound of the floor creaking just outside the apartment door. I quickly scooped up the gun I'd had in my lap and pointed it at the door as the knob began to turn.

As the door opened slowly, the nose of a 9mm became visible before a hand, followed by a sleeve of a gray tailored suit that definitely didn't belong to Brenna. I waited patiently, gun aimed, as my visitor was finally revealed.

The door swung open all of the way, revealing Dario Moretti, the don's enforcer and right-hand man, and standing right behind him was Nicoli. Both took in the carnage one body at a time. Dario's gun moved with his coffee-colored eyes until they both ended up fixed on me as he came further into the apartment. He didn't lower his weapon. So I didn't lower mine. I may have trusted Nicoli a tiny bit, but Dario, I did not.

Dario was a good-looking Italian man, with his dark brown hair that was short, spiky, and buzzed on the sides and back. He and Nicoli were about the same height, but Dario carried more muscle. His features were rugged compared to Nicoli's refined looks. Tattoos covered his hands and peeked out from under his collar on his neck and chest. Pretty exteriors didn't guarantee someone was pretty on in the inside, though. Dario was a killer known for strangling his enemies with a rosary he kept wrapped around his wrist.

Nicoli had his hands stuffed in his long coat's pockets as he moved to stand next to Dario. Nicoli stared at Amelia's body in the kitchen longer than the rest. When his attention finally landed on me, he took in the chains around my waist and the baby sleeping in my arms. He didn't even acknowledge the gun I had pointed at them.

The corner of his mouth lifted, and he stepped over the lackey's body, then Buck's. He eyed the couch with a hint of disgust before sitting on it. He leaned forward slightly and rested his arms on his knees as he faced me.

I stared back at him with my gun still pointed at Dario, who still stood near the lackey's body. I raised a brow and waited for an explanation.

Nicoli smiled, but it didn't reach his eyes as his gaze bounced all over me. "You look terrible."

"Just what every girl loves to hear," I said.

Nicoli's smile turned genuine. "Don't worry, princess, even beaten and bloody you're still sexy as hell."

Out of my peripheral, I caught Dario move slightly so his side wasn't exposed to the hall that led to the rest of the apartment. My arm was beginning to weaken from pointing the gun at him. I narrowed my eyes at Nicoli. "Why are you here?"

"I was curious." He glanced at Buck's body. "And I thought you might need help."

"I don't need help," I said.

Nicoli's eyes dropped to the chain around my waist. "Are you sure about that?"

Again, out of my peripheral, I caught movement, but it wasn't Dario who'd moved. "She's sure," said a sweet, feminine voice I knew belonged to my cousin.

At the same time, Nicoli and I looked toward Dario. Behind him, with a Beretta M9 pointed at the back of Dario's head and another pointed at Nicoli, stood Brenna. Despite being seventeen, she looked fierce. She was wearing a double vertical shoulder holster over a black, long-sleeved bodysuit. Her jeans were ripped and tucked into laced-up black combat boots. She exuded the confidence of an experienced killer with her finger hovering over each trigger of her guns as she looked from Nicoli to me to the back of Dario's head. "Were you going to shoot my cousin, Moretti?"

The corner of Dario's mouth tugged up. "The future of the Quinn family has been chained up and left smack dab in the middle of our territory." He shrugged. "I'd be lying if I said the thought hadn't crossed my mind."

Brenna stepped closer to him. "Did you not look around the room? She may be chained up, but there aren't any Aryans left in our territory or yours."

Dario turned his head slightly to grin at her over his shoulder. "Old feuds die hard, little Quinn."

"Be that as it may, I wouldn't have let him shoot her," Nicoli said.

"Not if you wanted to collect that reward money, you wouldn't," I grumbled.

Nicoli smirked at me. "I thought that was off the table?"

I lowered my gun as I gave him a look that screamed I wasn't a fool.

Nicoli relaxed back against the couch, threw an arm across the top, and rested an ankle over his knee. "I give you my word.

I really just came here because I was curious. I had a feeling there would be carnage." He eyed the bodies again. "And you did not disappoint." He reached into his suit and pulled out a flask from the jacket's inner pocket. He unscrewed the cap and took a sip. "However, this scene isn't as brilliant as when you hung four of them on a bridge before blowing up your city." He stood and came to me with the flask held out.

To free up my hand, I set my gun in my lap before taking the flask and sniffing at what was inside. I recognized the smell of whiskey right away. "What an honor it is to be the don's entertainment," I grumbled and took a sip.

That made him chuckle before he took a seat back on the couch. "Not just my entertainment. You wiped an entire gang off the game board. If there was anyone left who didn't know that Stefan's daughter had become a player in the crime world, they do now."

"I feel like you're trying to warn me about something, Nicky." I took another swig. "Whatever it is will have to wait until I've showered, eaten a cheeseburger, and slept for at least a week."

Brenna took that as her cue to move things along and help me get out of here. She pushed her gun into the back of Dario's head hard enough to make it dip forward. "Drop it."

"Make me," Dario taunted.

I glanced at Nicoli and saw that he was watching them with an amused look on his face. He didn't appear to want to intervene and if I was honest, I was curious to see how Brenna would handle Dario.

"Fine," she said with a hint of irritation, and shoved the gun she had been pointing at Nicoli into one of the holsters that rested between her arm and ribs.

"Giving up already?" Dario continued to taunt.

Brenna smirked. "No."

She kicked the back of his leg, making it buckle at the same time she grabbed the wrist of his gun hand and forced him to aim skyward. Cursing, he dropped to the carpet on one knee. Still holding his wrist, she kicked him again, but this time in his exposed ribs. He let out a grunt and tried to yank his wrist out of her hold. With the butt of her gun, she knocked his out of his hand. The moment it thumped to the carpet, she kicked it out of reach.

Dario cursed Brenna in Italian before he twisted his wrist in her grip, grabbed hold of hers, and pulled her closer until he could get his other arm around her waist. He yanked her off her feet and brought her to the floor. Dario rolled on top of her, quickly grabbed the hand she held the gun in, and pinned it above her head. Brenna twisted her other wrist free from his grasp and punched him. So close to him and pinned to the floor, she couldn't hit him hard enough to do much damage. Still, Dario's face was forced to the side with the hit. He looked back down at her slowly. Brenna smiled an evil little smile and went to hit him again. He caught her wrist and pinned it above her head, too.

Brenna didn't struggle beneath him. In fact, she held still, waiting. I didn't know if Dario or even Nicoli noticed, but Brenna wasn't putting much effort into the fight. I'd watched her spar with Asher, Dean, Finn, and even Jamie and Louie. Brenna was a fast learner, almost a natural when it came to fighting, and had put both Dean and Finn on their asses back at the cabin before I'd been taken by Buck. The way she would calculate her opponents' moves was extraordinary and the way she moved when she fought was almost like a dance. According to Asher, she would surpass what they could teach her a lot sooner than expected.

Brenna chuckled. "What now, Moretti? Are you going to use your mommy's beads to strangle me?"

Dario glared down at her.

She gave him a haughty look. "Did I hit a nerve?"

Dario let go of one of her wrists to grab her throat. I had the urge to reach for my gun. But if he was squeezing tightly, Brenna didn't let it show.

Dario snarled in Italian, "Mouthy little brat."

Brenna reached down her side as she replied in Italian, "Would that be the mouth you can't stop staring at, old man?"

Dario went tense and surprisingly, so did Nicoli. I peeked to the side to get a look at the don. His attention was completely captured by Brenna and his enforcer.

Dario switched back to speaking English. "Don't flatter yourself, child." Then he began squeezing her neck, forcing from her a small broken gasp.

Nicoli shot up from the couch. "Dario—"

Before Nicoli could say more, Brenna had a knife at Dario's throat. She didn't say anything. Neither did Dario. At least not with words. As they stared at each other, it was obvious they conveyed something.

"Enough," I said.

"Yes, enough," Nicoli agreed firmly.

Dario released Brenna's neck and pushed off of her. Brenna sat up, smirking at him, and slid her knife into her boot. "Were you even trying? I didn't even see spots."

"Did you want me to kill you?" he seethed at her.

The gleam in her eye told me she had a witty retort. I cut her off before she could say it. "Stop toying with him, Brenna."

She looked over at me and within an instant she became serious. "Probably for the best." She climbed to her feet. "I'm pretty sure we'll have company soon if we don't get out of here."

"You were followed?" I asked.

She shook her head as she made her way over to me, stepping right on Buck's body as she did. "Tracked. Vincent called me as I was parking outside and told me Jameson was twenty minutes behind me."

"Tracked how?" I asked.

Brenna locked eyes with Nicoli as she passed him to squat in front of me. "I'll tell you in the car," she said to me in a low voice. She noticed the sleeping baby in my arm and a flicker of sadness flashed in her eyes before she was able to mask it.

I was so exhausted, it took effort not to let my frustration show. "If Jamie shows, I'll figure it out."

Brenna tugged on my chain, searching for a way to take it off. "Let's at least get you unchained so they won't see you like this." She took the gun from my lap and moved behind me. "This will probably wake the baby," she warned before a shot rang out.

The baby startled and began crying. I immediately brought him to my chest and began to soothe him. I felt the three of them staring at me after I calmed him back to sleep.

Nicoli, who held a schooled expression, asked, "Whose baby is that?"

I pulled the chain away from my waist and tossed it to the side. "No one's. Not anymore."

Nicoli's eyes shifted toward the kitchen. Whether he put two and two together or not, he didn't comment on it. Instead, he moved closer and held a hand out to me.

I handed him back his flask. He took it with a small smile and put it back in his pocket before holding out his hand again. I slid my hand into his and tried to brace for the pain as he pulled me to my feet. I was able to keep myself from crying out, but I grimaced. The room began to tilt the moment I was up. I staggered. Both Nicoli and Brenna caught me. With my free hand, I grabbed onto Brenna tightly and closed my eyes for a moment as I waited for the room to stop spinning.

"The back of your shirt is wet with blood," Nicoli said.

My eyes snapped open to a room that was a lot less sideways. "Don't worry about it," I said as I took a step.

Brenna took that step with me, then another. "Maura," she said with a hint of unease.

I kept walking. "I'm fine, Brenna."

She didn't argue and let me use her arm as I walked.

You can do this, Maura. I just had to step over the lackey and then it was a handful of steps to the door. I lifted a weak leg to step over the Aryan and my legs gave out on me. Brenna caught me with an arm around my lower back and threw my free arm over her shoulder.

"I'd be more worried about the De Lucas seeing you like this than our family," she grumbled as she helped me step over the body.

I let out a weak laugh and glanced at Dario, who was watching us. "What was the first thing you saw when you walked in?"

His eyes narrowed, clearly confused by the question. "The bodies."

"And what did you think when you finally saw me?" I asked him.

"I was impressed," he answered honestly.

"What did you think when you saw me after taking in the scene?" I asked Brenna.

"Not going to lie, Maura. You look like hell. I stopped thinking about the bodies when I saw you," she answered.

"Worry or fear paired with love can sometimes make us do stupid things," I said as we walked through the apartment door, into a hall that was long and even more disgusting than the apartment. Debris and trash littered the floor. Graffiti decorated the stained walls in between more doors that led to other apartments.

"Jameson is a prime example of that," she mumbled as she steered me in the direction of the exit all the way at the end of the hall.

"Where the fuck are we?" I asked.

"Probably the most run-down apartment building in the shittiest part of the city," Dario said as he and Nicoli walked behind us. "Mostly junkies and prostitutes live here."

As we approached the exit door, it opened. Jamie walked inside, gun in hand.

We locked eyes and my heart began to race.

Fuck.

CHAPTER SIX

I dropped my arm from Brenna's shoulder and made myself stand straighter. Jamie stepped farther inside, his gaze traveling over me from head to toe, taking in every visible injury. His hand lifted toward me.

"It's done."

My words made him still before he could touch me. Understanding showed through his guarded expression.

His hand fisted before he dropped it to his side. "I'm sorry you had to do it alone."

Of all the things I'd expected from him, he said something that I'd never considered. It left me too stunned to respond.

Dean, Asher, and Rourke slid inside from behind him, guns drawn. They took in the situation, from me and Brenna to Nicoli and Dario behind us.

Rourke whistled as he looked me over. "Looks like we missed the party."

I glanced back at Jamie. He wasn't staring at me anymore, but at what I held. His gaze jumped back up to meet mine with heavy emotions I couldn't stand to see swirling in his eyes. "Is that *his* baby?"

I didn't need to answer, yet I still did. "Yes."

He moved closer, his expression schooled once again. I felt the strong urge to back away. Not for me, but for the baby. That sense of threat I felt from Jamie and the nearly consuming need to protect shocked me. As his hand came up, I found myself holding my breath. He pulled the blue blanket that obstructed his view away from the baby's face. He stared down at him, unblinkingly, unmoving. Jamie had lost what I had lost. Did he feel the same hatred as I had when looking at the baby? Would he seek his vengeance through this child?

"Why do you have him?" he asked in a low voice.

I didn't know how to answer that. Nor would I until I figured it out myself. I looked to Asher and Rourke. "The apartment down the hall is going to need a cleanup."

"I can take care of that," Nicoli said before Rourke and Asher could respond.

Jamie's shoulders tensed up as he looked behind me at Nicoli.

"Thank you for the offer, Nicky, but it's best to clean this mess ourselves," I said over my shoulder.

"Then we'll leave you to it," Nicoli said and headed for the door.

Dario came to stand next to Brenna and held out her Beretta M9 that he had knocked out of her hand when they'd...sort of fought. Brenna eyed the gun, then him, before taking it. He gave her a small smile and followed his don.

After Nicoli and Dario left, Asher and Rourke headed down the hall toward the apartment. Jamie and Dean stayed with Brenna and me. Dean holstered his gun as he eyed Brenna's arm that was still wrapped around my lower back with his signature grumpy frown. He walked over to my other side and went to put a hand on my back above Brenna's arm. I tensed up, bracing for pain.

Before he could touch me, Brenna smacked his hand. He gave her a glare that clearly screamed, *What the fuck?* She shook her head slightly. Dean craned his head to look at my back. His eyes widened before they flicked to mine.

"Not here," Brenna snapped at him before pointedly glancing at Jamie.

Jamie noticed and his face hardened. "You should have told us you knew where she was."

Brenna didn't cower under Jamie's harsh gaze. Instead, she looked bored. "I don't answer to you."

The muscle in his jaw twitched.

"Do you need to see that he's dead?" I asked, taking Jamie's attention off Brenna.

He glanced down the hall and I could see that he did. I would have, too.

"Go. Get whatever closure you can from it. We'll meet you downstairs."

Jamie looked torn but gave in to the need. "I'll just be a minute," he said and headed for the apartment.

I waited until Jamie disappeared inside before whispering to Brenna and Dean, "Time to go."

"We're on the second floor. We'll move quicker if Dean carries you," Brenna said, already on board with my unvoiced plan.

I turned to Dean. Without having to be asked, my grumpy best friend scooped me up. The feel of his arm around my back as he lifted me bridal-style forced from me a pain-filled, guttural noise. Dean stilled at the sound. I wrapped my free arm around his neck and buried my face in his shoulder, trying to will away the pain and the urge to throw up. "Go," I forced out through clenched teeth. Dean and Brenna rushed through the exit, which led to stairs that took us to the ground floor.

"Jameson is going to be pissed when he realizes you manipulated him," Brenna commented as we made our way out of the building.

I would've felt bad, but I had zero fucks left to give.

Two Escalades and my little Audi were parked outside. Dean set me in the backseat of one of the Escalades, then rushed to the driver's seat.

"I'll meet you there," Brenna said and shut my door.

Dean quickly got us on the road heading toward New Haven. "Is there a reason we ditched him?"

"It was undoubtedly a bitch move, wasn't it?" I said as I adjusted my hold of the tiny, sleeping being in my arms.

Dean didn't respond.

I smiled a little to myself. "Did you become friends while I was away?"

Through the rearview mirror I saw him roll his eyes. "He hasn't relaxed since you were taken. He's been doing everything to find you. I don't know how he's still standing."

I stared out the window. "I can't let him save me. Even if it's driving me home. I don't trust him not to lord it over me. Him and Stefan."

Dean didn't say anything to that, but I could sense something was off.

"You think I should forgive him?"

"When you choose to forgive him is up to you," he grumbled. "I figured you should know."

"I know he loves me, Dean. I've never doubted that. It's the trust that's broken between us."

The drive was quiet after that as we made our way to a home I'd run away from not once but twice. The first time, Stefan had let me go for six years. The second, I'd run away for almost four months. Somehow, the four months away felt longer than the six years. Everything felt different now.

"Pull around to the guest house," I told Dean as he drove up the long cobblestone driveway of Quinn Manor. Brenna followed us in my Audi.

"I can walk," I told Dean after he parked and opened my door. He stepped back so I could slide out of the car on weak legs. I just needed to get into the house, deal with seeing Stefan, and then I'd kick everyone out so I could finally breathe.

Each step I took was brutal as I made my way to the front door of the guest house. Everything fucking hurt. The only thing keeping me going was that I was almost to a hot shower and a comfortable bed.

When the door was within reach, the back door of the main house opened. Stefan and Brody came out in a rush. I paused for only a breath before continuing on. I didn't have the energy to just stand there and wait.

"Maura," Stefan called me.

I made it three steps inside before my legs gave out. Brenna and Dean caught me by my upper arms and helped me to the room I had claimed before I'd taken off. Sitting on the edge of my bed, I focused on breathing for a minute so I wouldn't throw up.

"I'll get you some water," Brenna said as she dashed out of the room.

Dean moved to stand against the wall and out of the way just as Stefan walked straight into my room with Brody right behind him.

Stefan's eyes bounced over the injuries on my face and neck and the blood that had dried to my skin and clothes. He knelt in front of me with his hand hovering over my face as if wanting to touch me, but refrained out of worry of hurting me. Instead, he ran his fingers through my messy, shoulder-length hair by my ear. "Christ, Maura."

Brody gently stroked the back of my head. "Dr. Ben will be here any minute."

Both of them seemed to see the baby in my arms at the same time.

"Whose..." Brody started to say before trailing off.

Stefan's forest-green eyes met mine and I could see that he quickly put two and two together. "Where's the mother?"

"Dead," I answered.

He didn't ask if I'd killed her. He probably didn't care. "And the father?"

"Do you think I would have called Brenna to come get me if he wasn't?" I snapped.

A beep went off in Brody's pocket. He pulled out his phone and read whatever message he was sent. "Dr. Ben is at the gate. I'll go escort him here," he said and left while typing away on his phone.

Stefan stood, frowning down at me. "Where is Jameson?"

I shrugged. "I don't keep tabs on your enforcer."

He stared at me with his ever-perceptive eyes. "I see things are still tense between you two."

Saving me from having to respond, Brenna returned with a glass of water in her hand. "Incoming," she mumbled as she handed it to me.

Jamie walked in a second later. He surprisingly looked calm.

"Where were you?" Stefan questioned him in a cold tone that I wasn't used to hearing him use with Jamie.

Jamie stuffed his hands into his pockets. "Maura was already on her way out when I got there. I stayed behind to determine if I was needed to help clean up the scene."

For the second time today, he had stunned me. Why had he just lied?

Stefan didn't look like he believed him. "I'm surprised you didn't insist on being the one to bring her home."

"She didn't need me to," Jamie replied.

Stefan's gaze flicked from Jamie to me, searching for the truth.

I didn't have the energy for this right now. I stood and took a step toward Brenna. "Can you take the baby into the living room? I want Dr. Ben to look him over first."

Brenna nodded as she took him from me.

I locked eyes with Dean. "Don't let anything happen to him."

He nodded and followed Brenna out of the room, leaving me with Jamie and Stefan.

"Ben will attend to you first," Stefan said, sounding as if he was losing patience.

"The baby wasn't properly discharged from the hospital, and I don't want there to be any surprises." I knew the kid was more than likely fine, but I needed some space...from everyone. As good as it was to be out of that shithole apartment, a part of me was still stuck there. I needed to process. I needed to do it alone because my darkness's ability to hold all of it back was wavering.

"That Aryan baby is not a priority—you are," Jamie said with just enough disdain to make me feel threatened again.

"He is to me," I snapped, stunning them both. "I will only say this once." A cold detachment laced my every word as I spoke. "If anyone hurts that baby, I will carve a shamrock into their skull and then hang them using their insides as rope."

They both stilled at my threat until Jamie's expression hardened. "I won't hurt him."

"A few days ago, I wanted to hurt him," I admitted, and I watched so many strong emotions he failed to hide show on his face—anger, sadness—before he closed his eyes for a few seconds as if to reel himself in.

I looked to Stefan. His brows rose a little. "I don't hurt children."

I set the glass of water Brenna had given me on the nightstand and I stiffly headed for the bathroom.

"Maura—" Stefan started to say.

"I'm taking a shower," I cut him off. "I just spent two nights in a junkie's toilet of an apartment and I am covered in blood that's not just mine."

Stefan moved with me as if afraid I'd fall. My legs wobbled a little and it was enough to make Stefan grab my wrist and put an arm around my back.

Jerking ramrod-straight, I let out a gasp. He pulled his arm away from my back and let out a curse. Before I could move another step, the back of my shirt was lifted.

Stefan and Jamie both sucked in a breath. Stefan's grip on my wrist tightened and I had to fight the urge to attack him.

"Let go of my arm," I tried to say calmly.

Stefan didn't seem to hear me. "They whipped you?" By his voice alone, I could tell he was horrified.

My heart started pounding heavily in my chest. "Stefan."

"Damnit, Maura," he snapped and pulled me to face him. His eyes bored into mine, frantic and searching. "Were you raped?"

Amelia's screams filled my ears and I knew I was at my breaking point. "Get your fucking hand off of me!" I snarled at him as I tried to yank my arm from his grasp.

He reeled back as his hand released my wrist.

I stormed toward the bathroom, tripping in the process. My hand snapped out and grasped the doorframe to keep myself from falling.

"Maura," Jamie called out to me just as I stepped inside.

Ignoring him, I slammed the door closed behind me. My chest rose and fell rapidly. My eyes blurred as they flooded. Using the wall for support, I walked over to the glass shower and climbed in.

Still in my dirty, bloody clothes, I turned on the water. I put my hands on the wall and stared down as the water poured over me. Blood and filth darkened the water as it swirled down the drain. I watched it wash away along with my tears.

Just for a minute. Just to take the edge off so my darkness can hold it all back again, I told myself as more tears escaped.

I needed to remove my clothes. Thinking of what it would entail to get my shirt off and the pain it would cause kept me from trying. The frustration I felt weighed against my resolve. I ached to scream, to break something, to unleash everything I'd been holding in—everything I had endured.

"Maura."

I glanced over my shoulder. Jamie was standing just outside the shower door.

"What are you doing in here?" I asked him.

He eyed my clothes that clung to me. "You look like you're moments from falling over."

The thought of sitting down had crossed my mind, but I was worried I wouldn't be able to get back up again.

His gaze felt intense and heavy and when it met mine, it was as if he could see every inch of my soul, all the damage, the lack of anything good, all the things I didn't want him to see— what he didn't deserve to see. Not anymore.

"Can you even lift your arms to take off your shirt?" he asked.

Fuck him. Fuck everyone else. Fuck! Fuck! Fuck!

"I won't think you're weak if you need help getting your shirt off," he said.

I glared at him.

He sighed with his eyes shut. "You know I didn't mean it like that." His eyes opened and locked with mine. "I've gotten hurt to the point of needing help and I wasn't too proud to accept it."

I turned to fully face him, seething. "I'm not being proud, Jamie. I don't want your help because I don't trust you not to use it against me."

He stared down with a clenched jaw. Then he climbed into the shower, clothes and all. Drops of water immediately started dotting his black suit. "You need to know that what I did and what I said had nothing to do with you. It was all me. I didn't know how to handle losing our baby and almost losing you, too. I felt like a failure, like I had no control of anything, and I wasn't confident I could keep you safe. None of that was a good enough reason to hurt you and I'm sorry." Remorse was sewn into his words. "I have never once thought you were weak. I was the weak one."

His apology didn't mend the broken trust, but it helped ease my anger toward him...some.

"Will you let me help you?" he asked.

The temptation to accept was there, but I couldn't let myself succumb to it. "No."

He didn't get angry. Instead, he nodded. "I can go get Brenna for you if you'll be more comfortable with her help." I almost jumped on that offer, until he added, "I'll have to take over caring for the Aryan baby, though."

He was so lucky I didn't have a gun on me. "A heartfelt apology followed by manipulation? Careful, Jamie, I might get whiplash."

"You're the one not comfortable with me around him," he said innocently.

I tilted my head slightly, studying his face, his posture,

finding it all unreadable. "When did we start playing the game with each other?"

"You started it when you used my need to see Buck dead in order to take off without me." His tone held a hint of anger. "But you and I are playing two different games."

"Is that so?"

He stepped closer, bringing us chest to chest. "Manipulation is the number one tool of the game. That's what Stefan has taught us. You used it to get what you wanted. I'm using it to help you."

"That's a shitty way of helping someone," I snapped.

"I did offer nicely," he snapped back. "Your stubbornness is blocking your rational thinking. You need help."

I reeled back a little. "So, what, you thought you'd try manipulation as a different approach?"

He smirked down at me. "Did it work?"

Strangely, I found him very attractive at that moment. It was probably due to exhaustion. On another, more rational note—and as much as I hated to admit it—he was right. I did need help. I'd prefer Brenna's over his, but that protective feeling inside of me kept me from choosing her. As fucked-up as it was, Jamie had just made it easier to accept his help. I sighed. There were other ways to handle my predicament, but I was too tired to think of them. "Fine."

He didn't show triumph in any way or look smug. He simply nodded and carefully began helping me pull my arms through my sleeves before pulling the shirt off of me completely. His jaw clenched as his eyes roamed over the bruises that marred my skin over my ribs and stomach. Without saying anything, he helped me out of the rest of my clothes. He didn't even attempt to remove his as he proceeded to help me wash my hair.

"You haven't asked about Louie," he said as he gently kneaded my scalp.

Hearing his name was like a punch to the gut. "I'm not ready to hear that he's dead."

"He's alive."

All the air left me as if someone had squeezed both of my lungs. Afraid my legs would give out, I grabbed onto Jamie's arm. "What?"

CHAPTER SEVEN

jamie

Maura stared up at me with such haunted eyes.

"He's alive," I repeated. "He's resting in the room across from mine in the main house."

She released a shuddering breath and looked down to hide the tears she thought the water had been masking. The soap in her hair began to slide down her forehead. I helped her turn toward the water to wash it away before it could get in her eyes.

With her facing away from me, I was given an unobscured view of her bare back. It was black, blue, and red. Not all, but a handful of lashes were split open and bleeding. Some were short and deep. The others were long and shallow. Her back was a canvas of brutality.

I grabbed her by her upper arms. "Was Buck the one who did this?"

She tensed up.

"Maura," I gritted out.

Her body relaxed a little. "Yes."

I rested my head on top of hers as I tried to rein in my rage. I was beyond relieved that she was alive and finally home, but I wished Buck was still alive so I could kill him myself.

"I'd like to be alone now."

The exhaustion in her voice matched what I felt down to my bones. Between Louie being shot and doing everything I could to find her in the past forty-eight hours, I was running on pure will alone.

I didn't want to let her go. If I was holding her, I knew she was safe. I knew it was my fear urging me not to let her go. I couldn't succumb to it. If I was going to repair what I'd broken between us, I had to prove I wouldn't make that mistake again.

I pressed my lips to her head before pulling away. "I'll make sure someone is nearby if you need anything," I said as I climbed out of the shower.

I grabbed a towel on my way out of the bathroom. In the bedroom I found Dr. Ben and Stefan waiting.

Stefan eyed my wet clothes with an unreadable expression. "How is she?"

I shut the bathroom door behind me. "How do you think she is?"

Stefan's brows rose at the irritation I couldn't hide. "More hurt than she's letting on and doesn't trust us to admit it."

I wasn't surprised he'd picked up on that. He knew his daughter better than anyone. I fisted the towel in my hands. "That's my fault."

Stefan stuffed his hands into his pockets. "It is."

His honesty made my guilt feel ten times heavier. It was what I deserved.

"But the fault doesn't just belong to you, or even Louie for that matter," Stefan said, looking away.

It wasn't everyday a boss, Stefan least of all, admitted fault and it was difficult not to show my surprise.

"I don't know what mistakes were made, nor is it any of my business," Dr. Ben said. He was visibly nervous, his hand gripping the strap of his medical bag hanging off his shoulder to the point his knuckles were white. "But she has been through a lot over the past few days. It could be that she's locked into survival mode, and it can take a while for someone to feel safe enough to come out of that. I think you should give her time before you take what she's doing personally."

What he said only made sense when it came to Stefan. I knew this because it hadn't been Louie or me she had called multiple times while she had been gone these past four months. She deserved more than just time from me.

After changing into dry clothes, I returned just as Maura was exiting the bathroom wearing a robe. Dr. Ben had her sit on the edge of the bed. He knelt down in front of her. "Will you tell me what happened? I need to know how you were injured."

Stefan and I gave them room and went to stand near the foot of the bed.

Maura stared at the doctor she often referred to as Fabio Jr. with a closed-off expression and tired eyes. "Point to which injury and I'll tell you."

He pointed to her face, where her cheekbone was puffy and cut, the area under her left eye was black, and the corner of her bottom lip was split.

"I was punched, backhanded, and slapped," she answered in a factual manner.

He lifted her chin to look at the finger-shaped bruises around her neck. "Here?"

"Choked."

Stefan had gone very still next to me. Seeing her injuries and hearing how she'd gotten them was far from fucking easy.

Dr. Ben grabbed her hands and inspected the tearing and bruises around her wrists. "Here?"

"I was handcuffed."

Dr. Ben's hand moved to her fingers on her right hand. There was a line of gashes across them. "Here?"

"I turned my handcuffs into my own version of brass knuckles," she said.

Dr. Ben looked over at Stefan and me. "I need her to open her robe."

Stefan ignored Dr. Ben's hint to leave and turned around, giving them his back.

I met Maura's eyes. "Do you want me to leave?"

She unfastened her robe. "You've already seen it, and this saves me from having to explain what happened later."

"This isn't telling us what happened, Maura," Stefan said, glaring at the floor.

Dr. Ben helped her stand and opened the robe wide enough so he could see the splash of bruises along her ribs and stomach. He felt around and pushed on her ribs. "Here?"

Maura jerked away from him a little while grimacing. "Punched," she forced out.

"I don't think they're broken," Dr. Ben said and moved his hand to her stomach. "Here?"

"Kicked and punched."

He nodded with a tight expression. "Are you hurt anywhere else?"

She turned around and let the robe slide down her back until it reached her butt.

Dr. Ben was quiet for almost a minute. "You were whipped?"

"Yes."

His fingers touched her back gently. "With what?"

She hesitated before answering. "A belt."

"Some of these lacerations are going to scar," he said.

"It doesn't matter," she mumbled with a vacant voice.

"Do I need to do a pelvic exam?" Dr. Ben asked.

The question seemed to startle everyone, because the room went quiet. I held my breath as I waited for Maura's response.

"No."

At Maura's answer, I finally exhaled, and I caught Stefan's shoulders sagging a little.

When Dr. Ben was done looking her over, he suggested that Maura go to the hospital just in case. She refused.

"Maura," Stefan said with a tone that told me that they were about to argue.

Maura didn't look in Stefan's direction as she put her robe back on. "You have two options, gentlemen. Either Dr. Ben can bandage me up or you can all get the hell out." Her voice was calm, almost too calm, and brooked no argument.

Stefan whirled around.

Before he could say a word, she said, "You're lucky I put my robe back on or we both might have been scarred for life." She slowly lowered herself back onto the edge of the bed.

"I'm glad you're able to find humor right now," he said caustically.

"Do you see me laughing?" she snapped, and the way she stared at Stefan was unsettling. It was as if he was nothing to her. I'd never seen her look at him with such intense detachment.

"You were badly beaten——" Stefan started to say.

"Yes, I was," she cut him off. "And if I felt it necessary to go to the hospital, I would have had Dean drive me there instead of here."

Stefan went quiet. He studied her, searching for what most of us couldn't see.

Maura stared right back at him, revealing nothing. "What do you think is going to happen when I show up to the hospital like this?" she asked him. "I've been dropping Aryan bodies from New Haven to New York. No amount of lying will hide what was obviously done to me. The last thing we need are police connecting dots."

"When Buck took you, I was taken in for questioning," I said. Then I glanced at Stefan briefly because he knew what I was going to tell her.

He didn't seem to be paying attention. He was staring at the carpet with a pensive frown.

I returned my attention to Maura and continued. "Detectives Cameron and Brooks interrogated me for hours on what happened. They asked about you. They said witnesses saw a redhead at the scene."

"What did you tell them?" she asked.

"I told them you were in Ireland," Stefan said, looking up from the floor with a schooled mask. "They brought you up after I showed up with our lawyer, Adam."

"So they're already putting theories together," she said.

"As a boss, I can't argue with your reasoning for not going to the hospital," Stefan said. "But as a father..."

"You can't be a father first this time, Stefan," Maura said.

"When will you learn, daughter?" Stefan said. "I have always been a father first."

The detachment Maura had been exuding cracked. If Stefan saw it, I didn't know, because as soon as he was finished speaking, he stormed out of the room.

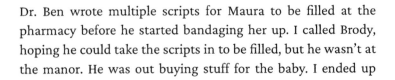

Dr. Ben wrote multiple scripts for Maura to be filled at the pharmacy before he started bandaging her up. I called Brody, hoping he could take the scripts in to be filled, but he wasn't at the manor. He was out buying stuff for the baby. I ended up having to ask Jeana, Stefan's personal chef, and she seemed more than happy to.

When Dr. Ben was done, I offered to walk him out. Stefan stopped us in the foyer of the main house and asked us to come speak with him. We followed him into his study.

As Stefan sat behind his desk, he gestured for Dr. Ben to take a seat in one of the chairs across from him. Wanting to have a visual on both of them, I sat on the couch in the seating area on the left side of the room.

"I'd like to hear your honest assessment of her injuries without Maura here to argue about it," Stefan said as Dr. Ben sat down.

Dr. Ben let out a sigh. "They're bad. If you're asking me if they're life-threatening, I'm pretty sure they're not. Only time will tell us for sure because she won't go to the hospital."

"She's very adamant about that," Stefan said with blatant irritation. "I'd force her if I didn't think she'd shoot anyone who came near her."

I could attest that she would and had the scar on my shoulder to prove it. "Even with the risks?"

Stefan ran a hand down his face, looking pissed-off and slightly torn.

"I wouldn't recommend forcing anything on her right now," Dr. Ben said very seriously. "Like I said earlier, she's still in survival mode. Victims of this type of trauma—"

"My daughter isn't a victim," Stefan snapped, cutting the doctor off. "And don't ever say that she is again, especially outside this room."

Dr. Ben stiffened and dipped his head with a single nod.

"Since she's refusing to go to the hospital, what do you recommend we do to make sure she's alright?" I asked, getting back to the point.

Dr. Ben looked from Stefan to me. "I don't think she should

be alone for a while. At least for a few days as we wait to see if anything more serious pops up."

She wasn't going to be thrilled about that.

"The baby appears healthy," Dr. Ben said.

"Of course he is," I grumbled.

Stefan's gaze flicked to me for a moment before he stood. "Thank you for coming, Ben."

Dr. Ben quickly stood as well, understanding that he was being dismissed. "Yes, of course. I can see myself out."

Stefan waited until the door closed behind the doctor before he spoke. "Do I need to worry about you when it comes to that baby?"

"No."

He sat back in his chair. "That baby didn't get to pick who his father was."

"I would never hurt a baby, Stefan." If I did, then I'd be no better than those who'd killed mine.

Stefan relaxed back in his chair as he studied me. "Then what's your problem?"

My eyes wandered and I stared at the wall without really seeing it. "I'm worried she's trying to replace the one we lost."

"I can see why you would think that."

I looked back at him. "You don't think she is?"

"I'm not sure. But what I do know is that she cares about him, and she hasn't cared about anything other than killing Aryans for the past four months."

I released a heavy sigh.

"We don't know what her plans are with him," Stefan said. "But if you're determined to make things right with my daughter, you need to figure out if raising your enemy's son is something you're capable of doing first. For your own sake and for my daughter's."

Louie's bedroom was dark when I entered. I walked through the room blind until I reached the window. I pulled back one of the curtains, letting in just enough light to make everything visible.

"Hey," Louie said, his voice laden with exhaustion.

I moved toward the bed where he was resting. Propped up a little by pillows, he watched me as I came to stand by the foot of the bed.

Like Maura, he should have been in the hospital. The bastard had lasted all of twenty-four hours before he'd unhooked himself from all the monitors, ripped out his IV, and made Brenna and Finn, who I had assigned to watch over him at the hospital, bring him to Quinn Manor.

"What the fuck?" I had said to him as he'd walked through the front door, barefoot and only in a hospital gown. His arms had been slung over Brenna's and Finn's shoulders. I'd been able to tell by Brenna's and Finn's strained expressions that they had been doing most of the walking for him.

"I hate hospitals," Louie had said as if that had been a legitimate reason as to why he'd left.

"You're a dumbass," Brenna had muttered under her breath as the three of them had made their way to the stairs.

"No one asked you, baby Quinn," Louie had said, his voice breathy and strained as they'd taken that first step up the stairs.

Brenna had grunted as they'd gone up another step. "Don't test me, Louie, or I will leave you on these fucking stairs."

"Maura really did help you find your backbone, didn't she?" Louie had grumbled.

Following through on her threat, Brenna had dropped his arm from her shoulder, stomped back down the stairs, and disappeared down the hall that led to Stefan's study.

Finn had let out a curse as he'd strained to support Louie. "You just had to be a dick."

"My bad," Louie had said. "I'm not the nicest when I'm in pain."

I'd rushed up the few steps and thrown his arm across my shoulders. "If you're in that much pain, you should have stayed in the hospital."

"I need to be here," had been his response.

Not wanting to argue because I understood, I had helped get him up the stairs. After Maura had run away, Louie had practically moved into the room across from mine. That was where Finn and I had taken him and that was where he had been since.

"She's home," I told him.

He sat up quickly. Before he could do much else, he hugged his middle with an arm and breathed between clenched teeth. "Is she hurt?"

I went over to his nightstand where a glass of water and multiple bottles of pills were, courtesy of Dr. Ben. I grabbed his pain meds, poured a couple tablets into my hand, and gave them to him with the water. "They beat her pretty bad."

After taking his meds, he handed me back the glass of water to set on the nightstand. "Did they…" he trailed off.

I shook my head.

He closed his eyes and relaxed back against his pillows. "How'd you find her?"

Stuffing my hands into my pockets, I began with how I'd received a call from the guards at the front gate that Brenna had just left the property in Maura's car.

Louie and I talked for a while. Most of what we talked about was Maura and the devil's spawn she had brought home with her. Louie didn't seem all that worried about him. Mostly he was intrigued.

"She just got back. You don't even know if the little guy will be sticking around," Louie said.

"What if she wants to keep him?" I asked.

He shrugged. "I haven't met him yet, so I can't answer that."

"I've met him and I still can't answer that question."

"Have you held him?" he asked.

I just looked at him.

He closed his tired eyes and mumbled, "You should try holding him for a while and maybe the answer will be easier to figure out."

It was nighttime by the time I found myself back at the guest house. Dean, Asher, and Brenna were all watching TV in the living room when I entered.

Brenna stood from the couch and blocked the hall that led to the bedrooms. "She wants to be alone, Jameson."

I stared down at her. "Dr. Ben says she can't be alone."

Brenna put her hands on her hips. "Then one of us will watch over her. The last thing she needs right now is you going in there and waking her up."

"I won't wake her, and I'll be gone before she wakes up in the morning," I said, doing my best to not lose my patience.

Brenna didn't look like she was going to back down.

"Let him pass, Brenna," Dean said. From where he sat on the couch, his back was to me.

Everyone looked toward him, surprised. He ignored us and kept his eyes on the TV.

Brenna sighed and stepped aside.

"Thanks," I said, trying not to sound irritated.

"I'm not letting you in there for you."

Dean's words made me pause. Maura's personal security genuinely cared for her, more so than anyone else's security in this family, even Stefan's. Because I loved her, I was happy she had people around her she could trust. At the same time, however, especially for the last four months, they were a pain in the ass.

The bedside light in Maura's room was still on when I entered. Maura was asleep in bed. She didn't stir as I came in or when I shut the bedroom door behind me. She was lying on her side facing a bassinet that was right next to the bed. As I got closer, I could see that the Aryan baby was awake inside. He was just lying there with a pacifier in his mouth, staring up at the ceiling with wide blue eyes. This was the first time I'd actually made myself really look at him. Before, when I had first seen him in Maura's arms, I hadn't been able to see past my grief.

The pacifier fell from his mouth, and a breath later, he started to whine. I glanced at Maura. She was so exhausted, she still didn't stir. Not that I wanted her to. After what she'd been through, she needed rest.

Shit.

Without letting myself think too much about it, I reached into the bassinet and scooped the baby up. In my arms, his whining got louder, and I retreated from the room quickly.

I ran into Brenna in the hall. She saw the fussing baby in my arms and stared up at me with an arched brow. "Where are you going with that baby?"

Great. She thought I was taking him. "I didn't want him to wake Maura," I said as I started to bounce a little, hoping that would calm him.

Her face relaxed as she watched me. "He's probably hungry. The formula and bottles are in the kitchen."

I nodded and went to take a step in that direction before stopping. "Do you know how to feed him?"

She folded her arms across her chest with a smirk. "Brody taught me how earlier."

The little brat was going to make me ask her.

My pride wanted me to just figure it out on my own, but the thought of fucking something up helped me ignore it. "Can you show me how?"

That damn smirk didn't drop as she headed for the kitchen.

CHAPTER EIGHT

MAURA

I opened my eyes to bright morning rays shining through the window. I felt rested, the clean sheets felt cool against my skin, the scent on my pillow smelled like home. Such things shouldn't be able to stir such strong emotions in me, yet they did. I sighed through my nose.

"Are you alright?"

Startled, I sat up and searched for the source of the voice I knew belonged to Jamie. Jolting upright sent a shockwave of pain through me, making me grunt and fist the blankets.

I found Jamie sitting in an armchair in the corner of the room. Seeing me in pain, his brow scrunched up. "I didn't mean to scare you."

"What—" I started to say. Then I noticed the baby in his arms and the fact that he was feeding him a bottle. That made me realize that I hadn't been woken once by the baby. "Have you been taking care of him all night?"

He glanced down at him with a guarded expression. "You needed rest."

I grabbed the bottle of pain meds Dr. Ben had prescribed me and a glass of water I had on the nightstand. I plopped a couple of pills in my mouth and chased them with nearly the whole glass of water. The moment the water hit my stomach, it growled loudly. It had been days since I'd eaten anything. Dean had tried to insist I eat something last night, but I had been so tired I'd just wanted to go to sleep.

Jamie pulled the bottle from the baby's mouth so he could free up his hand to reach into his pocket. "I'll ask Jeana to bring breakfast." He typed out a quick message on his phone, then shoved it back in his pocket after he sent it and returned to feeding the baby.

"Brenna could have helped me with him last night," I said.

"We both know you wouldn't have had her help you," he said. "Besides, I wanted to."

I didn't believe him. "I saw how you looked at him yesterday."

"Louie said I should hold him."

He talked to Louie about him? "Why?"

He locked eyes with me. "What is your plan with this baby, Maura? Are you planning on keeping him?"

"You're asking me questions I don't have the answers to. His parents have been dead for one whole day."

Jamie pulled the now-empty bottle from the baby's mouth and stood. I watched as he walked over to the bassinet and placed him inside carefully. I leaned over and peeked in to see that the baby was asleep. The little guy looked downright angelic when he slept.

"I can see how you look at him," Jamie said, throwing my words back at me in a low voice.

Feeling like I'd been caught doing something wrong, I pulled away from the bassinet.

Jamie sat on the edge of the bed. "Does he have any relatives?"

"He has an aunt, but she's a prostitute and junkie."

"He can go into the system. He's a baby. They might be able to find him a home pretty quickly," he suggested.

I opened my mouth to answer, then shut it. I didn't like that idea. What if he was placed in a bad home?

Jamie's eyes never left me. "I think you know what you want to do. You just don't want to admit it to yourself yet."

"This isn't a good home for him, either." Jamie opened his mouth to say something, but I spoke before he could. "You still didn't answer my question."

"You know why, Maura."

I knew, but it didn't matter and sadly, I wasn't sure if it ever would.

"You told me not to give up on us if you were enough," he said. "You've never not been enough for me, but you just added a baby into the equation. I know I said I'd be open to other ways to have children, but I didn't think you'd bring home an Aryan baby. And not just any Aryan baby, either."

Hating how he made me feel things I wasn't ready to feel, I climbed out the other side of the bed, needing space. "I haven't made any decisions when it comes to this baby, nor have I forgiven you. You're talking like everything will be fixed between us tomorrow."

Jamie stood and faced me. "I know things won't be fixed tomorrow, but I will make it right between us."

I had the urge to tell him not to bother and that it had been a mistake to ask him not to give up. I couldn't find my way back to myself. So how the hell were we going to be an *us* again?

I was saved from having to respond to him when there was a knock on my bedroom door. Brenna poked her head in. "Breakfast is here." She looked from Jamie to me and the bed between us. "Everything okay?"

"Yes," I said.

She didn't look like she believed me, but she didn't call me out. "Want me to bring you a plate?"

I nodded and she left, but not before she gave Jamie a stern look.

"Your little protector is going to kick me out when she gets back," he said, clearly annoyed.

"That's because I told her not to let anyone in the house. Did you sneak in last night?" I asked him.

He just smirked and headed for the door.

A handful of days passed by in a blur. I spent the majority in bed resting or taking care of the baby. I had told my goons not to let anyone in the house, but I quickly realized how that order had gone in one ear and out the other. Brody stopped by every day to fuss over me and fawn over the baby. Stefan visited at least once a day. Every time, he asked how I was feeling. Every time I answered evasively, and he knew but didn't push for the truth. He didn't ask what had happened while I'd been gone for four months, either. I appreciated his patience as much as I was highly suspicious of it. It wasn't in Stefan's nature not to push for answers.

Jamie snuck in every night to watch over me and help with the baby. I tried once to make him leave. It didn't work. Every night after that, I'd pretended to be asleep when he'd show up. A few times, it was highly entertaining listening to him interact with the baby.

Last night Jamie had let out a tired sigh. "Why won't you go back to sleep? It's two in the morning."

The night before, as I had lain there listening, I'd had to turn my face into my pillow to hide the smile that had threatened to stretch across my face as Jamie had cursed. "Do you spit up on everyone else or do you wait until I show up?"

Yesterday, before Jamie had left that morning, he had brought up Louie again. "He asks about you."

"I know what you're going to ask me and I'm not ready," I had said. It had been the truth.

When Jamie had just nodded and left with zero argument, I'd realized then that the two pushiest, pain-in-the-ass men in my life were being way too understanding. In the end, because they were giving me what I wanted, I didn't insist to know why. I didn't have it in me to care, either.

Other than the short and quiet cry I'd had in the shower the day I'd arrived home to take the edge off, I'd been just existing with my darkness holding everything I had yet to deal with— Louie, what I'd gone through when I'd been taken, and everything that had happened in the past four months—at bay. It wouldn't last, though. I'd eventually have to face the music and that made me feel like a ticking time bomb counting down to zero.

Today my time ran out. I knew as soon as I woke up, feeling like chains were wrapped around my middle. It was just the blankets, but I still kicked them off in a panic and sat up.

"Everything okay?" I heard Brenna ask.

I found her sitting in the armchair with a textbook in her lap. I was a little surprised not to see Jamie there. Stefan must have called on him early this morning to do mob shit.

I exhaled heavily. "Yeah."

As the day went on, I felt my darkness less and less as memories kept hitting me unexpectedly. The baby's eyes reminded me of Amelia's, and it was like falling down a rabbit hole. I couldn't stop remembering her standing in the kitchen, the look on her face.

After that, I called Brody and asked if he would take the

baby for a while. He had errands to run and was happy to take the baby along with him. The idea of Brody leaving the property with him made me feel uneasy, so I sent Dean and Asher with them just in case.

Knowing Brenna had schoolwork to do, I convinced her to do it somewhere else in the house so I could watch TV.

The moment she left the room, I felt like I could breathe a little. I turned on the TV that was mounted to the wall just for show and I tried to relax. I couldn't. The noises on the TV agitated me to the point I had to turn it off. The silence was worse. Panic was rushing toward me.

The sound of Buck's belt echoed in my head. The pain of the first lash. Amelia begging. The sound of the table creaking.

I pulled my knees up to my chest and rested my forehead on them. I began rocking as Amelia's screams played over and over in my mind.

"Maura?" I heard Brenna say before a hand touched my arm.

I jerked from her touch and fisted my hair with both of my hands. I just wanted the screaming to stop. "Go away, Brenna."

"I—"

"Go!" I yelled. My thoughts pulled me to the hospital. I could see myself standing in front of Amelia's hospital room door. I'd known in my gut that it had been a trap. I'd just wanted Buck dead so badly, I hadn't cared. The guilt hit me like a freight train as I remembered myself walking through that door. Then I could see Louie running for me. The memory of the gun firing and him hunching over made me pull on my hair and cry out.

Arms wrapped around me. Blinded by tears I hadn't known I was crying, I fought whoever it was. In my attempt to get away, I lunged off the bed, but before I could fall to the floor, the arms caught me by my middle. Whoever it was lowered me to the floor on my hands and knees.

Stefan's voice filled my ear. "It's me, Maura."

I shook my head violently. "I can't—! I can't—!" I couldn't stop. I couldn't hold it back any longer.

Stefan's arms tightened around me. "Just let it out. I know you need to." There was nothing more than reassurance in his voice and it gave me what I needed to let go.

I lowered my head to the ground, and I roared into the carpet. I kept roaring until it hurt and then I roared some more. I needed to hurt. My guilt demanded it.

After I couldn't scream anymore and all I could do was sob, Stefan sat on the floor next to me with his back against the bed. Then he pulled me to his chest. We were like that for a while. He didn't say anything as I cried. There was nothing he could have said. He just held me until I must have fallen asleep.

I was in my bed when I woke. It wasn't as bright out, so I assumed it was evening.

"How are you feeling?"

Stefan was sitting in the armchair watching me. He looked rough. My always put-together father wasn't so put-together. His suit jacket and tie were nowhere to be seen. His dress shirt was wrinkled and the sleeves were rolled up. I only ever saw him this way when I was hurt. It was unfortunate because I liked it when he looked human.

"You've asked me that every day." My voice was hoarse.

"And every time you've avoided answering," he said with a hint of frustration.

It'd be a waste of energy to pretend to be fine now. "I wish you hadn't seen that."

"Why?"

I stared up at the ceiling as I let the truth flow freely. "Because now that you've seen how fucked-up I am, you'll probably never let me leave the house again."

"That idea is appealing," he said, making me look back at him. He was staring at me with such a serious face. His eyes, though, held a hint of sadness. "I already knew you were hurting, and you were doing your best not to let it show. Which meant you weren't dealing with it. It's why I asked every day."

"But you didn't push. You always push."

"I couldn't push this, Maura." I was getting ready to ask why when he continued, "You came home looking at me like I was your enemy."

"You're not the enemy, Stefan." I could see why he thought that.

"Have you noticed that you call me Stefan when you want to distance yourself from me?" he asked. "You haven't referred to me any other way since you've been home."

I didn't know how to respond because I couldn't exactly tell him the truth.

"I don't know everything that happened to you when you were taken." He got to his feet. "But what did was obviously bad enough to make you forget that everything I have done and will do is for you."

"I didn't forget. I just haven't been able to feel it," I blurted. When my darkness was in full control, I could look at Stefan and know that I loved him and that he was important, but I couldn't feel it. Now that my darkness was back to coexisting within me like it had been these past four months, helping me move while I battled the shit I couldn't escape from, I could.

He frowned. "Care to tell me what you mean by that?"

I couldn't tell him about my darkness. He'd probably have me committed if I did. "I see how you, Jamie, and everyone stares at me. You're searching for the Maura you know, but she isn't there."

He was quiet as he waited for me to explain.

"All that's left of who I used to be is pain, guilt, rage, and...a darker part of myself who finds it way too easy to pull the trigger...if that makes sense," I tried to explain. "Everything else, what was good in me, the daughter you can't see when you look at me, is gone. Who I am now is who I needed to be to pick myself up four months ago."

"If who you were was gone, Maura, you wouldn't feel guilt, you wouldn't feel pain. You have to care to feel those things," he said and stared down at his feet, pensive. "I haven't been through what you have, but I have experienced my own hell. I know what it is to close off, to harden to spare yourself from pain. And I know what it's like to tap into your worst self to keep moving, and because of that choice, I did things that I'm not proud of."

I didn't blink the entire time he spoke. It was rare for Stefan to admit something so vulnerable.

"I don't think my daughter is gone, but I do think she's been changed by what she's been through." He stepped toward the door. "You should get some more rest."

After he left, I just lay there, and I braced myself for things I knew it was time to face.

CHAPTER NINE

Around dinner time, Brenna came to see me. She stood in the doorway with a tray in her hands. "Hey."

I sat up in bed and gestured for her to come in.

Her posture was a tiny bit stiff as she walked in and placed the wooden tray over my lap. "Jeana made Grandma's cottage pie." She announced that as if it would cheer me up.

I stared down at the tray of food and I found that it didn't. Noticing Brenna lingering, I glanced back up at her. She looked hesitant, like she had something to say.

"I shouldn't have yelled at you earlier," I said.

The tightness in her body seemed to ease. "I didn't take it personally, Maura. I just didn't know how to help you."

"Is that why you went and got Stefan?" I wasn't mad at her for doing it. I was just trying to understand why.

"I didn't go get him." She sat on the edge of the bed. "Like he's done every day, he came to check on you."

Even though it made me uneasy, it probably had been for the best that it had been Stefan to help me through that moment.

"Unfortunately, when Stefan showed up," Brenna said,

looking like whatever she had to say next wasn't easy, "Jameson was with him."

That unease I felt multiplied in an instant. "What did he see?"

"When you told me to leave, I ran into them in the hall. They heard you crying before I could say anything. They both rushed into your room. Stefan took one look at you and told Jameson to get out. Jameson didn't argue and as soon as he was in the hall, Stefan slammed your door shut. Jameson stood outside your door listening, and when you started screaming…" She trailed off with a sad look on her face. "He grabbed onto the wall as if he needed it to stay upright. And the more you screamed, the more upset he got. It was like hearing your pain was breaking him."

I exhaled heavily. *What a fucking mess.*

"If it means anything, I don't think you should worry about him using what happened as a way to control you," she said.

"First Dean and now you," I grumbled as I took my tray off my lap and laid it on the other side of the bed. The idea of eating wasn't very appealing at the moment.

"I have always hoped you, Jameson, and Louie would make things right, but that has never meant that I'm not on your side. If you decide to kill them tomorrow and need help hiding the bodies, I'll grab a shovel. So would Dean." She gave me a small smile. "You also don't see what we see. During the day, if Jameson's not working for Stefan, he's helping take care of Louie. Then he's here all night helping with the baby. I don't know when he's last slept."

Needing a break from the current topic, I deflected. "What happened right after I was taken?"

"It was chaos. A lot happened and very quickly. I'll give you the CliffsNotes version." She scooted farther onto the bed and sat facing me, cross-legged. "Dean and Asher chased after you and the Aryans. Jameson stayed behind with Louie and reported to Finn, Vincent, and me that Louie had been shot. We called EMS, but doctors from the hospital got to Louie first and took him into surgery right away. Detectives Cameron and Brooks took Jameson down to the police station for questioning in handcuffs. Finn, Vincent, and I stayed at the hospital with Louie. Not long after that, Dean and Asher returned without you. Dean was freaking out. He wouldn't sit still. He paced the halls. We all voted that it was time to call Stefan."

"Who was the one brave enough to make that call?" I asked.

She smiled. "I volunteered. I figured he was less likely to kill his young niece."

As I stared at her, a little bit of guilt washed over me.

"What?" she said, her smile dropping.

Realizing that I wasn't hiding what I was thinking very well, I schooled my face. "I forget sometimes how young you are."

A look of understanding took over her face. "Jameson, Dylan, and Rourke all had to kill at sixteen. Even you killed at seventeen."

"Mine wasn't a test to see if I could do it," I pointed out.

"No, it wasn't," she said sullenly. "As terrible as the circumstances were, it made you more badass than the guys because you went off and did that voluntarily. It feels like an obligation when it's a test."

"I made you feel obligated?"

"Yes and no. I wanted to do it, but when the time came, it became real and I had to figure out if I was capable of pulling that trigger or not," she explained. "Did you have that moral moment when you killed for the first time?"

I thought back to the moments that had led up to killing Zack and Tyson. Memories of Jamie and Louie picking me up from the party, the relief I'd felt when Louie had agreed not to tell anyone what had happened, the way Jamie had held me as

I'd fallen apart took over my thoughts. They were bad memories, but it was easier to look back on them and see a tiny bit of good. Louie and Jamie had both been there for me. Remembering those moments and what it felt like to have unwavering trust in them made me envy my younger self. "No. I didn't have a moral moment," I told her. "All I felt was anger that someone would kill them for me."

"See. Badass," she said, her smile returning. "Besides, I'm going to be eighteen soon."

"In less than a month," I said. "And what would you like for your birthday?"

"A motorcycle," she answered seriously.

"You really are rebelling from your previous obedient life," I teased as I eyed her low-cut top and ripped jeans. Very slowly and subtly, she had been making changes to her style. She'd used to dress very modestly, almost Stepford-daughter-like. I would've been concerned, but I felt who she'd been before I'd taken her from Dylan was how her father, Samuel, had demanded she be. Since I'd taken her into my care, I'd noticed over time that she'd learned how to be comfortable enough to test out who she wanted to be. Given what she had been through, it was an amazing accomplishment for her.

"Is that a no on the motorcycle, then?"

I shook my head with a tiny smile. "Let's get back on track. What happened when you called Stefan?"

"I found out that he was already on his way. He knew about the shoot-out at the hospital but didn't know that you were missing. That wasn't the easiest thing to tell him. Then he showed up with Uncle Conor and Rourke and they took over and had Vincent taken back to Quinn Manor to help find you. After Louie got out of surgery and we were told that he was going to live, Stefan ordered Asher, Finn, Dean, and me to stay and watch over him while he went to go get Jameson."

"What do the police think happened?"

She shook her head. "I don't know. I haven't been included in those discussions."

I supposed I'd find that out later.

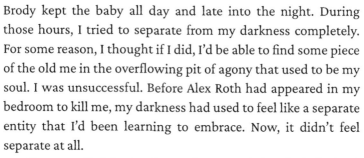

Brody kept the baby all day and late into the night. During those hours, I tried to separate from my darkness completely. For some reason, I thought if I did, I'd be able to find some piece of the old me in the overflowing pit of agony that used to be my soul. I was unsuccessful. Before Alex Roth had appeared in my bedroom to kill me, my darkness had used to feel like a separate entity that I'd been learning to embrace. Now, it didn't feel separate at all.

Close to midnight, Jamie was the one to bring the baby back to me. I watched as he walked into my bedroom with a diaper bag hanging from his shoulder and the baby in his arms. It was very domestic given the criminal he was and for some reason that irritated me.

He looked exhausted. By the length of scruff on his face, I'd say it had been a while since he'd last shaved. It bothered me that he was running himself ragged, which just added to my irritation.

His brows rose a little when he saw me sitting up, awake in bed. "Hi," he said as he set the diaper bag on the dresser.

I forced my voice to sound calm. "Hi."

He gently placed the baby, who was asleep, in the bassinet. As he tucked the baby in, I got angrier and angrier by the second. I should have felt relieved that he didn't seem like a threat to the baby anymore. Instead, it upset me that he now cared for him.

Jamie met my eyes for a moment, and I did what I could to

mask what I was feeling. He appeared like he wanted to say something to me, but he looked away and made his way over to the chair in the corner of the room. He sat down with an exhausted sigh.

"You don't need to be here. You should go get some sleep in your own room," I insisted for his sake, for more than one reason.

He rested the back of his head against the chair and closed his eyes. "You sound like you're worried about me."

"You look like hell," I grumbled.

He opened his eyes with a smirk that made me want to smack his stupid handsome face.

I couldn't do that from all the way over here, so I used words instead. "Fine. Do what you want. But know that running yourself into the ground isn't earning you brownie points."

His smirk dropped and he lifted his head. "You think that's why I'm here? That the only fucking reason is to earn your forgiveness?"

"Yes, I do." As soon as the lie left my mouth, I braced for a fight I didn't even want, yet couldn't help but start.

He seemed to see through my lie. Instead of getting riled like he normally would, he ran his hands down his face tiredly. "What do you want from me, Maura? You're the one who told me not to give up on us."

Knowing that I needed to get away from him, I ripped off my blankets and began climbing out of bed. "So, what? You think that just because you're not giving up, the road to my forgiveness is going to be smooth fucking sailing?"

Jamie got to his feet at the same time I did. "No, I didn't expect it would be easy, but you're acting like you don't want me to try to fight for us at all."

"Maybe I don't," I said under my breath and headed for the

bathroom before I made shit worse.

Jamie grabbed me by my arm, stopping me. "There you go running when shit gets too heavy to deal with between us," he growled. "That's the only thing that hasn't seemed to change about you."

I lost it. The rage inside me needed an outlet and he had just given me one. My hand flew. The sound of the slap bounced off the walls. Jamie's face was knocked to the side and his cheek was already reddening. He slowly turned his head back to stare at me, eyes burning.

"That's why I run," I seethed and tried to yank my arm free from his grasp to no avail. "So I don't fucking kill you."

His hand on my arm tightened and he leaned closer, bringing his face inches from mine. "You can't kill me, baby."

"There you go again, *baby*," I mocked his term of endearment. "You're underestimating me."

He gave me a sardonic smile. "I'm not underestimating you. Despite what I've done, you still love me, no matter how much you wish you didn't."

With my free hand I shoved him back. All my push did was make his shoulder move a little. "You're right. I do love you," I snapped and shoved him harder. This time he moved back a small step. "But I also hate you." I shoved him again, forcing him back just a little more.

"No, you don't. You just want to hate me," he snapped back.

"Yes, I do." I slammed my fist on his chest. "I hate you for what you did to us." I started smacking his face, his chest. He tried to block my hits by holding up his arm, but at this point it didn't matter. I didn't care where I hit him. I just had to hit him somewhere. So I settled for his arm. "You did this. You broke the last piece of me." Jamie caught my wrist to stop me from hitting him. "You, Louie, our daughter were my everything." My voice broke. "Losing her was my fault, but you broke our family and I hate you for it."

He released my arm and slid his fingers behind my neck, pulling me to his chest and forcing me to look up at him. His other arm wrapped around my lower back, careful of my wounds that weren't fully healed. "You're right. It's my fault. Not Louie's. Just mine. I was spiraling and I pulled him down with me," he said with disdain. "But losing our baby wasn't your fault."

I shook my head and tried to pull away. He wouldn't release me.

"You killed who was at fault, Maura." His words were filled with so much conviction. "If you didn't believe that to be true, you wouldn't have spent the past four months killing every one of those Aryan fucks. You did what most couldn't, and I am so fucking in awe of you."

With his eyes locked with mine and his beliefs boring into me through them, I wanted to believe what he was saying was true.

He moved his hand from the back of my neck to cup my cheek. "Let go of that guilt, baby."

I turned my face away from his hand. "Let me go."

He released me and I backed away. I looked down in an attempt to hide what I was feeling. "Just get some fucking sleep," I grumbled and started for the bathroom again.

"Are you sure you hate me?" he asked, making me pause.

"If I truly did, it'd make me a hypocrite, wouldn't it?" I said over my shoulder. I didn't know why I said that. Maybe it was because I was overwhelmed with the rawness of everything that had just happened or maybe I just didn't care about the consequences anymore. Either way, what I had said was true. Jamie, I, and even Louie were all guilty of hurting each other. At least what they had done had been out of fear and the need to keep me safe. Louie had gotten shot because of my need for revenge.

"What do you mean by that?" Jamie asked.

I turned slightly so I could see in his eyes that he knew exactly what I meant. "If you insist on not leaving, I'll get up with the baby tonight," I said and went into the bathroom.

CHAPTER TEN

The next morning, I was woken by the baby fussing and the sound of a male voice. I opened my eyes just in time to see Stefan scoop the baby out of the bassinet. Stefan handled the tiny human with ease and clear experience as he rocked and bounced his arms a little. Even though Stefan was my father and that was evidence enough that he had experience, I still found it odd seeing him like that.

He caught me staring and a small smile tugged at the corner of his mouth. "I remember when you were this little."

I sat up in bed, feeling stiff, but not in much pain today. "He's hungry."

"A bottle is being made," Stefan said as he watched me reach for my pain meds on the nightstand. "I've asked Brody to hire a nanny."

I twisted the pill bottle in my hand as I debated if I should even take them. "Why?"

"I have your bottle, little man," Brody cooed as he walked in with said bottle in hand. He gave me a smile. "How are you feeling today, Maura?"

"I'm fine," I said as I watched Stefan hand the baby off to him.

Brody's smile turned tight, and he met Stefan's eyes. They seemed to communicate something with the look they exchanged before Brody took the baby over to the chair in the corner so he could feed him.

I stared at Stefan expectantly. He had yet to answer my question.

Stefan read that I was waiting. "You need to be focusing on healing and Jamie needs to sleep before he falls over, or worse, gets himself killed."

"I tried to get Jamie to go to his own room last night. The stubborn bastard refused to leave," I grumbled. "I got up with the baby through the night so he would get some rest at least."

"That's not good enough," Stefan said.

"I still don't think it's necessary to go through all the trouble of hiring someone if the baby might not be sticking around," I said.

I caught Brody looking from me to Stefan, who was staring at me intently. "Have you decided what you plan on doing with him, then?" Stefan asked.

"I can't keep him, Stefan," I said.

Stefan's eyes narrowed. "Why do you feel like you can't keep him?"

Feeling the intensity of his stare, I wanted to look away. I knew I couldn't. "That baby deserves better than this life."

"Then shall we drop him off at a fire station and hope he gets placed in a good home?" Stefan was goading me. When I didn't fall for it, he pushed some more. "You felt the same way about your baby, yet you were going to find a way to do it."

He might as well have gut-punched me, bringing her into this. "This isn't my baby."

"You care for him like he is," Stefan pointed out. "Our life may not be ideal, Maura, but don't forget that this baby was born from a criminal far worse than us."

Brody spoke first before I could argue. "You don't have to make any decisions right now, Maura. If you want to research other options, then fine. We won't deter you from doing that. In the meantime, as you come up with your decision, we will be getting a nanny to help out." Brody locked eyes with Stefan and this time I could see that he was conveying to my father to stand down.

Surprisingly, Stefan did. "Brody's right. Nothing needs to be decided right now."

"What you should decide right now is a name for him," Brody said, staring down at the baby with a smile. "Personally, I think he looks like a Hunter or an Emmet."

I couldn't stop my nose from scrunching, making Stefan huff a laugh. "She doesn't like those."

"Take some time to think on it, but not too much time. I'm going to need one to give to the nanny when we hire one," Brody said and stood. "I can take him again today to let you rest."

"Are you planning on leaving the manor with him?" I asked.

Brody looked like he was trying not to smile. "I figured we'd go for a walk and get some fresh air after I got him dressed."

I reached toward my nightstand for the new phone I'd had Dean get me because Buck had destroyed mine. I shot a text to my goons.

"I have security that can go with them," Stefan said, figuring out what I was doing.

"I only trust my goons," I said.

Stefan rolled his eyes. "You don't trust anyone else because you think I'll use them to spy on you."

I gave him a look that dared him to deny it.

"What are you going to do when you're healed?" he deflected. "You need to have all of your security protecting you."

I'd cross that road when I came to it.

"How about a compromise?" Stefan asked. "You send one of yours and I'll send one of mine with Brody and the baby."

Asher and Dean appeared in my doorway at that moment.

"Brody wants to take the baby on a walk for some fresh air," I told them. "Can one of you go? You'll be accompanied by one of Stefan's goons."

"I'll go," Asher volunteered.

"It's settled, then," Brody said, heading for the door.

"Wait," I said, stopping him. "Since I have you all here, I want to hire the best fighting teacher there is in both weapons and hand-to-hand."

"For you?" Stefan asked.

"For Brenna," I said, making Dean and Asher smirk knowingly.

"I can reach out to your old self-defense instructor," Brody offered.

I had to fight not to smile. "Brenna is too advanced for him." I glanced at Stefan and found him staring at me with confusion showing on his face. The corner of my mouth lifted a tiny bit.

He took in my tiny smile with a slight tilt of his head. "You've been training her?"

"Did you think I'd let her continue to be docile? In this family?" I shook my head.

Stefan seemed impressed. "I'd thought it stupidly stubborn of you to call on a seventeen-year-old girl to come and help you. Now I see that wasn't the case."

"That seventeen-year-old girl killed three out of those four Aryans we hung from that bridge. She also helped me play target practice outside that bakery in Hartford," I said.

Stefan's face became schooled. "Let me assign security to the baby and I'll find Brenna a teacher."

Of course he'd use this to get something he wanted. "Fine, but after you find the best teacher for her. If you need help narrowing down the right one, ask Asher, Dean, or Finn. They've overseen her training so far."

Stefan nodded and he left with Brody, the baby, and Asher. Dean lingered in my doorway.

I arched a brow at him.

He nodded at the pill bottle in my hand. "Did you take those?"

I shook my head and set the bottle back on my nightstand. "I don't have much pain today."

He reached into his pocket of his black cargo pants and pulled out a joint and a lighter. "Then do you want to get some fresh air, too?"

I snorted.

He tilted his head toward the hall behind him. "Let's go into the living room. It'll give you a change of scenery."

I climbed out of bed and followed him into the living room. We both took a seat on the couch facing each other. Dean lit the joint and took the first couple of puffs, then held it out to me.

I took it. "I like your idea of fresh air."

He smiled a little. "I figured you'd prefer this over a stroll along the property line when you need to de-stress."

I took a hit and released it slowly. "Apparently I've become transparent."

"Anyone with eyes can see that you've been keeping shit bottled in."

I handed him the joint. "I'm processing in my own way."

"What happened when you were taken or all of it?" he asked.

"All of it." I laid the side of my head on the back of the

couch. "Being back home feels different, yet the same. It's because I'm different."

He blew the smoke through his nostrils and relaxed back against the couch with me. "You've been through hell. You can't expect to jump back into your life like nothing has happened."

He was right.

The sound of shuffling feet came from the hallway. Dean and I both glanced in that direction. Brenna was zombie-ing her way toward the kitchen in black cotton sleep shorts and a matching black crop top. She was rubbing her eye as she let out a big yawn. Her blonde shoulder-length hair was a mess.

Dean and I watched quietly as she grabbed a mug from a cabinet and went over to the coffee maker. After she filled her mug, she turned around and leaned back against the kitchen counter. She took a sip with her eyes closed. With a sigh, she finally looked over at us. "It's eight in the morning. Don't you think it's a little early to smoke weed?"

Dean and I responded at the same time. "No."

***

The weed this morning had been nice. I was feeling more relaxed than I had in a long fucking time. I should have just spent the whole day getting high. However, that first joint gave me the munchies, and those munchies took me to the kitchen where I saw the liquor cabinet. The idea of a buzz sounded too good to pass up. So I traded eating junk food for a nice finger of whiskey in a crystal tumbler. After three of those, I went from feeling relaxed to feeling weightless. All my worries, guilt, heartbreak lifted off of me. They were still floating nearby in a sense, but I wasn't carrying them at the moment.

I actually got dressed. Since I'd been home, I'd been wearing nothing but sweats or pajamas. I put on jeans and a green T-shirt and immediately I felt somewhat human. Forgoing the glass, I began drinking the whiskey straight from the bottle. I went into the living room and connected my phone to the stereo system. As soon as the music started, I turned the volume almost all the way up.

I didn't just want to be weightless. I wanted to feel good. I wanted to feel joy and dancing was something I'd used to enjoy. I took a swig of whiskey as I swayed and bounced a little, trying to find the rhythm.

Dean and Brenna came into the living room at the same time, both wide-eyed. Once they saw me, Dean frowned, and Brenna looked like she was trying not to laugh. I gestured for Brenna to come to me. She ventured over. Once she was close enough, I grabbed her hand and pulled on her to dance with me. I saw rather than heard her laugh because the music was so loud. She held her hand out for the whiskey bottle.

I handed it over as I mouthed, "Just a sip."

She rolled her eyes and brought the bottle to her lips. The moment she tasted the whiskey, her nose scrunched up, making me chuckle. I grabbed the bottle back from her, took another drink, and got back to dancing. Brenna swayed with me at first until the stiffness left her and she began to dance more fluidly.

Many songs passed, a good amount of whiskey was drunk, and Brenna and I hadn't stopped dancing. Dean hadn't stopped or interrupted us, either. He stood in the kitchen, arms crossed over his chest as he watched us with his resting bitch face. At some point Asher had returned and joined him in the kitchen.

I bumped into Brenna a few times and actually laughed about it. That seemed to surprise her in a good way because after the shock wore off, she smiled brightly.

I was riding a good buzz, feeling tiny sparks of joy, when

suddenly the music was turned off. I whirled around to see who had done it. Jamie was standing in front of the stereo.

"Oh, joy, you're here," I said caustically.

Jamie eyed the whiskey bottle in my hand with a tight jaw. Then he looked at Brenna and my goons. "Can you give us a moment?"

"She's just having a little fun, Jameson," Brenna said. "She deserves it."

Jamie met my eyes. "You know what will happen if you mix pain meds and too much alcohol."

I did know. That was why I hadn't had a drink the whole time I'd been home. I hadn't taken any pain meds today. Jamie didn't know that, though. Given he'd ruined the slightest bit of fun I'd had in I couldn't remember how long, I felt like being an evil bitch. "What I do is none of your business."

"It becomes my business if you do something that will hurt yourself," he snapped.

I gasped and I put my hand to my chest in mock disbelief. "I had no idea." Silence filled the room, and I could feel all of their surprise. "So how do you plan to stop me?"

Anger burned in Jamie's eyes at my challenge. When he didn't answer, I gave him a sardonic smile before turning and leaving the living room.

I felt him behind me as I stepped into my room. He followed me in and slammed the door closed. I spun around to face him.

He held his hand out. "Give me the bottle, Maura."

I held the bottle out of his reach. "If you want it, you'll have to take it from me."

I could see that he was considering it.

"There he is," I taunted. "How are you going to force your will on me, the dumb woman, this time?"

"This is different and you know it," he seethed.

It was, but I didn't care. I wanted him to snap, to stop being patient, and I was curious how long I'd have to push him to see it happen.

He tried to snatch the bottle from me, and I stepped out of reach just in time. He tried again and again. I moved away from him each time. Clearly fed up, he stormed toward me, and I retreated backward until my butt ran into the dresser, then I moved to the side until I was backed up against the wall. I stared him down with a smirk as I let him take the bottle from my hands. He slammed it on top of the dresser and caged me in by putting his hands on the wall next to my shoulders.

This moment felt like a power play. I wouldn't let him win. I slid my hands over his waist.

Beneath his clothes, I felt his body stiffen. As his eyes bounced all over my face, the anger in them extinguished. "What are you playing at?"

"Afraid I'll kick you in the balls again?" I goaded, bringing up the last time I'd come onto him after he'd found Brenna and me dancing in a club.

His face hardened and he surprised me when his hands dropped from the wall to the backs of my thighs. He lifted me up and I locked my legs around his waist. He held me up with one arm under my butt and his other hand went back on the wall by my head.

I ran my hand over his shoulder to the back of his neck. My fingers slid into his short, brown hair and fisted it. "I guess you were."

He leaned into me, pushing his body against mine. His hand dropped from the wall, and he cupped my jaw and throat, holding my face still as his mouth hovered over mine. "Is this what you want, baby?"

I pushed my mouth closer until it lightly touched his. "I don't think you can handle what I want, *baby*."

He snapped, but in a different way than I'd originally

planned. His mouth slammed down onto mine. His lips devoured mine with four months of pent-up intensity. For a split second, I had a moment where I knew I could choose to push him away or I could give in to that intensity.

I kissed him back, stroking my tongue with his. He let out a small groan like me giving in felt like the best fucking thing in the world. He pushed against me even harder, grinding himself between my legs. My back rubbed against the wall, making me tense up and wince.

He ripped his mouth from mine and pulled me from the wall. "Damnit!"

"It's fine. Keep going," I assured, and I tried to kiss him again.

He pulled away with his eyes squeezed shut. He let out a frustrated breath. "Why are we doing this, Maura?"

Well, that killed the mood. I unlocked my legs from his waist. "Why do you have to ask questions right now?" He set me on my feet, and I moved over near the bed to put some space between us. "The whole point is to not think."

"So you were using me?"

I pinched the bridge of my nose. "Do you want to fight or do you want to fuck, Jamie?"

"You're drunk, Maura," he snapped.

I was buzzed, not drunk, but right now, I was beginning to wish I was.

He put his hands on his hips. "You were being reckless."

"Christ, Jamie! I haven't taken any pain meds today," I snapped.

He went quiet for a moment as he frowned at me, confused. "Then why didn't you say anything?"

"I. Do. Not. Have. To. Explain. Myself. To. You." Looked like we were going to fight. Fortunately, I could get pleasure from that, too.

"You do if you want to fuck me," he snapped.

"I'll blame that lapse of judgment on whiskey." I looked him up and down, unimpressed. "Good thing you stopped. If that kiss was anything to go by, I was saved from a boring time of lovemaking."

"And how would you have wanted me to fuck you, Maura?"

"Like you fucking hate me, Jameson." Although the thought of him doing that sounded like a good time, it was a lie to save face.

The look he gave me told me he couldn't decide if he wanted to kill me or fuck me, and either way it excited me. Now I was a tiny bit bummed he'd chosen to fight over bumping uglies.

"Well, I don't particularly like you right now," he said.

"The feeling is mutual, buddy." Needing one more jab, I smirked. "See, I told you that you couldn't handle what I wanted."

He let out a curse and came to me in just a few strides. His hand grabbed me by the back of my neck and he pulled me to him, molding the fronts of our bodies together. His mouth captured mine with a brutal kiss, forcing from me a moan that should have been embarrassing.

Jamie pulled away from me again just as my legs were beginning to go weak. This time he was the one who put space between us. "Why do you want me to fuck you like that?"

I sighed in frustration. Both emotional and sexual.

"Why ask that of me now when you're hurt?" he asked. "Are you hoping I'd hurt you more?"

"I find this good-guy side of you a real mood-killer," I said dryly. He had it all wrong.

He stared at me with his stupid perceptive eyes, and I knew I was about to regret all of this.

"What did you mean last night about being a hypocrite?"

That had the same effect as an ice-cold shower. "Get out."

He ignored me. "Why haven't you gone to see Louie? You've been home a week."

"Why are you asking questions ya already know the fucking answer to?"

He ran his fingers through his hair. "You pulled this shit with Louie at the cabin."

I shook my head. "This is not the same, Jamie."

He didn't seem to believe me. "I don't have any room to lecture you and I haven't endured nearly as much as you have since we lost our baby," he said in a tone that was as gentle as it was firm. "But I know what it's like to spiral and you're spiraling."

I kept my voice calm. "I'm not spiraling, Jamie."

"Then what was this?" He gestured from me to him. "Or what was that between you and Louie at the cabin? You want us to hurt you to satisfy your guilt. I wouldn't be surprised if you weren't all that upset over the beating Buck gave you."

"No, I'm not upset over that—"

He interrupted me with a curse. "You went into that hospital room knowing it was a trap, didn't you?"

Since my talk with Stefan yesterday, I had done my best to let myself feel, instead of burying myself in my darkness. Right now, though, I was tempted to retreat back into it and feel almost nothing again. "Are you ready to listen now?" I asked him calmly. When he didn't respond, I took that as an answer. "One, I am not spiraling. If I was, I would have taken my pain meds and drunk a hell of a lot more whiskey. Two, yes, I wanted Louie to hurt me to satisfy my guilt. We had just killed Alex and I was in a fucked-up place. Three, I'm not upset over what Buck did to me. Not because I felt like I deserved it." Anger seeped into my voice with what I said next. "He didn't deserve anything from me but the death I gave him. I'm not broken over being whipped and beaten because I had accepted what might happen to me when I walked into Amelia's hospital room. Which brings us to four: yes, I did go into that hospital room knowing it was a trap, and because of that decision, Louie almost died. I haven't gone to see him because I knew I needed to face my guilt first and it nearly tore me apart yesterday. Someone I love almost died because of me again and that is the worst feeling in the world." I took a deep breath to calm myself. "Lastly, five, I don't know what is happening with us. I just know that I'm angry with you and I have so much rage in me that needs an outlet. I just look at you and it comes out of me without thought. You deserve some of it and the rest is just me being cruel. I love you, Jamie. Even though you hurt me, I never stopped. I want more than anything to forgive you, but I am terrified to trust you and I am so mad at you for that." As that vulnerability left my mouth, I itched to be cruel to him all over again.

The muscles in his jaw clenched as he processed everything I had said. Before he was ready to say anything at all, his phone in his pocket started ringing. He didn't reach for it right away, nor did he look away from me. After three rings, he reached into his pocket and read the contact lighting up the screen of his phone, which I could see was Stefan. He declined the call and put his phone back in his pocket. "I need to go," he said and headed for the door. As he reached the doorknob, he stilled. "Go see Louie. He took a bullet for you. It's the least you can do." With that said, he walked out, slamming the door behind him.

I went into the bathroom and splashed cool water on my face in order to calm down. With water dripping off my chin, I stared at myself in the mirror. The bruising on my face and neck had faded to yellow. My vision glazed out as my thoughts took over and I tried to find the nerve to do what I needed to. When nothing seemed to change, I blinked. "Fuck it."

I left the bathroom, then my bedroom. I passed Dean in the living room.

"Everything alright?" he asked.

"I'm going to the main house for a while," I said over my shoulder as I walked out of the guest house.

I stormed through the main house, passing cameras and goons. I ran into Stefan in the foyer.

He paused when he saw me. "Maura?"

I didn't say anything to him as I passed and began my way up the stairs. If I stopped to talk to him, I'd find a reason to turn back.

Jamie had said Louie was in the room across from his and that was where I ended up. I debated knocking for a second, then just grabbed the doorknob and twisted it to open the door.

I walked in, finding only half of the curtains drawn back. There was just enough light to see that his bed was empty. At that moment, the door to the en suite opened and Louie came out slowly, stiffly, and clearly in pain.

He was in nothing more than gray sweatpants. His middle was entirely wrapped in thick bandaging. Two steps into the room, he noticed me.

He took me in from head to toe and back up again. A tired but genuine smile graced his face. "Hello, beautiful."

Hearing his voice drowned me in guilt. Tears filled my eyes and with a broken voice I blurted, "I'm so sorry."

CHAPTER ELEVEN

louie

I was finally strong enough to walk to and from the bathroom on my own. Sure, it wore my ass out each time, but it was worth it. Before, Jameson or one of the house staff had had to help me, which was not only inconvenient, it did a number on my pride.

Downside to my newest achievement was that it pointed out how I wouldn't make it if I tried to go see Maura. She had been home a week now and it was killing me not to see her. I felt like a broken record asking Jameson everyday about her and how she was doing.

"She's focusing on healing," was his answer almost every time. I could tell that he was holding shit back from me, and ever since yesterday, I'd known without a doubt. Jameson had come to see me early in the afternoon looking fucking broken.

"She doesn't trust me. She has every right not to trust me," he had said as he'd stared out the window.

"Did something happen?" I had asked.

"Shit came to a head today and I had to just stand by and do nothing. I don't know how to help her. She won't let me help her." He had sounded so frustrated and helpless.

In that moment, I would have given anything to go see her. I had been tempted to say fuck it and go. I would've crawled to the guest house if I'd had to. Then I'd remembered that Stefan had threatened to send me back to the hospital if I left my room before Dr. Ben cleared me.

"You can't give up, Jameson." Encouraging him had been all I could do on my end, and I had to hope that it'd be enough.

Pulling myself back to the present, I dried my wet hands on a towel before opening the bathroom door. I took two steps out of the small room and noticed I wasn't alone. Maura was standing in the middle of my room. It was a shock because for a moment all I could do was stare at her, hoping she was real. I took in every gorgeous inch of her just to make sure. I spotted the yellowish bruises on her face and neck right away. The evidence of what Buck and the Aryans had done to her pissed me off, but the relief of seeing her stand there smothered it. I wanted so badly to touch her, hold her, and not let go. Before I gave in to the urge to do that, I tested the waters with a smile. "Hello, beautiful."

Her reaction wasn't what I expected. Her brow scrunched up as tears filled her alluring green eyes. "I'm so sorry." Her knees buckled and she dropped to the floor.

Out of instinct, I rushed to her, hoping to catch her. The feeling of pain and pulling in my abdomen made me grit my teeth as I knelt on the floor in front of her. Her hands were fisting her hair as she stared at the carpet. I grabbed her wrists and gently tugged on her hands to release her hair before taking the back of her neck and pulling her to my chest. I hugged her the best I could without touching her back.

I felt tears drip and slide down my chest. Her body shook. "I'm so sorry," she said again.

I kissed the top of her head, then her temple, breathing her in as I did. Having her in my arms made me realize how starved I was of her. "Shh, it's okay."

"No, it's not." She pulled her head from my chest, bringing us face-to-face, her mouth a breath from my own. She stared at me with sad eyes, and I just wanted to take that sadness away.

"It's okay," I assured and pressed my lips to hers with a brief kiss, then another, and another. In between each kiss, I told her that it was okay, and each time she softened against me and kissed me back until our kisses stopped being brief. Her hands moved up my chest, behind my neck, and her fingers slid up into my hair. She clung to me and kissed me with needy desperation, which I reciprocated. I had missed her so much and if we didn't stop soon, I'd fuck her on this floor. I didn't care how badly it'd hurt. I'd find a way to find pleasure in it.

Maura's hands dropped back to my chest, and she pushed a little as she tore her mouth from mine. "I can't. You don't understand."

I brushed some of her hair from her face and tucked it behind her ear. "What don't I understand?"

"I knew, Louie," she said, her eyes full of what looked like guilt. "At the hospital, deep down I knew it was a trap and I went into Amelia's room anyway."

Silence stretched between us as I absorbed what she'd said. She tried to pull away. I grabbed her arm and gave her a stern look. She wasn't going to pull that running-away shit with me.

"You could have gotten yourself killed," I practically growled.

"I didn't care."

"Obviously," I snapped. "You didn't care about anything or anyone." What I found surprising was, I understood why she had done it. I wasn't even mad that I'd been shot. Well...no, I was pissed about that, but I didn't put that on her. It was her complete self-disregard that made me livid.

I let her go and struggled to stand. She tried to help me. "I got it," I snapped and got to my feet. I put a hand over where I'd been shot as I walked back to the bed. "The shitty thing is that I don't feel like I can be mad at you right now because I feel like I owe you for the shit I pulled," I said angrily as I ripped back the blankets and fixed my pillows.

"You're allowed to be angry at me," she said from where she stood on the other side of the bed.

I huffed. "Thanks for the permission." I winced the whole time as I climbed into bed. Maura watched as I got settled. "You've lost your high ground with this, Maura. All three of us have fucked up and have ended up hurting each other. We need to work on how to repair us. Especially you and Jameson."

She folded her arms over her chest. "You want me to forgive him?"

"Yes." I wasn't going to ask her if she forgave me, because after the shit she'd pulled, we were fucking even. Not that it was a competition. What I had done didn't compare to what she had done, and I'd use that to my advantage if it meant that I could fix things between all three of us.

"Forgiving him isn't the issue," she said.

She didn't trust him. Trust was the issue. "Apply that intense need for revenge you felt to the fear Jameson and I felt after we lost the baby and almost you. Maybe then you might understand."

She looked away from me, clearly seething. I could see that she wanted to tell me to fuck off, but she held it back. "How do I know you two won't do it again?"

"How do I know you won't go do something reckless like purposely walk into a trap again? We still haven't figured who betrayed the family," I said. "You're not the only one who needs to learn how to trust again. At least I'm willing to try."

"What if trust isn't the only issue?" she asked. "What if

everything has changed us too much?"

I knew she was talking about herself. Out of the three of us, the change in her was the most notable. She was colder, withdrawn, and so serious all the time. I missed her sass and warmth. "If we've changed, we still need to give each other a chance."

She looked uncertain.

"You need to try, Maura, and I want you to come visit me every day until I'm healed," I said.

She gave me a defiant look. "And if I don't?"

"Then I'll tell Stefan about your suicidal tendencies."

Her mouth dropped open. "You're blackmailing me?"

"You bet your perfect ass I am." I pulled back the blankets on the other side of the bed. "Now lay down with me for a while."

She looked ready to argue.

"Don't test me, princess," I told her.

She exhaled heavily through her nose, and I wouldn't have been surprised if there had been smoke with how pissed she looked. Reluctantly, she lay down flat on her back. Staring up at the ceiling, she grumbled, "What now?"

The corner of my mouth lifted. "You might be more comfortable if you took your jeans off."

The glare she gave me warned me not to push it. It made me chuckle. The moment my body started to shake, pain erupted in my abdomen. "Don't make me laugh," I groaned.

I woke when I heard the bedroom door open and then close. I lifted my head from behind Maura's to see. Jameson was walking toward the bed with the baby I had yet to meet in his arms. He looked from me to Maura, who was still asleep.

I had put the TV on not long after she had climbed into bed next to me. Within a half hour of the TV being on, she had fallen asleep. Since then, she had migrated to the center of the bed, the place she had always slept between Jameson and me.

"Looks like you're getting along with the baby," I whispered.

Jameson ignored my comment. "What happened?"

I shook my head slightly. "Don't worry about it." Jameson didn't need to know about my deal with Maura.

Trusting me, Jameson didn't push to know. Instead, he lay down on the side of the bed Maura had vacated and adjusted the baby so that he was lying on his tummy on Jameson's chest. The little guy's head was turned to face me. He was sucking on a pacifier with a teddy bear on it. I noticed his bright blue eyes first and how they caught sight of Maura right away.

Maura, who I had thought was asleep, reached up and ran her finger over the baby's cheek, adoringly. Jameson's eyes met mine and I knew what he was trying to convey. Maura cared for this baby, more than she wanted to admit, according to Jameson. Right now, he was making sure I saw the evidence of that.

"Can I hold him?" I asked.

I felt Maura still against me for a second. Then she sat up and I did the same, just a lot slower. She took the baby from Jameson and when I was ready, she placed him in my arms. "Make sure you hold his head," she instructed.

"I know. I read the baby books," I said.

"You read the baby books?" Jameson asked, sounding like he didn't believe me.

As I stared down at the baby, feeling extremely grateful the kid looked more like his mother than his father, I answered, "I downloaded them on my phone and read when I could."

Both Maura and Jameson had gone quiet, and I saw they were trying to mask the sadness they were feeling.

"Does this little guy have a name?" I asked, changing the subject.

Maura sighed. "No."

I reached over and grabbed my phone off the nightstand. The small movement still made me wince, but I pushed through the discomfort. I looked up baby names on the internet. "Pick a letter?"

Maura thought about it for a second. "K."

I clicked on K and started listing off names. Maura vetoed almost every name I said. Things got interesting when Jameson turned down a name.

"I like the name Keegan," Maura grumbled.

"His name isn't Keegan," Jameson said.

"What about Kieran? It means 'little dark one,'" I suggested.

"It's quite fitting," Jameson muttered.

"I really like the name, but not the meaning. I don't want him thinking we named him that because of who his father was or the gang he was born into." Maura held a distant, sullen look as she spoke.

I glanced at Jameson, and he was watching her, taking in what I'd already seen.

"It doesn't matter what the meaning is if you really like the name," he said to her.

"Or we could apply the meaning to him being a mobster's son," I said.

Maura tensed up and I realized my mistake.

"I'm tired of going over names," she said as she took the baby from me.

Jameson and I watched as she clambered out of the bed and headed for the door. I ran my hand through my hair frustratedly. "Shit."

Jameson sighed, sounding just as frustrated, and left to follow Maura.

CHAPTER TWELVE

maura

Another week passed. During that time, a lot happened. I visited Louie every day. At first, I told myself that the only reason I was visiting him was because I owed him and because he was blackmailing me. After two days of visiting, I caught myself looking forward to seeing him. Stefan found a teacher for Brenna, and she had already started training with him. Brody hired a nanny, who would be moving into the manor in two days to help us take care of baby Kieran. I'd ended up choosing that name, despite its meaning. Jamie and Louie had seemed pleased I'd decided on that name as well. Part of me felt like I shouldn't feel good that they were pleased about anything, but apparently the rest of me was a masochist. Jamie still stayed overnight in my room to help with Kieran. Thanks to Louie, all interactions I'd had with Jamie had been civil. A little too civil, apparently, because he kept staring at me like I was up to something. That made me assume Louie hadn't told Jamie of our deal.

It was the middle of the night, and the baby woke both of us. Jamie got up with him and was able to get him back to sleep pretty quickly. I couldn't fall back to sleep. Instead, I found myself watching Jamie. He still looked exhausted as hell, and with how he was rubbing his neck, the chair was evidently a shitty place to sleep.

I sat up and scooted out of the middle of the bed to one side. "My neck is hurting just watching you. Sleep in the damn bed, Jamie," I said, sounding put off as I grabbed a pillow and put it in the middle of the bed as a barrier between us.

Jamie didn't get up from the chair.

"Now who's being stubborn?" I goaded, and it worked. He went to the other side of the bed, toed off his shoes, and slid under the blankets. I lay on my side, giving him my back.

It didn't take long for his breathing to even out. I ignored the temptation to roll over for as long as I could, but I eventually gave in. I turned over and stared at his sleeping face. For a little while, I allowed myself to remember us—something I'd done my best to avoid for months. Before, I hadn't been able to handle the pain on top of everything else. It had been easier to focus on the anger. I wasn't angry with him or Louie anymore.

I lay there until the early morning hours. When sleep clearly became a lost cause, I got out of bed and ventured to the main house. There was somewhere I needed to go, and I couldn't put it off any longer.

As I approached my old bedroom, my feet slowed to a stop. Memories overwhelmed me. I stared down at the carpet in the hall. Any evidence that I had been lying there bleeding and dying was gone.

I closed my eyes to steel myself for what I was about to do. No. What I had to do. When I opened them again, I was determined, and I'd found strength.

I opened my bedroom door. Inside, I expected to see destruction. I had heard Jamie had trashed the room after the attack. As I walked in, everything for the most part was where it should be. A few pieces of furniture had been replaced. So had the lamp I had broken—the one I had shattered with a log of wood to make the room completely dark so I could hide from Alex Roth.

I looked around and faced the memories, the pain. It wasn't easy, but it wasn't as hard as it had been when I'd woken up in the hospital to Jamie and Louie holding each of my hands. Jamie had been the one to tell me what we had lost. There had been so much sadness in his eyes, yet he had been so strong as he had delivered the news he'd known would break me.

As I looked around my old room, I tried to think back to before the attack. The time after I'd killed my cheating boyfriend. There had been ups and downs, loyalties earned, love and death. It hadn't been a large span of time, but it had been pivotal. It had showed me who I really was. These past four months had made me accept it.

I went over to my closet and opened the door. I stepped inside and eyed all of the designer suits Stefan had bought me. I ran my hands over the tailored fabrics until I found the one I was looking for. I took it down from the rack and went back into the bedroom. I laid the suit on the bed. As I stared down at it, I pulled my phone from the pocket of my pajama pants. I dialed Dean's number. It rang three times before a tired and grumpy voice answered.

"Hello?"

"Good morning, Grumpy."

There was silence for a heartbeat or two. "What time is it?" he asked.

"It's time to get back to work."

I had Dean, Asher, Brenna, Finn, and Vincent meet me in my bedroom in the main house. Dean, Asher, and Brenna arrived first because they lived in the guest house. Finn and Vincent had to travel from their homes. Dean and Asher had their own homes, too, but ever since Alex Roth had snuck into the house, they'd pretty much moved in to help keep me safe. At first, everyone was surprised where I had chosen to meet, and I caught each of them glancing around.

Brenna was the quickest to get over the shock. "So who are we killing today, cousin?"

Dean turned his grumpy attention on her. "Why do you think we're killing someone?"

Brenna looked at me with a smirk. "Why else would she call all of us here?"

I was standing in front of the fireplace, the same place I had stood as I'd warned Alex Roth what would happen if he killed me. Only he hadn't killed me, and I'd still followed through with my threat. Brenna, Vincent, and my goons were either standing around or sitting on the couch and chair in the small seating area in front of me.

"She wants to attend the family meeting today," Asher said. "Grounds security was informed of it a few days ago."

"How'd you find out?" Brenna asked.

"To keep Maura safe, I make it a point to always be aware of what is happening in this very large house at all times. If there ends up being anything worth mentioning, I inform Maura," Asher replied.

Today's family meeting was only part of what I'd called them here for. "I'm pretty sure I know who sent the Aryans after me."

Silence fell upon the room for a few heartbeats.

"Who do you think it is?" Vincent, the nineteen-year-old hacker genius, asked. He had dyed his hair lime green since I'd last seen him, which had been before I'd been taken. I hadn't seen Finn since then, either. Brenna had told me they had tried visiting the day after I had returned to Quinn Manor, but I had been sleeping. I'd called them the next day to tell them that I'd been alright and to enjoy their time home. After being away for so long, I'd known Finn was eager to be with his son, and Vincent was a major introvert.

I met Brenna's Quinn green eyes. After a moment of staring at each other, I saw the flicker of understanding in them. "It's Dylan, isn't it?" she asked.

I caught the way Dean and Asher looked at each other with worry. They both knew what it meant for me if Dylan had betrayed the family again.

"That makes sense," Finn said.

"How sure are you?" Dean asked me, his voice sharp with agitation.

Having heard it, too, everyone's heads turned toward him.

Brenna looked from Dean to me. "What's going on?"

Dean didn't answer. He expected me to.

"In order to spare Dylan from being executed along with your father, I took responsibility for him," I said.

Finn let out a curse and Brenna's face went a little pale.

"What does that mean?" Vincent asked.

Dean leaned forward on the couch and set his elbows on his knees before he ran his hands down his face. "Stefan threatened to kill her if Dylan destroys the family."

"What?!" Brenna blurted, then shook her head quickly. "He wouldn't do that."

"He hasn't destroyed the family, but his mistakes are my mistakes, and I will have to answer for them if we don't handle this discreetly," I said calmly. I went on to tell them the conversation I'd overheard Buck and his fellow Aryan having when I'd been captured.

"Other than Stefan, Dylan is the only other male with the Quinn last name here in New Haven." Brenna said what I had already deduced. "We have distant cousins who have the surname Quinn, but they're all in Boston."

"Samuel was the one who oversaw the new security systems that were put into the manor, his house, and many other properties that belong to the family. It's how we found out where he was storing the money he'd been stealing," Vincent said. "I wouldn't doubt that the contractor who installed all of the security systems created plans or blueprints of where everything, such as the cameras, wiring, and the system's main hub, would be placed in the house. There's a possibility that Samuel had a copy of those plans and Dylan had access to them."

"That could explain how Alex Roth got into this room without being seen," Asher said.

"Vincent, I want you to look into Dylan. I want concrete evidence," I ordered. I didn't want to have any doubts that it was him. The last thing we needed was to get it wrong and be blindsided by the real traitor.

"Stefan already has Aiden's security firm investigating everyone. I don't think I'll find anything they haven't," Vincent said.

"With a large investigation like this, they look at call history, GPS in the car, emails, web searches, bank accounts," Asher said.

"Which means they aren't being creative in their searches. Your searches are," I said to Vincent.

Vincent nodded and pulled his laptop from his computer bag he carried everywhere.

I looked to Dean, Asher, and Finn. "I need you three to go retrieve Dylan."

Dean stood from the couch and the three of them left.

It had been over an hour since I'd sent my goons to go retrieve Dylan and I hadn't heard from them. Family meeting was due to start in thirty minutes.

"Want me to call them?" Brenna asked from where she stood, leaning against the doorframe watching me get ready in front of the bathroom vanity. We were back at the guest house.

I paused in the middle of covering up any lingering bruises on my face. "Yes. Find out what the holdup is."

Through the mirror, I watched as Brenna took her phone out of the back pocket of her jean shorts and began dialing. She went into my bedroom as she brought the phone up to her ear. Someone must have answered, because I could hear her talking.

A few minutes later she returned with the phone still held to her ear. "Dean's saying Dylan isn't home. My mother, who's using again, is claiming she hasn't seen him. I guess she's so strung out she has no idea when she last saw him or even what day it is." The anger in Brenna's voice when she spoke of her mother was hard to ignore. I'd make sure to listen to her vent about it later.

"Why hasn't grounds security at your house reported Dylan missing?" I asked.

"There wasn't any security at the house when they got there," she answered. "They want to do more digging around and question the house staff."

I looked at my phone's clock. Dean and Asher wouldn't be here in time for the meeting. I glanced at Brenna and came to a decision. "Tell them to do what they need to. You'll accompany me to the meeting."

Brenna appeared stunned for a second, then quickly recovered and passed on what I said to Dean.

After she hung up, she stared at me, a little panicked. "I don't have anything to wear."

"Raid my closet. If I don't have anything here, you'll have to check my bedroom in the main house."

"Stefan and the leaders won't be thrilled with me attending the meeting. They'll view me as a liability," she said.

"Act like you're supposed to be there, and I will handle the rest."

She nodded and dashed out of the room. I gripped the edge of the bathroom counter with both hands, closed my eyes, and just breathed.

Up until now, I'd been naive, reckless, and arrogant. All three were sure ways to get anyone killed in a world of crime and blood money, where the most dangerous beings thrived or died trying. I'd understood that. I'd grown up learning it and yet I'd still fucked up. I couldn't make those mistakes again.

What Brenna ended up wearing was one of my more modest suits. It was midnight blue and formfitting. Her heels were black satin Louboutins and also mine.

"I can't wear a holster with this," she complained, staring down at her outfit.

I turned around and lifted up the back of my suit jacket, revealing the pistol I had tucked in the back of my pants.

"But I can only carry one gun that way," she grumbled.

I snorted. "We're going to a meeting, not a shootout, Brenna."

"You never know," she said as she placed her gun in the back of her pants. "Oh, before I forget." She reached in her jacket pocket and pulled out a joint and a lighter. "Dean told me to give this to you. He said it's if you can't decide if you need to have sex or smoke a cigarette, whatever that means."

I took them from her with a small smile. "It means if I'm stressed." It was good to have a best friend, even if he was an asshole. I put the lighter and joint in my pocket. "Are we ready?"

Brenna nodded and we headed to the main house.

Goons were already lined up along the hall walls outside the chamber when Brenna and I approached. Brenna walked ahead of me to get the door. It felt like it had been forever since I'd last attended a family meeting, but nothing had changed. As soon as I stepped into the room, voices stopped and heads turned my way.

My spiked burgundy pumps clacked on the floor as I made my way toward my seat. "Gentlemen."

Everyone appeared surprised to see me. Stefan and Jamie were the only ones to quickly mask theirs. Louie's seat was empty.

Rourke smiled at me and leaned back in his chair. "Done slaughtering Aryans, I see."

I took a seat in my chair as Brenna went to stand behind me. I met Stefan's eyes. "Sorry I'm late."

He studied me with a blank face for one heartbeat, then another, until he eventually said, "We were just about to start."

"We were going to discuss all the havoc you've caused in the past month," said a voice to my left.

My attention flicked in that direction. Sean Kelly, who'd used to oversee the Boston area for the family, was the biggest weed supplier on the East Coast, and had taken Dylan's spot at the table, was looking down his nose at me.

"Me?" I said innocently. "What havoc do you mean?"

Rourke snorted. He knew the truth, as I was sure Conor did.

They had yet to accuse me of something, though. So I'd be damned before I admitted to being guilty of anything to Sean.

Sean held his hand out to his enforcer behind him. The enforcer handed him a newspaper. Sean took it and slammed it down on the table in front of me. It was dated back to the day we had hung the Aryans and blown up their properties. "You hung four Aryans with giant shamrocks on their chests from a bridge and blew up four properties that belonged to the Aryans. You've brought a lot of attention on the family with this shit."

The news about the hangings took up the front page. I scooped up the paper and looked it over with a blank face. "Who still reads the paper?" I flipped to the next page to read about the explosions. "I have to say that I'm quite touched, Sean." I folded up the newspaper and laid it in my lap. I wanted to keep it.

He gave me a confused frown. "What?"

"That you think I could do all of that," I said. "But whoever did this...I like their style." I held Sean's yellow-flecked green eyes. "It screams, 'If you fuck with me, I will destroy everything you care about, and when I'm done killing you, I will desecrate your carcass so that everyone else will know who you fucking crossed.'"

The room fell silent.

Sean looked positively enraged. "Did you just threaten me?"

I sat back in my chair with a smirk and dismissed his question by glancing around the room. "Does anyone else at this table have any issues with me or the vacation I took?" I looked from Rourke to Conor. I noticed that Conor was eyeing Brenna.

Conor's attention flicked to me when he felt my stare. "Why is my baby niece standing behind you?"

"Because she isn't a baby anymore, Uncle," I said, holding Conor's eyes.

It took a moment for him to understand what I was saying, but his brows rose slightly, and he glanced back at Brenna.

"A child shouldn't be present for these meetings. It puts us at risk," Sean protested.

He'd had no problem accusing me of murder and arson in front of her one minute ago. *Jackass.*

"If you have an issue with her being here, remove her from the room yourself," Jamie said. The irritation in his tone was blatant and amped up the tension in the room.

Rourke looked from Jamie to Sean with a mischievous grin. "I've heard some interesting rumors about my littlest cousin. I'm kinda hoping you try to remove her."

Sean had lifted his arm to gesture for his enforcer to do it, but paused after hearing what Rourke had said.

I locked eyes with Stefan. "Neither I nor Brenna will be held responsible if she kills him."

Stefan looked around the table, reading those sitting at it. "She stays." The *Ri's* decision was final and not even Sean went against it. "Now let's get on with this meeting."

CHAPTER THIRTEEN

I lit the joint Brenna had given me as I listened to Conor talk about how he was going to meet with his contacts who supplied his pillar, weapons.

"When do you meet with them?" I cut my uncle off after taking a puff.

Everyone glanced at me.

"Tomorrow morning," Conor answered.

I nodded as I blew smoke through pursed lips. "I'll be joining you."

"I don't know if that's such a good idea," Conor said. He shot a glance at Stefan, who was doing his best to mask his surprise, before continuing. "Those Irish bastards get real nervous—"

"Then you will explain to them that Stefan's daughter and heir to this family, which happens to be their biggest buyer this side of the pond, will be tagging along." My tone was firm and brooked no argument. I turned my attention on Rourke. "I'm assuming you will be reaching out to your buyers next?"

He nodded.

"Who will you be reaching out to first?" I questioned.

Rourke grinned. "I'm meeting up with a local MC this week-end." He pointed behind me. "I'll tell your little secretary the time and place after the meeting so you can join me."

I glanced over my shoulder and saw Brenna typing on her phone. She looked up at Rourke with a blank stare before her gaze met mine.

I looked back at Rourke. He leaned back in his chair with laughter in his eyes.

I took another puff and looked to Sean. "By Monday I want your books and I want a list of your buyers and dealers."

Sean's mouth opened and I cut him off before he could protest. "Within the next month, plan on me going with you to Boston. I expect to have a full tour of your facilities and meet every employee. Before I return to New Haven, I better know all things weed."

The tension Sean put off was palpable. "I don't answer to you. I sit at this table—"

"Actually, you do," I cut him off. "I run the drug pillar in this family. Your business is marijuana, which falls under drugs. Therefore, you answer to me. As for this special table...well, you're sitting in Dylan's seat if you want to get technical. He answered to Samuel, who ran drugs, and again, that's my job. If those explanations aren't good enough for you, let me ask you this: Whose fucking chair do I sit in?"

Sean looked ready to lose it and I was ready.

"Be very careful with what you say next, Sean," Stefan said in a quiet and deathly calm voice.

I was equally surprised as I was disappointed that Stefan had come to my defense. I was one more push away from Sean damning himself and I would've been justified in killing the bastard.

"When does the cocaine shipment come in?" Stefan asked me.

"In a few days." Before he could ask, I added, "I will set up a meeting with the don as soon as the shipment is in my possession."

"I think that's enough for today," Stefan said, dismissing everyone. As I went to stand, Stefan stopped me. "Maura, a word?"

I told Brenna to leave without me, and as I went to turn back around in my chair to face Stefan, I noticed Sean was watching Brenna. His eyes were fixed on her like a hawk tracking its prey as she walked out of the room.

As soon as the door closed behind the last person to leave, Stefan asked, "If I ask you how you're feeling, will you actually answer?"

I got up and walked over to the liquor trolley that was up against the wall, opposite from the doors. I stubbed out my joint in the glass ashtray that was on the middle shelf. "How long did you succumb to your worst self?" When he didn't answer right away and I could feel that he was thinking of a way to deflect, I grabbed the crystal decanter of whiskey and poured a finger each into two glasses. "When you've spent so long as your darker self, it becomes harder to let it go."

Stefan watched me as I walked over and set a glass down in front of him. "Is that what it is to you? Your darker self?"

I took a sip from my own glass as I made my way back to my chair. "Something like that."

"We all carry darkness in us. What sets us apart is how much we let it consume us," he said as he picked up the glass in front of him and twiddled it in his fingers. "To answer your question...I never let my darker self go. There isn't me and that side of me anymore. It's very much a part of who I am today."

That explained why he could detach so easily.

"I think I take after you a little too much," I said before taking another sip. Stefan had been right. I wasn't gone. Not completely, anyway. There were still broken pieces that remained hidden beneath all the pain and rage. During this past week, I'd come to realize that I might not ever be able to glue those pieces back together. I could, however, use my darkness to hold them together, which cemented the fact that my darkness wasn't going anywhere. "It's been hard finding a balance. It's so easy to be an unfeeling, coldhearted bitch."

"Give it time," he said.

"As for how I'm feeling...I've been worse."

He finally took a sip of his whiskey. "Are you sure you're ready to be back?"

"The crime world won't wait for me. Besides, I'm tired of laying around." I scooped up the newspaper Sean had brought to the meeting off the table and stared at the picture of the bridge on the front page.

"Are you ready to talk about it?" Stefan asked, eyeing the newspaper in my hand.

I set the paper down and leaned back in my chair. "Where would you like me to begin?"

"From when you left," he said.

I told him pretty much everything that had happened up until I'd gone to the hospital to see Amelia. I left out the part where I'd had a feeling that it had been a trap, yet gone into her hospital room anyway. With how Stefan's eyes narrowed as he listened to me go over that part, I was pretty sure he knew.

He listened quietly for the most part. Then I began talking about what had happened when I'd been taken. Stefan began to get tense after that. He finished the rest of his whiskey and got up to refill his glass when I got to the part where I'd thought I was going to be raped.

I didn't continue until he returned to his seat. Toward the edge of the table, I ran my finger along the top, feeling the crevices. "When he was whipping me, trying his best to make me scream, I thought of you. Exactly as we are now, at this table, is what I saw, and you just sat there with me."

"You dissociated."

I nodded. "I suppose if anyone could keep me strong in that moment, it would be you."

I finished telling him the rest of what had happened up until I'd killed Buck. I left out the part about what I'd overheard about Dylan. That'd be a conversation for another day, hopefully years from now.

Just as Stefan was beginning to question me on what happened after I had killed Buck, the door to the chamber opened abruptly and Dean walked in. He leaned down and brought his mouth close to my ear. "Dylan and all of his security disappeared the day you returned to Quinn Manor," he whispered. "And Vincent found proof that Dylan was working with the Aryans."

Fuck.

Looked like the Dylan conversation was going to happen a hell of a lot sooner. I closed my eyes for a few seconds as I steeled myself for what I had to do. "Wait for me outside," I told Dean.

He didn't move. Instead, he glanced at Stefan, then back to me. I could see unease in his eyes and if I could see it, so could Stefan.

"Go," I ordered.

Dean reluctantly left the room. I sat there quietly as I tried to form a plan. I was pretty sure my father wouldn't kill me, but I knew I'd be punished. It would make Stefan look weak if he didn't.

"Whatever you have to tell me must be bad if it has your security nervous to leave you alone with me," my father said as he stared at me intently.

Fuck it. Here goes nothing. "I know who in the family hired the Aryans to kill me."

Stefan sat straighter in his seat. "Who?"

"Dylan."

Stefan went still. He didn't react or say anything for the longest time, but I could feel his rage. He eventually reached into his pocket and pulled out his phone. As he powered it on, his voice was laced with barely contained anger. "I'm guessing you sent your security to go obtain him and that is why Brenna was standing in for Dean. You planned to kill Dylan before anyone found out about his betrayal."

I didn't need to confirm that. He knew it was true.

"Seeing as you are telling me now, your security was unable to bring Dylan to you, which means he is on the run, making him an unpredictable threat to the family."

Again, I didn't need to confirm anything for him.

"You took responsibility for Dylan," he snarled. "Do you have any idea of the position this puts you in, or me for that matter?"

"Yes," I said.

"Why did you tell me now instead of trying to find Dylan first?" he questioned.

"Because I would rather the family be prepared in case Dylan does something rather than be blindsided and end up with someone getting killed."

"Even if it means you'd be punished?"

I didn't look away or cower under his intense stare like most would. "Yes."

"At least there's that," he grumbled as he typed on his phone and brought it to his ear. "Call your uncle and tell him he needs to come to the manor today, as soon as he can."

I had a feeling he was talking to Jamie.

After Stefan hung up and put his phone back in his pocket, he said, "Tell me everything you know."

CHAPTER FOURTEEN

"W hy didn't you tell anyone when you returned home that you suspected Dylan?" Jamie asked me. He, Stefan, Vincent, Dean, and I were all in Stefan's study waiting on Aiden to arrive. I had just finished explaining, again, what I'd overheard Buck and his lackey discussing. Like Stefan, Jamie wasn't pleased with me at the moment.

I was currently pouring myself a big drink at Stefan's liquor trolley. I took a huge gulp before I turned to face the room. Stefan was sitting behind his desk, Vincent was sitting stiffly in one of the armchairs in the lounge area that took up the left side of Stefan's study, Dean was standing by the door, and Jamie was standing right behind me when I turned around.

"She took responsibility for Dylan, Jameson," Stefan reminded him. "She didn't want to risk anyone finding out."

I took another drink. "Sure, we'll go with that."

Stefan gave me a disapproving look. "Care to enlighten us as to why you didn't tell anyone sooner?"

I wouldn't admit to him that I had been in too much pain and too exhausted to remember when I'd first arrived home or that, because I hadn't been left alone for one fucking minute, I hadn't been comfortable enough to allow myself to process what I had gone through, so I'd shut out what had happened. I would rather be whipped again right now than tell any of them that when I had remembered and put two and two together that it was Dylan, it had nearly destroyed what tiny pieces I had left of myself. Dylan was my responsibility. His mistakes were my mistakes. The guns the Aryans had stolen fell on me. The men that Rourke had lost fell on me. The loss of my baby fell on me.

Jamie stared at me, and I swore he could read my mind even though I was revealing nothing. He stepped closer. "I know you don't trust me, but despite that, you know if you had told me I would have taken care of him without anyone knowing."

"It's nice to know that both the children I raised would have tried to hide this from me," Stefan said dryly.

Jamie turned slightly to face Stefan. "To protect her, I would have."

Stefan did nothing to hide the anger burning in his eyes. "To protect her from the family or from me?"

Jamie didn't answer, but his silence was answer enough.

Stefan's gaze flicked to Dean and then Vincent. "I need to speak with Jameson and my daughter alone."

Vincent and Dean looked to me before they moved, which didn't help Stefan's mood. I nodded and they both left the room.

The moment the door closed, Jamie said, "You threatened to kill her."

"Yes, Jameson. I'm aware of my fuck-up," Stefan snapped.

Jamie's shoulders relaxed a little. "Rourke and Conor won't hold Maura responsible for Dylan's actions."

"Conor will forgive the loss of the guns, but I'm not sure about Rourke," I said and threw back the rest of my drink. "He was close to the men he lost."

"As of right now, no one knows someone within the family was working with the Aryans," Stefan said. "That has been something that has stayed between Jameson, Louie, Aiden, and me. We didn't want the rest of the family finding out that we were investigating them. We'll keep it that way. We'll find Dylan and take care of this mess without anyone knowing."

I turned back to the trolley. "And if they find out?"

"I will handle Conor and Rourke," Stefan said.

"Sean can't find out," Jamie said. "He'll use this to make you punish her severely, and if you don't, he'll use it against you, Stefan."

I refilled my glass with more whiskey. "I get that we were hurting for support here in New Haven after we removed Samuel and his men, but there had to be better options than Sean."

"There weren't," Stefan grumbled.

"He's the type that will never be satisfied with what he has. He has a seat at the table, but he wants to run drugs. I am an obstacle to him and once he finds a way to remove me, it won't be long before he starts gunning for your position," I said as I stared at the painting on the wall above the trolley without really seeing it. I couldn't let a threat like Sean remain, but I couldn't outright slit his throat, either. It might piss some people off in the family. I'd have to make sure it was justified, at least to criminal standards.

"Many want the power my position holds," Stefan said.

I turned back around. "I don't."

Stefan's brows rose. "It didn't look that way at today's meeting."

"That wasn't me being eager to learn everything because I'm excited to be the big bad boss one day," I said and took another big gulp of whiskey. "That was me doing what I can so when my ass has no choice but to plant itself in your chair, I am prepared." The alcohol was starting to make me warm. "Honestly, I'd be happy running drugs for the rest of my miserable life. Jamie should be your heir."

"You're meant to lead this family, Maura," Jamie insisted.

I gave him an incredulous look. "Are you sure about that? I fucked up with Dylan, which resulted in our people getting killed, guns stolen, and there was one more. What was it?" I snapped my fingers. "Oh, yeah. Because I let Dylan live, our daughter never got to take her first breath."

Jamie looked away from me. My words might as well have been a slap to the face if his expression was anything to go by.

I glanced at Stefan. "Still think I should be your heir?" My words tasted as bitter as they sounded. I grabbed the bottle of whiskey off the trolley and went to go sit on the couch.

"You're chasing the rabbit," Stefan said.

I poured myself another drink. "I outran that fucking rabbit months ago." I set the whiskey bottle on the coffee table in front of the couch and settled back against the comfy leather upholstery.

Jamie stormed over to me, took my glass from my hand before I could take another sip, and tossed it across the room. The crystal tumbler shattered when it hit the floor.

I crossed my legs and laid an arm across the back of the couch. I stared up at Jamie, taking in his clenched jaw and his intense gaze that was bearing down on me. "Did that make you feel better?"

"Are you done having a pity party?" he asked.

My eyes dropped from his. He was right. I leaned forward, put my elbows on my knees, and cradled my head with my fingers snaked into my hair.

Fuck. I'm going to cry.

"I did this," I strained to say.

Jamie sat on the coffee table in front of me and his legs

framed mine. He grabbed my wrists and pulled my hands from my hair. "Maura."

"I'm so fucking sorry, Jamie." My voice wobbled as I fought to hold my tears back.

His hands cupped the sides of my face and he made me look at him. "Don't you say that to me."

A tear fell down my cheek and his thumb wiped it away.

"Losing her isn't your fault. It's his," he said vehemently. "He's a dead man walking, baby. We're going to find him. We're going to kill him, and we'll do it together."

I nodded and he pulled me to him by the back of my neck. I laid the side of my face over his heart and let the sound of it calm me. Letting him hold me, feeling the warmth of him around me, made me realize how achingly cold I had become.

After I calmed down, Jamie and I pulled apart and we noticed that Stefan wasn't in the room. Neither of us had noticed when he had left.

I went to the bathroom to make sure I didn't look like I'd been crying and once I returned to Stefan's study, everyone was back in the room. Vincent was sitting on the couch, Dean was standing up against the wall near the liquor trolley, Jamie was sitting in one of the leather armchairs next to the couch, and Stefan was back behind his desk. I could feel all their eyes on me as I took a seat on the couch next to Vincent. Just as my butt touched the cushions, there was a knock on the door. Brody walked in. By the tight expression he held, I could tell he was irritated. Brody stopped walking just past the door and gestured for someone in the hall to come in.

"Thanks for the escort," Aiden said to Brody with a wink as he swaggered in. Smirking, Aiden walked straight toward Stefan's desk.

I glanced back at Brody and saw that he was glaring at the

back of Aiden's head. "Where's Kieran?" I asked, because Brody was supposed to be watching him for me.

As Brody's attention moved to me, his expression instantly softened. He pulled a small, screened device out of his pocket, which took me a second to recognize as a baby monitor. "He's napping." He glared one last time at Aiden before he left and closed the door behind him with a little more force than necessary.

It had been many years since I had last seen Aiden. He and Jamie were the same height and build and they had the same eyes. The similarities ended there. Aiden had blond hair with a little bit of gray. He also wasn't as stoic as Jamie could be. Aiden was more personable, but every time I'd interacted with him in the past, it had felt like a facade.

"You called?" Aiden said to Stefan with a smile that came off as flirtatious.

Stefan's eyes instantly flicked to me for only a second before returning to Aiden. "Yes, we need your assistance with something."

Aiden finally spared the rest of us a glance. He greeted his nephew with a nod. "Jameson." When he saw me, he appeared surprised at first. Then something darker showed beneath that charming personality he had. "Maura. You've been a hard woman to track down."

"That's because I didn't want to be found," I said.

That charming energy of his slipped a little bit more. "My people normally can find anyone."

The corner of my mouth lifted. "I have better people."

"One of them is mine, and one of my best, I might add," he said.

Ah. He was mad that Asher belonged to me now. "He's not yours anymore." When I'd made the decision to go after the Aryans without the help of the family, I'd given everyone who'd come with me the choice to stay or join me. I hadn't forced any of them and they'd all chosen to help me. It had been Asher's decision to cut ties with Aiden's security firm in order to make sure we weren't found.

"I have an agreement with Stefan that poaching my people—"

"You didn't make that agreement with me," I said, cutting him off.

"He's the head of your family." Although Aiden was irritated, he kept calm. I could respect that.

"Yes, he is," I agreed. "And what did he say to you when you brought this matter to him, I wonder?"

Aiden's silence was answer enough. I glanced at Stefan, and I could see mirth in his eyes. I was pretty sure Stefan had told him to take it up with me.

I looked back at Aiden as a wicked smile slowly stretched my mouth. "Asher is a grown man. He makes his own decisions. If you want him back, well, it sounds like you need to have this conversation with him."

Aiden held a frown as he stared at me as if seeing something he found interesting. When he was done, his face relaxed as he turned back toward Stefan. "She's just like you." He took a seat in one of the chairs in front of Stefan's desk. "Why am I here?"

Stefan explained that Dylan was the traitor. Dean went on to tell everyone what he, Asher, and Finn had discovered at Dylan's house. According to the security footage, Dylan had last been seen leaving his house with his enforcers and all of his security on the evening of the day I'd returned to Quinn Manor four months ago.

Vincent took his turn explaining what he knew next. "The morning of the day Maura returned home, Dylan and a few of his enforcers were in New York. I used facial recognition to search a ten-mile radius around where Maura was being held.

Dylan showed up on a camera inside a gas station two blocks away, purchasing a coffee with cash." Vincent typed away on his laptop as he spoke. "Using the station's cameras and traffic cams surrounding it, I was able to see that Dylan and two of his men stopped at that gas station at eight fifty-three in the morning. Dylan went inside to purchase his coffee, which is where my system pinged him. Then at nine, Buck and another Aryan arrived at the same gas station." He turned his computer around in his lap so we could see his screen. First he showed us footage of Dylan's Escalade pulling into the station. We watched as Dylan and his enforcers exited the vehicle and Dylan walked inside the station's small convenience store. Vincent typed something that gave us a view from behind the register of Dylan coming up to the counter to pay for his coffee. Vincent typed something again and showed us when Buck had pulled up next to Dylan's Escalade, then a shot of Buck and Dylan talking.

Vincent turned his computer back toward him. "They spoke for a while."

Aiden got up and as he walked over, he pulled a card from his pocket and held it out to Vincent. "When you tire of working for the Quinns, call me."

Clearly nervous, Vincent took it. The moment Aiden turned to walk back to his chair, Vincent held out the card to me. He hadn't even spared a glance at it. I snatched it and shoved it into my pocket. Everyone saw but Aiden. Grumpy Dean, who was facing us on the opposite side of the room with his arms folded over his chest, smirked. Stefan and Jamie looked like they were both fighting not to smile.

Aiden took a seat again. "So I'm assuming you need my help finding Dylan?"

Stefan nodded. "Discreetly."

Aiden grinned at Stefan. "I'm always discreet." Something told me he meant more than just work.

Stefan didn't react. The unreadable expression he held was locked in place. "Vincent will be helping us look for him as well." He looked from Aiden to Vincent. "Whoever finds him first, I will triple your pay."

Aiden chuckled. "Making this a competition?"

Before Stefan could respond, the door to the study ripped open and Brody stormed in quickly. He rushed to Stefan and whispered in his ear. Stefan's eyes went to me, and I got a bad feeling.

I leaned close to Vincent. "Go hang out in the guest house with Brenna."

Vincent shut his computer and left the room, no questions asked.

"Aiden, I need you to go with Brody. Jameson, the police are pulling up," Stefan said.

Jamie got up and briskly walked out of the room.

Aiden stood, smiling at Brody, and gestured for him to walk ahead of him. "Lead the way."

Brody rolled his eyes and led Aiden out of the room.

"I'm guessing they're here to speak to me," I said as I got to my feet and went to sit on the front edge of Stefan's desk.

"I believe so," Stefan said behind me. "You've been in Ireland visiting family for a little over a month." He gave me the date I'd left for Ireland and the time my flight had departed.

"When did I arrive home?" I asked and noticed Dean, which reminded me of Detective Brooks.

"Two weeks ago, same day you actually returned home," Stefan answered.

"Dean, why don't you—" I started to ask him to leave when there was a knock on the study's door.

Fuck.

"Come in," Stefan said loud enough for Jamie to hear.

Jamie came into the room first. Detectives Cameron and Brooks followed in right behind him. Jamie veered off to the side to stand against the wall next to Dean.

"Detectives," Stefan greeted them without getting up from his desk. "What can we do for you?"

The Detectives stopped walking when they were a few feet from me. "We're here to speak to Miss Quinn," Detective Cameron said.

CHAPTER FIFTEEN

"What are you here to accuse me of today?" I asked the detectives.

Not at all pleased with me, Detective Cameron, the more seasoned of the two, frowned. "Are you aware of the event that took place at Yale New Haven Hospital that resulted in Louie Dupont being shot?"

"My father informed me of it," I answered.

"We had witnesses who said they saw a redheaded woman at the scene and that she was being kidnapped," Cameron said.

I noticed his use of the word *had*. "Let me guess, you think that redhead was me?"

"Is there another redheaded woman that has a connection to Jameson Coleman and Louie Dupont?" Detective Brooks asked.

Between the two, Detective Brooks gave me the most unease, especially with Dean in the room. I had underestimated the baby cop initially. Turned out that he'd recruited Dean to go undercover and infiltrate our family. Dean, despite being a cop, liked the dark side we Quinns had to offer and hadn't given Brooks shit. Well, I'd had him give Brooks information to incriminate my mother, who apparently was still alive. If anyone found out that Dean was a cop, I wasn't sure I could save him, and if the family found out that I'd given a cop information, even if it was on an enemy, Stefan really wouldn't be able to save me.

I folded my arms across my chest. "I don't keep track of the women in their lives, and besides, I was in Ireland at the time."

Cameron surprised me when his eyes dropped to my chest. "Yes, I'm aware of that." His eyes jumped up to meet mine. "How'd you hurt your hand?"

I didn't have to look down to know what he was talking about. The cuts across my fingers from the handcuff were closed, but still pink. "I accidentally slammed my hand in a car door."

Cameron's eyes narrowed in disbelief. "Do you know what's strange?" he asked. "The witnesses who said they saw a redheaded woman all changed their story when we followed up with each of them with more questions. Every single one insists that the woman's hair color was brown. Why do you think that happened?" I watched as his gaze shifted to Stefan behind me.

"It sounds to me that the first time you interviewed these witnesses, you only heard what you wanted to hear," I said.

Cameron glared at me. "What's even weirder is that all the footage the cameras recorded in the hospital during the time of the shooting was erased."

As Cameron droned on about the hospital's cameras, I caught Detective Brooks staring at Dean with a smirk. Dean was so still as he glared back at him, I didn't think he was breathing. I pushed off the desk and moved to block Stefan's view of Brooks. "As much as I love a good mystery, do you have any more questions to ask me?"

Cameron's gaze dropped to my hand that was now hanging

at my side. "I think this visit isn't going to be any more informative."

"If you have what you need..." I heard Stefan say, but I stopped hearing him when I saw Jamie notice the way Brooks and Dean were staring at each other. I watched as he took them in and questions began to form in his eyes, then suspicion.

"We'll see ourselves out," Cameron said.

"Jameson will escort you," Stefan insisted, and Jamie pushed off the wall.

The detectives walked ahead of Jamie as they headed for the door. Cameron walked out of the room first, but before Brooks stepped out of the room, he shot one last glance at Dean. Jamie paused, having noticed.

Shit! Shit! Shit!

I waited until Jamie left the room before I too headed for the door. "Let's call it a day, Daddy. I need to get the baby from Brody," I shot over my shoulder.

Dean pushed off the wall and followed me.

"Will you come to dinner?" Stefan asked me.

"Yup," I answered without thinking. As soon as Dean and I were in the hall, I grasped Dean's arm and pulled him close. "I want you to track down Vincent and have him pull up everything he can find on Brooks. Tell him it's just as important as finding Dylan and to be discreet about it."

Dean nodded.

Jamie had just shut the front door as we stepped into the foyer. He turned and noticed me but locked his sights on Dean. I gave Dean's arm a slight push to urge him to keep going without me. Jamie's eyes followed Dean as he crossed the foyer and disappeared down a hall.

I moved toward the stairs. "I was going to go up to see Louie."

Jamie's attention flicked to me and all I saw was suspicion in the way he stared at me.

"Want to come with?" I asked as I began heading up.

He didn't respond, but he followed me.

As we made our way toward the west side of the house, Jamie broke his silence. "Is there something I should know about Dean and the cop?"

I kept my body relaxed as we turned down the hall that led to Louie's room. "I don't know what you mean."

My upper arm was grabbed and I was dragged into an unoccupied spare bedroom. I stumbled a little in my heels when Jamie released me to shut the door. Everything about his demeanor was serious, closed-off, and angry as he towered over me. If I'd been someone else, I might have been intimidated. However, I wasn't someone else and I found his deadly mobster attitude kind of hot.

"You know something." He sounded so certain, I knew I wouldn't be able to convince him otherwise.

I spun on my heels toward the rest of the room and made my way over to the bed. As I walked, I unbuttoned my suit jacket. I pushed it open enough to reveal my see-through, black lace bralette underneath and took a seat on the foot of the bed. I leaned back a little on my hands, just enough for my chest to push out, revealing everything, and crossed my legs.

Like I knew they would, Jamie's eyes dropped down to my breasts. I saw a flicker of heat spark in them before they narrowed and jumped up to meet mine.

"Have you been with anyone else since we've been apart?" I asked.

For a breath, he appeared taken aback by the question. By the next breath, anger had hardened his features. "Have you?"

I smirked. "Do my fingers count?"

Glaring, he came closer until he was standing before me.

"Now who's manipulating who?"

I leaned back on my elbows so I didn't hurt my neck staring up at him, lifted a leg, and set a high-heeled foot on his lower stomach. I gave him the same smirk he had given me in the shower the day I'd returned home and asked, "Is it working?"

In that moment, I couldn't tell if he wanted to strangle me or fuck me. The thought of him doing both at the same time warmed me from the inside out. My heart raced with the feeling and that stunned me a little.

"Do you even want to fuck me?" He grasped my ankle. His firm grip told me that he was struggling to contain himself.

"If I didn't, I would have killed you instead."

His hand at my ankle moved my foot to the outside of his hip before he began trailing that hand up the back of my calf until he reached the back of my knee. He leaned down, hiking my leg over his hip as he did, and he used his other hand to reach around my waist to the small of my back. I felt him grasp the gun I had hidden there. He took it and, without even sparing it a glance, he tossed it farther up on the bed.

A small smile tugged at the corner of my mouth. "Scared I might change my mind?"

He brought one knee onto the bed next to my hip as he grabbed the back of my neck. His grip was firm and kept me where he wanted me as he leaned closer until his mouth was inches from mine. "Getting shot by you once was enough."

My smile dropped. "Don't ever make me do it again."

"I won't," he said, and slammed his mouth down on mine.

I was ready for him. His lips moved with mine as I kissed him back. He licked at the seam of my mouth, demanding that I open for him. I happily obliged and greeted his tongue with mine.

I was breathless when his mouth traveled down my neck. His lips or tongue never left my skin as he helped me shed my jacket. Multiple times, he went over the spot on my neck he knew would make me shiver.

When my shivers weren't enough for him, he scraped his teeth over that spot, making me groan. That seemed to ignite a short sexual fuse in us, and the rest of my clothes were stripped from my body very quickly. As soon as the last of my clothes hit the floor, Jamie stared down at me, taking in every visible inch of my body. His gaze froze below my belly button and the heat in his eyes dimmed a little. I knew what he was staring at and even for me, it was impossible for it not to taint the moment.

He grabbed me by my hips as he bent down. I gasped when he pressed his lips to the scar that would always serve as a reminder of what we had lost. I fisted the blankets underneath me as I fought to control my emotions.

Jamie moved down and knelt on the floor. He pulled me by my hips until my ass was at the edge of the bed, threw my legs over his shoulders, and dove between my thighs. My back arched off the bed at the first hot swipe of his tongue. He feasted on me as if he was a starved man. His torturous tongue flicked at my clit to the point my legs shook uncontrollably. He kept me on the edge of coming. I snaked my fingers into his hair and tugged as I rocked my hips, seeking release.

He pulled away, making me growl out of frustration. "You know what I want," he said as he slid two fingers into my pussy and began pumping them in and out. His tongue returned to my clit and he quickly got me back to the edge of the fucking cliff, but wouldn't push me over.

When I couldn't take it anymore, I gave in. "Jamie, please." Those two words were a simple plea, but relinquished all of my control to him, and that was what he always craved in the bedroom. Control over me. The bedroom was the one place I never had an issue granting him the power. He just had to make me first.

Now that I'd given him what he wanted, he attacked my clit with vigor, and what sent me hurtling off the cliff was when that perfect fucking mouth began sucking on that little bundle of nerves. I threw my head back, crying out as intense pleasure exploded from my core. I shuddered and thrashed as that pleasure rippled through my body.

As I came down from my orgasm, Jamie stood and began taking off his clothes. Without taking my eyes off of him, I scooted toward the middle of the bed. I didn't want to miss a single second of him revealing his sculpted body and the tattoos that decorated his skin. I slid my hand between my legs when he shoved his briefs off and wrapped his fist around the base of his hard cock.

I spread my legs open so he could see my fingers working my sensitive clit.

His fist stroked his cock from base to tip. "You're as perfect as I remember."

I began kneading my breast with my free hand. "Are you just going to stand there and watch?"

He released his cock and climbed onto the bed, up between my legs until he was braced over me. I held his hazel eyes as he reached between us, aligned himself with my entrance, and thrust in. I moaned as I stretched around him.

He let out a curse as he rocked his hips. "Four fucking months since I've been inside you."

That amount of time sounded shorter than what it felt like. As I began to relax around him, his thrusts picked up the pace.

He fucked me like those four months were catching up to him. My nails dragged along his skin, my body writhed beneath him, and my moans of pleasure couldn't be contained. Release came hurtling toward me so fast I wasn't prepared for it. I nearly blacked out from the intensity.

"This is it, baby," he said before he kissed me and swallowed my screams. Jamie's hips began to stutter, and his mouth ripped from mine as his own release came.

I watched his face as he came undone. Seeing that vulnerability and feeling the intimacy between us made me feel different, yet familiar. Through the pain and rage and darkness to the broken pieces, I felt a flicker of something else. It was warm and heavy and good.

I grasped the back of Jamie's head, pulling him close enough to kiss him. I put what I was feeling into that kiss.

When we pulled away from each other, he stared down at me, astonished. His hand cupped my face. "There you are."

"It won't last," I warned.

"Then I'll have to bring you back again," he said. "I'll bring you back over and over again until you stay."

I smiled. "That sounds like a lot of orgasms."

He returned my smile with his own and his hips began rocking again.

My breath hitched. "Already?"

"We have four months to make up for," he said.

Jamie kept his pace slow and gentle as he took me for a second time. It was obvious that he wanted to take his time, savor the moment, until I was shattering underneath him again.

The feel of Jamie's chest stiffening beneath my cheek woke me before a voice said, "Would you look at that?"

I opened my eyes and saw Louie standing at the foot of the bed, Kieran in his arms. He was grinning down at the two of us.

"Did you know that my room is next to this one?" he asked. "Imagine my surprise when I heard...familiar sounds that I haven't heard in quite some time coming through the wall."

I sat up from where I was lying on top of Jamie. Louie's eyes dropped to my naked chest, and he did nothing to hide the desire in his eyes. "I have to admit that I was getting jealous by round number four," he said. "I was tempted to come and join you, but Brody and Stefan showed up with the baby looking for you. Apparently, you were supposed to relieve Brody of baby duty hours ago. They could hear that you were occupied." Louie let out a chuckle. "I've never seen Stefan so uncomfortable."

Shit! "What time is it?"

"Dinner time," Louie answered. "They didn't want to interrupt the two of you, so I offered to take him." Louie glanced down at Kieran with a warm smile. "We've been hanging out since then."

I ripped off the blankets and began looking for my clothes that were scattered everywhere.

Jamie sat up in bed. "What's the matter?"

"I told Stefan I'd be at dinner," I said as I dressed.

Jamie climbed out of bed and began collecting his clothes. "I haven't forgotten about Dean and the cop."

I was almost dressed when I looked over at him. "I need you to let it go, Jamie. I know it's a lot to ask you to trust me when I say I have it handled."

He frowned as he finished zipping up his pants and appeared ready to push the matter.

"If you pursue this, you will not only risk Dean's life, but mine as well," I said.

He went still. They both did as they stared at me.

"Please, Jamie, let this go," I pleaded.

He debated long enough to make me nervous. "Will you eventually tell me what's going on?"

I thought about it and considered the risks.

"You're asking for trust, but you don't trust him in return, or me for that matter," Louie pointed out. "You know we love you, and even though we've fucked up, it was out of the need to protect you."

I nodded and slid into my suit jacket. "I'll tell you when I can." I grabbed my gun from where I'd stashed it under the pillow, tucked it into the back of my pants, and held my hands out to take the baby from Louie.

He didn't hand him over. "You might want to pop into the bathroom before you head out." His voice had gone serious. "I don't like the idea of anyone seeing what you look like when you've been thoroughly fucked."

I didn't argue and headed for the connected bathroom. After flipping on the light, I took in my appearance in the mirror. My hair was wild and my makeup was smeared. Using my fingers and a little bit of water from the sink, I got to work on making myself a little more presentable.

"She seems..." I overheard Louie say in a low voice.

"Less cold," Jamie finished for him.

"I was going to say less pissed-off and scary, but that works, too," Louie said.

The corner of my mouth twitched as I finished up by quickly running my fingers through my hair.

I returned to the bedroom. Louie looked me over before handing over a sleeping Kieran. "He just fell asleep."

Jamie came to stand by me and put his hand on my back. "Are you coming down for dinner?" he asked Louie. It was then that I noticed Louie was dressed in a dark blue, long-sleeved shirt and jeans instead of sweats.

"I need to see more than that room and I'm feeling strong enough to do it," Louie said.

With that said, the three of us and baby Kieran headed downstairs to the dining room.

CHAPTER SIXTEEN

S tefan was already seated at the head of the table when we entered the dining room, and he wasn't alone. Brenna, Rourke, my uncle Conor, and my aunt Kiara were also sitting at the table. When everyone noticed us, Rourke and Conor greeted us with hellos.

My aunt Kiara stood from where she sat at the opposite end of the table from Stefan. With a smile, she walked toward me. "Maura, honey, how are you?" As soon as she was close enough to touch, she tried to hug me, but stopped when she saw that I had a baby in my arms. She was shocked for one whole second and by the next she was excited. "Oh my goodness! Who is this?" she said cheerfully as she took Kieran right from my arms and walked away with him.

I was left standing there, stunned for way more than a second, wondering what the hell had just happened. "I'm fine," I finally answered her, not that she was paying attention to me anymore.

"He's so precious I could just squish him until he pops," Kiara gushed as she took Kieran over to Conor.

"Come sit down, Maura," Stefan said.

I looked toward the other end of the table, where Stefan was watching me. Jamie and Louie had already taken their seats, leaving me standing near the dining room entrance alone. I did as Stefan asked and went to go sit at my spot at the table. Right as my ass touched my seat, Kiara let out a gasp, making me jump back up in a panic.

"Look at those pretty blue eyes," she gushed, obviously waking Kieran up. She held the baby close to Conor so he could see as well. "Look how handsome he is, Conor. Oh, this makes me think of Rourke when he was this tiny. He used to be so cute and squishy like this little guy."

"Are you saying I'm not cute anymore?" Rourke asked.

Kiara was so entranced with Kieran that she didn't even hear her own son. Conor gave Rourke a small smile from where he sat across from him at the table. "I'm sure your mother still thinks you're cute, son."

"Maura, sit down," Stefan ordered. I glanced at my father, finding him already staring at me expectantly. "The baby will be alright with your aunt."

Not if she squishes him. I sat back down. "You could have warned me that it was a family dinner," I whispered to him.

He relaxed back in his chair. "When could I have done that? You rushed out before I could because you were in a hurry to get to the baby." He was calling out my lie.

Louie snorted and quickly tried to cover it up with a cough when I shot a glare at him. Jamie put his elbow on the table and rubbed his top lip to hide his smile.

"I got sidetracked," I said.

"Oh, I know you did. For hours," he said, sounding equally annoyed and disgusted.

Louie's face was downcast and his shoulders bounced a little. Jamie's brows furrowed as he met my eyes from across the table.

I was about to straighten the silverware on my place setting, but stopped myself. It would show him that I was uncomfortable, which would give Stefan the upper hand. I straightened my shoulders and stared right at my father. "Well, Stefan, moving forward, I'll be sure to schedule all future dick appointments so this won't happen again. Sadly, it will take the spontaneity out of the act, but as long as there are orgasms still involved, there really isn't any reason to complain, now is there?"

Stefan grimaced and I took that as a victory.

"Whoa now, what about dick appointments?" Rourke asked, having just tuned into the conversation.

Louie lost it and erupted with laughter. Then Brenna, who had been sitting right next to me, quietly listening the whole time, started laughing.

Stefan let out a sigh, but he didn't appear to be annoyed anymore.

Noah and Jeana came out of the kitchen with food, interrupting the laughter. They delivered a plate to each of us and when Jeana saw the baby in Kiara's arms, she offered to make him a bottle in case he got hungry, too.

Jeana had made a delicious steak dinner that everyone dug into. I offered to take the baby from Kiara so she could eat without having to hold him, but she refused to give him back.

"I've asked Brody to set up a nursery here in the main house for Kieran to stay in," Stefan said, nonchalant.

I froze as I was about to take a bite. As calmly as I could, I set my fork down on my plate. "Kieran stays with me."

Stefan wiped his mouth with his cloth napkin. "The nanny won't be able to help you take care of him at night if she must walk from the main house to the guest house and barge into your room to get him. Kieran needs his own space. I've chosen a room next to Jameson's."

I glanced at Jamie to see if he knew about this. He was staring at Stefan, appearing just as blindsided as I was.

"I have agreed to hiring a nanny. I agreed to you picking out his security, but I did not and do not agree to this." The idea of Kieran being that far away from me at night, in this house, made me anxious and that anxiousness pissed me all the way off.

"You and Jameson have dangerous jobs. Being exhausted puts you both at risk and I can't allow that." Stefan's voice was firm.

I didn't respond right away. If I had, I would have lost control. I more than likely would have said or done something I couldn't take back—cold-blooded and dark things that came to the forefront of my mind way too easily. "I understand your concern, but when it comes to Kieran, I make the decisions. Not you."

The table went silent, and I could feel the tension coming off of everyone.

"Yes, I do," he said in a tone that brooked no argument, but I didn't fucking care.

"No, you do not," I said in the exact same tone.

Stefan held my eyes with a disappointed frown. "He will be moving into the main house tomorrow."

I was going to lose it if he didn't let this go. "No, he won't, Stefan."

"Yes, he will, Maura. I expect you to bring him to me first thing tomorrow," he ordered in a raised voice, which was something he rarely ever did.

"I will not, and if you try to take him from me, you will regret it," I threatened.

"Why?" he questioned.

"Because he is mine!" I yelled. "Not yours, Stefan! He will not spend one goddamned night in this house without me. I have already lost one baby in this house, I will not lose another, and I swear to God, Stefan, if you try to take him from me, I will burn this fucking manor to the ground!" I shoved my chair back from the table and stood.

Before I could storm over to Kiara to take Kieran, Stefan grabbed my hand. "Okay," he said, his voice gentle.

He appeared calm, like he hadn't been angry at all. It was then that I realized what he had done. He had played me, and I'd fallen for it.

I yanked my hand from his grasp and stormed over to Kiara. As she had done to me, I took him from her arms without asking. Just as I left the room, I heard Stefan say, "Don't look at me like that, Jameson. She needed the push."

"Maybe, but you didn't have to use her fear of losing another baby to do it," Jamie said, his tone riddled with barely contained anger.

I didn't hear anything after that because I kept walking. I returned to the guest house with Kieran. Dean and Asher were in the kitchen washing dishes from their own dinner.

Dean noticed me first and he greeted me with a frown. "Did something happen?"

"It's just been a long fucking day," I grumbled as I walked by, heading toward the hall that led to my room. "I'm going to call it a night."

About an hour later, after getting the baby to bed, I drew myself a bath. With a large glass of wine, I relaxed back in the claw-foot tub and soaked in the hot water, doing my best to unwind. I was almost finished with my wine when I felt a presence standing by the door behind me. I had left it open so I could listen for Kieran in case he woke.

"Are you just going to stand there and watch?" I threw over my shoulder.

"I was thinking about it." The voice belonged to Louie.

I was a little surprised it wasn't Jamie. He normally showed up at this time. The fact that Louie was here instead of Jamie gave me the feeling that Louie had been a little more jealous than he had let on earlier. I smiled down at the water. "Shall I lay the other way to give you a better view?"

"Only if you're trying to seduce me."

I turned around in the tub and lounged back, facing him. Louie was leaning against the frame of the bathroom door with his hands shoved into the front pockets of his jeans. His beautiful sapphire-blue eyes dropped to the water where my nipples were visible just below the surface.

I sat up a little, bringing my breasts out of the water, and rested my arms along the rim of the tub. "Are you really going to just look and not touch?"

"Do you want me to touch you, beautiful?"

"How else will I know if I've seduced you?"

He pulled away from the doorframe and pushed up the sleeves of his shirt as he came to me. Holding the edge of the tub, he knelt stiffly next to it and grasped the back of my neck, so I was forced to look up at him as his mouth descended upon mine. His touch may have been rough, but his lips were gentle. He broke our kiss, leaving me breathless. "Bend your legs," he ordered.

I did as he asked, and my knees rose out of the water. Without letting go of the back of my neck, he put his hand on top of my knee closest to him. Very slowly, that hand slid down the inside of my thigh.

I let out a little gasp as his fingers slid over my pussy to my core. He pushed two fingers inside of me and began stroking them in and out. I grabbed hold of his arm when he pressed his thumb on my clit and started rubbing that as well.

The water splashed as I thrashed from the pleasure. My breathing turned into pants as pressure between my legs built.

The closer I got, the more my pants turned into moans. As I reached the edge, Louie's mouth slammed down onto mine and his tongue matched the strokes of his fingers until my release hit me. He pulled back to watch me as I squeezed around his fingers and my body shook in his arms.

"You're so fucking beautiful when you come." He withdrew his fingers from me and slid his hand up to cup my breast.

Climbing to my knees, I threw my arms around his neck and kissed him like I was starved for more. His arm wrapped behind my back and his hand gripped the back of my thigh before he pulled me out of the tub. I squealed as I fell against his chest and he rolled onto his back on the floor with me on top of him. He let out a grunt.

"Are you okay?" I asked as I straddled his waist. Water rolled off of me, soaking him and the rug beneath us.

He smiled. "I'm fine, but you're going to have to help me take off my clothes."

I got to work on that. First I lifted the bottom of his wet shirt and then scooted down to his thighs so I could help him sit up. He let out a groan like an old man on his way up.

"Are you sure you're okay?" I asked as I helped him take his shirt off completely.

He pressed his naked chest to mine. A smile pulled at his mouth as his hand came down on the left side of my ass and a loud *slap* echoed in the small room. I let out a gasp.

"Just keep stripping me, beautiful," he ordered.

I shook my head as I unfastened his pants and released his hard cock. I made sure I gave it a few teasing strokes before working on getting his pants off. He helped me get his pants down to his knees before he grabbed me by my waist.

"Can't wait any longer," he said and pulled my hips so I hovered over his shaft.

I aligned him with my entrance and locked eyes with him as

I sank down on him. His brow furrowed as if pained and he let out a curse. Enjoying his reaction and needing to move, I rolled my hips. His grip at my waist encouraged me to do it again. I threw my arms over his shoulders and obliged. It didn't take long until I found the perfect motion of lift, roll, and grind that made us both pant.

His fingers dug into my hips and he slammed me down on his cock each time I would lift up. Moans tore from my lips. I molded my chest with his and held onto his neck tightly as I felt my orgasm building.

"I'm going to come," I cried.

Louie kissed and bit along my shoulder. One of his hands reached between us and he rubbed his thumb over my clit, making me explode. Taking control of my hips, he continued to thrust into me, chasing his own release as I contracted around him.

He let out a groan with one last thrust and then the two of us were falling. Louie landed on the rug on his back with me on top of him. Breathing heavily, I went to roll off of him, but he wrapped his arms around me, keeping me where I was.

He kissed the top of my head. "Give me thirty seconds and we'll go again."

I wiggled his arms off me and sat up. "Again?" I asked as I stared down at him.

"Yup. At least three more times."

He really was jealous of my afternoon with Jamie. "Are you trying to break my vagina?"

He smiled and put his arms behind his head. "No, but I'd settle for you walking funny tomorrow."

I couldn't stop myself from smiling and I lazily ran my fingers down his chest to his stomach. When I felt a bandage, I glanced down to where he had been shot. His whole abdomen wasn't wrapped anymore, but his wound was covered with a bandage the size of my hand. "We got this wet."

He reached up and cupped my face. "Don't worry about it." With how gently he said that and how he was staring at me, I wondered if he meant more than the bandage.

The sound of Kieran crying poured in from the bedroom.

"Little man and I need to have a talk about sharing Mommy," Louie grumbled.

His words made me tense up.

He felt it and sat up so he could wrap his arms around me. "I didn't mean to upset you."

"You didn't."

He searched my face, which I kept blank. I could tell he didn't believe me, but he didn't push. "Alright." He gave me a quick kiss and released me.

I stood and went to grab my robe that was hanging on the door.

"Am I allowed to sleep over?" Louie asked as he finished removing his jeans and got to his feet.

I slipped on my robe and tied the sash. "Because you asked, the probability of you getting three more rounds just went up."

He gave me a saucy look that made me laugh as I left the room.

CHAPTER SEVENTEEN

I t took effort not to feel irritated as Sean and one of his goons pulled into the parking lot of Show 'n Tail right after we did. The bastard insisted on being at the exchange with the don today and had followed us from Quinn Manor. On the plus side, he still didn't know where I'd stashed the cocaine. Finn and Dean were in charge of transporting that and arrived at Show 'n Tail a few minutes before Asher, Brenna, and me. Unlike the last time we'd done an exchange at Show 'n Tail, I was going to let Brenna come in.

"Sean gives me ick vibes," Brenna said in a low voice as we climbed out of the Escalade.

"I'm sure every woman who's met him would agree with you," I grumbled.

Asher snorted as he held out his hand for me to climb out.

Brenna and Asher walked behind me as I made my way toward the front door, where Dean and Finn were waiting with an extra-large duffel bag in each of their hands. Once I was a few feet from them, Dean nodded his head toward Sean and his goon making their way over. "Are we waiting for them?"

I glanced over my shoulder at Sean to gauge how long it

would take for them to catch up and found Sean staring at Brenna again. I glanced back at Brenna. She was already staring at me with an annoyed expression. I arched a brow at her.

"I know," she said in a low, disgusted voice. She walked ahead of me, muttering, "Nasty Irish bastard." She opened the door to the club a lot calmer than expected. "Under the Influence" by Chris Brown poured out of the open door. As she held the door open, Brenna gestured for us to walk in. "I vote we don't wait."

Dean and Finn seemed to agree with her. They picked up the bags and walked in. I followed next, with Brenna and Asher right behind me. The door closed behind us for a few seconds before it was ripped open again and an annoyed Sean walked in.

The club was empty of customers. A few strippers were dancing on one of the stages. Nicoli and Dario were sitting at a table watching as a handful of their goons stood around the room.

The moment Nicoli and Dario noticed that we'd entered, they stood. Having done this exchange many times, Dean and Finn went to Nicoli's goons, who had our money. Brenna, Asher, and sadly Sean and his enforcer followed me as I made my way over to Nicoli.

"Tequila or whiskey?" was how Nicoli greeted me as he gestured for me to take a seat.

"Whiskey," I answered as I pulled out a chair.

Nicoli's brows rose as he scooped up a bottle of expensive whiskey and poured me, Dario, and himself a glass each.

"Bad day or is it due to unwanted company?" he asked as he slid my drink closer to me.

I scooped it up. "I bet you can guess." As I took a quick sip, my gaze drifted to Dario. "This is the first time you've come to an exchange."

"Maybe he missed us," Brenna commented as she walked past the table we were sitting at. I caught the sly smirk she gave Dario as she did, and I had to hide my smile by taking another sip. I could tell even Nicoli was fighting not to grin. The mirth in his eyes gave him away.

Dario didn't react to Brenna's little jab. Instead, he watched her as she got closer to the stage the strippers were dancing on. She watched them with a schooled expression, but I knew she was fascinated.

"Go get her," I heard Sean say in a low voice behind me before he came closer to our table. "I apologize for Brenna's rudeness, Nicoli."

Dario's head whipped around and he eyed Sean with an unfriendly expression. Nicoli stared at Sean, looking unimpressed. I kept my face emotionless and was about to tear into Sean when Dario abruptly stood from the table, his focus back on Brenna. I looked in that direction just in time to see Sean's enforcer grab Brenna by her wrist, which she easily yanked free. The way she stared at Sean's enforcer, I knew she would kill him if he went to touch her again.

"Brenna," I said just loud enough for her to hear me.

Our eyes locked and I didn't have to say another word. She walked around Sean's enforcer and headed back over.

When she was within reach, Sean made the stupid move of grabbing her roughly by the arm. He yanked her to face Nicoli. "Apologize for—"

He didn't get to finish because Brenna spun on her heel and rammed her elbow right into Sean's nose. Blood spewed from both of his nostrils. He released Brenna's arm to cover his nose with both of his hands. Brenna took that opportunity to kick him in the chest, which was impressive because she was in a tight suit and at least four-inch heels. Sean went stumbling backward until he fell into a chair. Brenna reached into her jacket and pulled out a pistol. She took large steps until she was back in front of Sean and she pressed the barrel of her gun to his forehead.

I stood from my chair extra slowly and smoothed away the nonexistent wrinkles on the front of my suit. I wasn't exactly in a rush to stop her. If she killed him...oh, well. I wouldn't lose sleep over it.

Before I could fully get to my feet, Sean's enforcer came up next to Brenna and pointed his gun at her temple. "Drop it," he ordered.

Nicoli stood and grabbed Dario's shoulder. "Stay out of it."

It was then that I saw Dario had his gun in his hand as he stared in Brenna's direction.

I sighed loudly and unhurriedly walked over to stand at Brenna's other side. Asher followed closely, his hand inside his suit jacket, ready to draw his weapon.

Sean's eyes flicked to me. "Tell her to stand down or I'll have Justin shoot her." With his hands still covering his nose, his voice was muffled and nasally.

I was impressed at how calm Brenna was. The only emotion she showed was a mean little smile.

"Can I kill him?" she asked me.

"That's a question you need to ask yourself," I told her. "But don't pull that trigger unless you know you can."

Sean put his hands out, revealing ribbons of blood rolling from his nose and dripping off of his chin. "If you shoot me, Brenna, Justin will shoot you. Lower your gun and no one has to get hurt."

"Such reassuring words," I said as I walked behind Sean's chair. "From an evil man."

Brenna's eyes flicked to me for only a second before returning to Sean.

"Never trust the words of evil men." I stuffed my hands into my pockets as I continued to walk around the three of them.

"Maura," Sean growled.

I ignored him. "Do you know what you can trust of evil men?" I asked Brenna as I moved around them. "Their pride and what it will compel them to do. If you stand down right now, what do you think Sean's pride will compel him to do?" I made a full circle and was back to standing behind Sean's chair. "You've embarrassed him. He will be compelled to make you pay for it. If you lower your weapon, he will have his enforcer drag you outside and they will beat you. Or at worst, they will rape you."

Brenna's smile dropped and anger seeped into her beautiful green eyes as she stared down at Sean.

"Don't get angry," I instructed. "It will cloud your ability to think clearly. Treat what I've just told you as a fact, because that's what it is. It's a reality of our world."

Brenna's shoulders rose slightly as she took in a deep breath to calm herself.

I nodded once. "You know your enemy. So what are you going to do?"

Brenna didn't move for what seemed like the longest handful of heartbeats. During that time, silence had blanketed the room. Even the music had been turned off as we waited to see what she would do.

Brenna lowered her gun from Sean's head slowly until it was pointing to the ground at her side.

Justin seemed to relax, and he moved his gun from her temple slightly as he held his hand out in front of her. "Give me your gun."

The corner of Brenna's mouth twitched. With his gun not pressed to her head, Brenna had room to move, and she did. We all saw it coming but Justin.

She dropped to the floor and kicked Justin's legs out from under him. Crouched on the ground, Brenna aimed her gun at Justin, who went to sit up after landing on his back. He was getting ready to aim his gun at Brenna, but he wasn't fast enough.

A shot rang out, sparks flared, the strippers on stage screamed and scurried out of the room. Justin let out an embarrassing yelp as his gun fell from his hand. Brenna pushed up to her feet, gun aimed at Justin, who was still on the ground. Sean went to stand, but Brenna quickly turned her gun on him.

"Sit down," she ordered.

Sean slowly and reluctantly sat.

Brenna walked carefully over to where Justin's gun had fallen. Without taking her eyes off either man, she squatted and picked it up. Aiming one gun each at Sean and Justin, she looked at me. As we stared at each other, I could see the question in her eyes.

A small smile lifted the corner of my mouth. "If you kill them, it might piss off Stefan. Not to mention there are quite a few witnesses around." I moved so I wasn't right behind Sean. Brenna was an amazing shot, but I still didn't want to risk it. "But I'll support whatever decision you make."

She let out an annoyed sigh as if bummed that she wasn't getting her way. "Get up," she barked at Sean and Justin. They both got to their feet. As she stared at the two of them, her evil smile came back. "Strip for me."

Seeing how we were at a strip club, it was fitting.

They didn't move.

"How pissed-off do you think Stefan will get? Because I think it'll be worth it to just kill them," she asked me.

Justin yanked his suit jacket off, then toed off his shoes as he undid his belt.

Sean still didn't move as his enforcer stripped.

"What's the matter, Sean?" I asked, unable to stop myself. "Don't tell me you're shy?"

"He must have a tiny dick," Brenna said, grinning like crazy.

"A tiny dick isn't worth dying for, Sean," I goaded.

Brenna snorted. "How should I kill him? A couple of rounds in the chest? Or one between the eyes?"

Red with embarrassment or anger or both, Sean yanked off his suit jacket. "Stefan will hear of this."

"Oh, I wish I could be a fly on the wall when you tell my father," I said.

We all watched as Sean stripped to his underwear, which is what Justin had done.

"Underwear, too, boys," Brenna ordered.

"You have got to be fucking kidding me," Sean seethed, his Irish accent coming out thick. He pushed the last bit of clothing he had on down his legs until it dropped to his ankles. Some of Nicoli's men whistled and catcalled.

Brenna pointed her guns toward the ceiling. "Thanks for the show. You may leave now."

Sean and Justin went to grab their clothes.

"Wait!" I said, making them pause. I pulled out my phone and quickly took a picture. "Okay. Now you can go."

Sean and Justin grabbed their clothes, used them to cover their privates, and walked out of the club quickly.

Nicoli and Dario came to stand next to me. "It's always entertaining when you're around," Nicoli said.

"You should have killed them," Dario said as Brenna came over. "As you said, his pride won't let this go."

Brenna holstered her gun and held out Justin's to Asher, who took it from her. Then she looked at me for guidance on how to respond.

"I know," I said.

"You sound like you're planning on it," Nicoli said.

"To kill a high-ranking member of my family, it must be justified," I explained. "And when he retaliates, it will be."

Dario's mouth dropped open slightly. "The two of you planned that?"

I shook my head.

"The opportunity sort of presented itself," Brenna said.

Nicoli smiled. "That's entrapment."

I shrugged. "He doesn't have to let his pride rule him. He can choose to let this go."

"Would you let it go?" Dario asked me.

No. But I was better at playing games than Sean was. I answered Dario with a smirk.

"Shall we get back to our drink?" Nicoli asked.

We returned to the table we'd been sitting at. Brenna pulled out the chair next to mine, across from Dario, and took a seat.

Dario picked up his drink and took a sip, his gaze never leaving Brenna as he did. "Shall I get you a juice box?" he asked her as he set his glass back on the table.

Brenna put her elbow on the table and rested her chin on top of her fist. "You seem really fixated on my age." She smirked at him like she was privy to something that he didn't want her to know. "I wonder why that is."

Dario glared at her.

Taking control of the conversation before their bickering got out of hand, Nicoli said to me, "You look better since I last saw you."

"It's been almost a month. I—" The sound of my phone ringing in my pocket interrupted me. I reached into my pocket to see that it was Jamie calling. I sent him to voicemail. Before I could put my phone back in my pocket, he called me again. "Excuse me a moment," I said to the table before getting up and walking out of hearing range.

Putting the phone to my ear, I answered, "I'm in the middle

of an exchange." I glanced back at the table. Nicoli and Dario were listening to something Brenna was saying, and whatever it was made Nicoli grin and Dario frown.

"Are you almost done?" Jamie's voice was calm, but with the phone calls back-to-back, I knew something was wrong.

"Is everything alright?" I asked, getting straight to the point.

"You need to come home." Something slipped into his voice then. It was subtle, but there was no mistaking the insistence spurred on by worry in his words.

I took in a calming breath to steel myself before I asked, "Is someone hurt or dead?"

He was quiet for too damn long.

"Answer the fucking question," I ordered.

"It's Stefan."

Everything in me stilled. "Is he hurt or dead?"

"We don't know."

I hung up on him and squeezed my phone in my hand. I gave myself five seconds to get a grip, to stop my pounding heart, to push back the panic that was building inside of me, and I sank into my darkness, letting it take over completely.

"Is everything alright?"

I turned to find Dean behind me. "Is the exchange done?"

His eyes narrowed as he stared at me. "It's done."

"Good. Let's get moving," I said and walked around him back toward Nicoli and the others. As I approached the table, I plastered a polite smile on my face. "I have to cut our drink short. Something back at home requires my attention."

Nicoli and Brenna stood at the same time. "That's too bad," Nicoli said. "I guess you'll have to make it up to me with that dinner you owe me."

"Of course," I said. "Until then, Nicky."

I could feel Brenna's and my goons' eyes on me, knowing

something wasn't right, as we left the club, loaded up our money, and climbed into our vehicles.

"What happened?" Brenna asked as soon as we got on the road back to Quinn Manor.

Asher's phone rang as he drove. I watched as he answered it. Not even five seconds into the call, he locked wide eyes with me in the rearview mirror.

"Something happened to Stefan," I finally answered her.

CHAPTER EIGHTEEN

Brody was waiting in the foyer when we arrived home. The moment he saw me, he looked relieved, but that relief didn't overshadow the fear in his eyes.

"They're waiting for you in the chamber," he said and walked with me as I headed that way.

"Where is Kieran?" I asked. Even though I knew he was with his nanny, whose name was Caroline, I still wanted to know that he was safe.

"I just checked on him," Brody said. "He and Caroline are in the nursery upstairs." The nursery that he only used during the day. At night, he was always with me, which was now in either Jamie's or Louie's room. We alternated each night. I hadn't slept in the guest house in over a week. Dean and Asher had moved back to their homes a few days ago. Brenna was the only one who remained living there.

Goons were already lined up outside as we approached the chamber. Brody stopped walking and watched us continue on. Asher took his post in the hall. Dean and Brenna followed me inside. Conor, Rourke, their enforcers, Jamie, and Louie were already inside. With stoic expressions, they all stood from their seats as I entered the room, which I found odd. They had never done that before. I noticed Sean was missing, not that I gave a shit at the moment. Seeing Stefan's chair empty made my chest feel a little tight. The moment I took my seat, so did the others.

I looked to Jamie. "Start explaining."

"Do you want to wait for Sean?" Conor asked.

"No," I said without removing my eyes from Jamie, who was doing a good job of holding an unreadable expression.

"Stefan meets quarterly with top officials in the state to play golf," Jamie explained without looking away from me. His words were calm and factual. "When he was on his way home, his Escalade got a flat tire. As soon as they pulled off the road, two utility vans drove up, men in black ski masks jumped out, and they began gunning down Stefan's security. They dragged him from the SUV, shoved him into one of their vans, and took off."

"How do you know this?" I questioned.

"Only one of Stefan's personal security survived the attack. He was shot three times. Two in the leg and one in the shoulder," Louie answered. He also spoke in a calm voice and did his best to keep what he was thinking from showing. His eyes gave him away, though. They filled with apprehension the longer he stared at me.

I had to look away from him. "I want Vincent and Aiden on this now."

"They already are," Jamie said.

I looked around the rest of the table. "What are our next steps?"

"News of this is going to spread like wildfire through the family, the city, and then our entire territory," Rourke said.

"Before anyone gets any ideas, we need to make it known that you've taken over," Conor said next.

I shook my head. "I'm not taking over anything. Until we have proof that Stefan is dead, he is still the head of this family."

The table went quiet, and I caught how they all glanced at each other.

Jamie leaned forward a little, his serious eyes locking with mine. "With Stefan missing, the entire family is vulnerable, Maura. He appointed you as his heir. If you do not assume leadership, others might try to take over."

"Others still might," Rourke grumbled.

"Not if we are united in our support of her taking over," Conor said.

"Sean won't be on board," Louie said. "From day one he hasn't hid his dislike of her."

The more they talked amongst themselves, the more my chest got tighter, and my darkness' hold wavered.

I didn't want this.

I wasn't ready.

"Maura?" Jamie said, saving me from my thoughts and granting me the distraction my darkness needed to strengthen its hold.

"I'll do it," I forced myself to say, because I had to. For the family and to make sure Stefan's place was still here for him when we found him.

All of them began talking again and I couldn't hear any of it. So many things were racing through my head. No one would support me—a woman. Scenarios and outcomes filled my head, overwhelming me.

I was losing it again.

I wanted to scream.

I wanted to leave.

I stood and everyone went quiet. "I need to pee," I said as I walked out of the room. All I could hear was my heartbeat in my ears as I stormed through the house. There was a battle of control happening inside me and it was making the walls around me feel like they were closing in. I had to get out.

I rushed for the garage. Keys for all the cars were in a cabinet just inside its entrance. I ripped that cabinet door open and grabbed the keys to my Audi—the only car without a tracking device on it, thanks to Brenna's help. When Brenna had come to get me from that shithole apartment in New York, she had said that Jamie was not that far behind her because they had tracked her. Apparently, Stefan had put tracking devices on all of the cars while I'd been on vacation. Brenna hadn't known about the tracker until Vincent had called her and told her when she'd been outside the apartment building I was being held in. When we'd returned home, she'd eventually told me, and I'd asked her to figure out how to remove the tracker from my car.

I tore down the cobblestone driveway and paused just long enough for the goons to open the gate. Then I floored it and didn't look back. I rolled down all the windows and sucked in the cool air that rushed in. At the beginning of my drive, I just drove around aimlessly until my darkness could take back full control. As soon as it did, an idea came to me, and I headed to New York.

Before I walked into Alessandro's—a restaurant owned by the De Lucas—I sent a text to Nicoli telling him that I was in the city and to come find me. Then I turned my phone off. When I walked in, I went up to the hostess. "Tell Nicoli that I'll be waiting for him at the bar."

The young Italian woman's eyes went wide at the mention of the don's name as she watched me walk away.

Alessandro's was an upscale Italian restaurant with rust-red walls, black linens, and silver fixtures that shined like jewelry. I had been here once before to use cocaine as currency in order to get help from Nicoli. I hopped up on one of the vacant stools at the bar. The bartender, who had to be about my age, came right over. "What can I get you?" he asked.

"Whiskey, top shelf."

He grinned. "I'm going to need to see your ID."

I reached into my suit jacket's pocket and pulled out my ID and a hundred-dollar bill. I set them both on the black marble bar top. He picked up the ID and looked it over. His brows rose for a split second before he held my ID out to me with a polite smile.

I took it. "I guess you recognize my name."

His smile turned strained. "Do you know whose restaurant this is?"

I set my elbow on the bar top and rested my chin on my fist. "I'm sure he already knows I'm here."

He nodded and picked up the hundred. "I'll bring your change with your drink."

"Don't bother," I said. "Just keep my drink full."

He nodded again and went to pour my drink.

I was on my third glass when someone sat on the stool on my left. "You sure love to play hide-and-seek in my city."

I smiled down at my glass. "I like to keep you on your toes."

Someone sat on the stool on my other side and said, "Nicoli is right. You are entertaining." The voice belonged to Dario.

"I try," I said as I threw back what was left in my glass.

As if sensing that I was in need of a refill, the bartender headed over, whiskey bottle in hand. He looked from Dario to Nicoli with respect in his eyes. "Can I get you something to drink, sir?" the bartender asked Nicoli in Italian as he poured me another drink.

"I'll have what she's having," Nicoli responded in Italian.

The bartender looked to Dario. "Same," Dario said in English.

As soon as the bartender finished pouring their drinks and left, Dario spoke. "It's risky coming into someone else's territory alone."

I saw a head of blonde locks lean close to Dario's ear before a feminine voice said, "Who says she's alone?" Dario went still as Brenna molded her chest to his back. I could see that she was holding something at the base of his spine. "In case you're wondering, that's the barrel of a 9mm."

Dario took a sip of his drink. "I thought you were just happy to see me."

Brenna cracked a smile for a split second before she forced it to drop. "You're in my spot."

"I didn't see your name on it," Dario said and spun his stool around partially so he could see her better. "But if you need to sit here, you're welcome to sit in my lap."

Brenna put her gun in the holster hidden in her jacket, then surprised us by hopping into his lap. Through his shock, Dario still wrapped an arm around her waist so she didn't fall. Brenna didn't seem to notice. Her attention was fixed on me. She leaned her face close to mine with a serious expression. "You shouldn't have left on your own." Her voice was low. "You are too important to take a risk like this."

"How'd you find me so quickly?" I asked.

"I've been behind you the whole time, you just didn't see me. Until they showed up." She tilted her head at Nicoli. "I was giving you space to process."

I nodded.

Nicoli rested his elbows on the bar and stared at Brenna and me. "Not that I'm not happy to see you ladies twice in one day, but why are you here?"

I took a sip of whiskey. "I wanted to drink somewhere less suffocating."

Something flashed across his face. Understanding, maybe? "Are you hungry?"

"No," I answered at the same time Brenna said, "Yes."

The four of us moved to a private table that was mostly blocked off from the rest of the restaurant with sheer black curtains. Nicoli sat at the head of the table. I sat to his left, Brenna sat to his right, and Dario sat on the other side of Brenna.

Brenna ordered me food even though I had no intention of eating.

"Did something happen?" Nicoli had asked only once. I hadn't answered. Instead, I'd downed another whiskey.

When our food came, Brenna, who'd ordered the same exact thing as Dario, switched her plate with his, then switched Dario's original plate with mine. The three of us watched her silently and when she was done, she made no move to touch the food she'd taken from me.

Nicoli picked up his fork, stabbed a bite of food from the plate in front of her, and ate it. "It's not poisoned," he said after he swallowed.

Dario huffed a laugh as he started eating from the plate Brenna had switched to him. Brenna picked up her fork and began eating. When I didn't and just kept drinking, she shot me a worried glance. Nicoli noticed.

"You don't get to count this as the dinner you owe me if you don't eat," he said to me.

I twisted my glass on the table in a circle. "To make it up to you, I'll give you two dinners. One can even be at my house."

I felt Brenna's gaze as I stared at Nicoli. His brows rose.

"Dinner at the Quinns'. How would Stefan feel about me coming to your home?"

I didn't react. I didn't so much as blink. "I'm sure he won't care."

Ivano, Nicoli's little brother, and a few men of the De Luca family showed up midway through the meal. Ivano looked surprised but delighted to see me and sat in the chair next to mine. "Having dinner with The Castrator and you didn't invite me, brother?" he said to Nicoli as he and his friends sat.

"It was a spontaneous thing," Nicoli said before taking a bite.

Ivano noticed Brenna and recognition lifted his brows. "You must be Brenna."

Brenna nodded as she chewed.

Ivano grinned mischievously. "I heard you've been keeping Dario on his toes."

Dario glared at Ivano.

That just made Ivano's grin brighten. "Nicoli said you knocked Dario on his ass."

"There's no way Dario got taken down by this girl," one of the two men who'd showed up with Ivano said in Italian.

"Maybe he got distracted checking her out," the other added in Italian, making them both chuckle.

Dario's glare turned murderous as he looked at the two of them and they immediately shut up.

"Such a scary face," Brenna teased as she twirled spaghetti on her fork.

His glare lessened just a smidge as his attention shifted to her. She took in the harsh look and smiled before taking a bite.

The waiter came. Ivano and his buddies ordered drinks and food.

"So what brings you to our territory?" Ivano asked.

Brenna looked to me to answer, but as she did, something caught her eye through the black sheer curtains behind me. I watched as her eyes followed whatever she saw. "Maura," she said, warning me of what I already knew was coming. Or rather, who was coming.

The restaurant went quiet and the men at the table noticed.

Jamie and Louie were the first to come into view, then Rourke and Conor, followed by Dean, Asher, and many enforcers. Nicoli's goons stopped Jamie and Louie before they could get close to our table. Jamie and Louie didn't try to push through them. They just stood there staring at me.

I downed the rest of what was in my glass and looked to Nicoli. He was taking in the entourage that had come to retrieve me. "I came to get drunk and to see I could truly trust Nicky," I finally answered Ivano's question.

I felt the men at the table look at me, but I only stared at Nicoli.

He set down his fork and pushed his plate forward. "Care to explain?"

"I came here alone, looking vulnerable, and trying to get drunk. I wanted to see if you'd take advantage of that," I said. "I'm sorry to test you, but things are about to change, and I need to know for sure who I can trust."

Nicoli stared at me, his eyes narrowing. "What do you mean things are about to change?"

"I would like to form a true alliance between your family and mine. Not through marriage, but through our friendship and trust," I said, making him go still.

"Shouldn't the head of your family be making that offer?" Dario asked.

"She is the head of our family," Jamie said from where he stood.

Nicoli's eyes widened for a split second. Had I not already been staring at him, I would have missed it.

I stood and Brenna stood with me. "Take the night to think on it and call me in the morning," I said and walked to Jamie and Louie.

Neither looked happy, but they followed me as I made my way out of the restaurant.

Jamie and Louie were angry with me. Not that I could blame them. I was angry with me—not for the same reason, though. I'd taken a risk, and they didn't like that. It was a risk I'd had to take and even though they didn't understand right now, they would later, and then I'd be the only one left regretting it.

Jamie was driving my Audi. Louie was riding in the front passenger's seat, and I was in the backseat alone. As we made our way home, my car was being escorted by four Escalades. Two drove in front of us and there were two behind us. When we had left Alessandro's, I had refused to get into an Escalade, which hadn't helped Jamie and Louie's mood.

"The Escalade is safer, Maura," Jamie had practically growled.

"Tell that to Stefan," I had retorted.

That had shut down the argument and Jamie had ordered a goon to go retrieve my car.

As we had waited, Conor had come to stand next to me. "The day your da learned that he was taking over, he got hammered," he'd said. "He didn't want it either, but he was excellent at it. I've seen that excellence in you. We all have."

"You're talking like we won't find him," I'd said.

For only a moment, his eyes had turned sullen. Then he'd blinked and the emotion had been erased. "As much as I loathe

the De Lucas, they are a powerful ally." Conor's voice had gone very low, so that only I could hear him. "If you gain this alliance, no one will oppose you taking over, and any enemies who might have taken advantage of us at this vulnerable time will think twice. But with this gain, there is a cost. The De Lucas will be forming an alliance with you, Maura. There isn't a guarantee the alliance will stick if we find Stefan and you hand the family back over to him."

Since my conversation with my uncle, I had been quietly mulling it over in the backseat. It was giving me a headache. There was nothing I could do to change or fix what had happened tonight, especially as buzzed as I was at the moment.

"I think I want to move back into my bedroom in the main house," I said. It was the first thing to pop into my head to fixate on.

Louie turned in his seat so he could look back at me. "What?"

"Yours and Jamie's rooms are too small. I have things scattered between my room in the guest house and the main house and both of your rooms. I need a designated place that is mine... or ours. If you're not comfortable with it, I was thinking we could remodel it or find a different area of the house and remodel that. I was going to ask Stefan...I suppose I don't have to ask anyone."

Jamie stared at me through the rearview mirror, "We can create a space that's ours."

I looked out my window to see that we were driving over the bridge I'd hung Aryans from, when Louie shouted, "Jameson!"

Jamie hit the brakes at the same time I looked forward to see a semi-truck, driving in the wrong direction in the next lane, swerve into our lane between the Escalade in front of us and our car. Before Jamie could do anything else, the truck hit us head-on, making the air bags deploy and the windshield shatter. The semi kept driving, pushing us backward. For a short time, I could feel the back of the car hitting things behind us, but we weren't stopping. Then we weren't hitting anything anymore and we were falling.

CHAPTER NINETEEN

jamie

W hen we hit the water, it was dark. Almost too dark to see. Ice-cold water began filling the car quickly and I knew if we went under, it'd be pitch black.

I glanced over at Louie and saw he was working to get his seat belt free. I tried to undo my belt and it wouldn't unlatch. I reached into my pocket for my switchblade I always keep on me. "Maura!" I yelled for her as I sawed at the belt.

She didn't answer.

Fuck!

Louie got his belt free right after I did. I crawled into the backseat. Maura was unconscious, bleeding from the side of her head, and the water was up to her neck. I quickly got to work on cutting her loose from her seat belt. The water reached the top of her head before I could. "Fuck!" I roared, and just when my panic started to kick in, the belt cut free. I yanked her up and did my best to hold her head above the water, but the more the car filled up, the faster we sank. Louie was on the hood of the car waiting to help me get Maura out. As I got us into the front seat, Maura and I were swallowed up by ice-cold darkness. I couldn't see. Feeling around, I tried to find the way out. Louie grabbed me by my shoulders and helped guide me and Maura through the windshield until we were out of the car. I swam up as fast and as hard as I could with one arm.

When we surfaced, I gasped for air. In the distance there was gunshots, but that wasn't something we could worry about right now. Louie helped me get Maura to shore.

"She's not breathing!" he said as we crawled up the muddy bank.

Once we had Maura mostly out of the water, I laid her on her back. I grabbed her shoulders and shook her. "Maura!"

She didn't respond.

I put my hands on her chest and began doing compressions. I did them until I reached thirty. Then I put my mouth over hers and gave her two breaths. When that didn't work, I did it again. "Come on, baby," I begged as I pushed on her chest.

I was almost to thirty compressions again when she started coughing. Water spilled from her mouth and Louie helped me roll her on her side.

Relieved, Louie let out every curse known to man.

As soon as Maura was done coughing up all the water, I pulled her to my chest and hugged her tightly. Louie leaned in and hugged her from behind. I moved an arm from around Maura, threw it over his shoulder, and held both of them close.

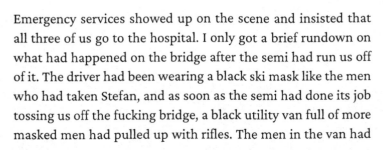

Emergency services showed up on the scene and insisted that all three of us go to the hospital. I only got a brief rundown on what had happened on the bridge after the semi had run us off of it. The driver had been wearing a black ski mask like the men who had taken Stefan, and as soon as the semi had done its job tossing us off the fucking bridge, a black utility van full of more masked men had pulled up with rifles. The men in the van had tried to help the guy driving the semi escape by opening fire on all of our people. We'd taken out two of theirs and thankfully, we hadn't lost anyone on our end.

Conor and Rourke looked over the two dead masked men, one of them being the driver of the semi, and found Irish tattoos on them. Rourke took their wallets just before the police and EMS showed up.

Louie and I only had a few bumps and bruises and were cleared to go home pretty quickly. Maura, however, had knocked·her head pretty good and with her drowning, the doctors kept her to run more tests. I called Brody, told him what had happened on the bridge, and asked if he could bring us dry clothes. He got to the hospital in record time. When he walked into Maura's hospital room, he looked distressed. It showed in his red-rimmed eyes and the way he stiffly moved. It seemed that as the hours had ticked by since he'd learned about Stefan, Brody had been slowly losing the battle to hold it together.

Maura, on the other hand, had been holding onto a hard, emotionless mask. When she looked at me, Louie, or anyone else, there wasn't any warmth in her eyes. Just cold, detachment, and determination. I didn't like it and neither did Louie. It felt like a huge backslide after weeks of hard work to get back glimpses of the woman we loved. I knew I couldn't focus on that right now. I had to reassure myself that Maura was doing what she had to in order to stay strong because too much relied on her right now. And if this was a backslide, Louie and I wouldn't give up. We'd fight like hell to regain the progress we lost.

As Brody walked into the room and Maura took in his distraught appearance, that mask she had been wearing wavered, and emotion scrunched up her brow. Brody rushed to her bedside, and they hugged each other tightly. Seeing that emotion come to the surface made every part of me sag with relief.

"I will find him," Maura assured Brody.

Brody stroked her hair, doing his best to hold on to his composure. "I know."

Not long after Brody arrived, there was a knock on Maura's hospital room door before it opened. Dean walked in, looking more pissed-off than usual. "Detectives Cameron and Brooks are here to see you," he told us and stepped out of the way for said detectives to walk in.

"Two attacks on the Quinn family in one day," Cameron said as he took in the room. "Don't you have one of your henchmen down the hall?"

He was referring to Stefan's attack this afternoon, only the police didn't know Stefan was missing. Only that our men had been gunned down. "We already gave our statements to the police," I told them from where I stood near the room's only window.

Cameron gave me a not-so-friendly look. "Well, we have a few more follow-up questions for the three of you."

I glanced over at Louie, who was sitting on one side of Maura's hospital bed, and Maura, who was holding Brody's hand. Maura asked Brody if he would go get her something to drink. He nodded, understanding that she was giving him an excuse to leave the room and taking it. As soon as Brody stepped out, Asher came into the room and shut the door. He and Dean stood guard by it.

The detectives began asking questions about what had happened, which we answered honestly at Maura's order. We recounted the semi hitting us and how we'd survived our car falling into the river. When they asked us if we knew anything about the shoot-out on the bridge, Maura took over.

"How would we know about anything that was happening

on the bridge if we were not on the bridge? And if there was a shoot-out, my family and our security would not have fired back had it not been in self-defense."

"Did you see who was driving the semi?" Brooks asked.

We all answered no.

"Interesting fact about that bridge," Cameron said. "About a month ago, four Aryans were hung from it and had shamrocks drawn on their chests."

"That same night, four properties that belonged to the Aryans exploded," Brooks said.

Maura didn't react. None of us did.

Cameron looked from me to Louie. "Weren't you two in a shoot-out with Aryans recently?" Then he looked to Maura. "And weren't you and your cousin, Rourke Murphy, attacked by the Aryans in a parking garage about nine months ago?"

"Sounds to me like tonight's incident on the bridge might have been retaliation by the Aryans," Brooks said as he stared intently at Maura.

"The attack earlier today could have been, too," Cameron added.

"If you believe that to be true, why aren't you speaking with the Aryans?" Maura asked, knowing that there weren't any Aryans left to speak to.

Cameron frowned. "We'll be speaking with them when we're done here."

"I'd love to know what they say," she said with a little spark of wickedness in her eye.

Before they could respond, I asked, "Are there any other questions we can answer for you, Detectives?"

They repeated a few questions to see if we'd change our answers. When we didn't, they decided to leave.

Cameron was the first to walk out. Brooks, though, lingered

in front of Dean. "You haven't been returning my calls," Brooks said to him.

The shock that took over Dean's face was unmissable. Brooks took it in with a smirk. "Have a good night, Officer Gallagher," he said and walked out.

As soon as the door closed behind him, Louie stood from where he was sitting. "Officer Gallagher?"

I glanced at Maura. There was true worry in her eyes, which told me that what Detective Brooks had said was true. Ice began to pump through my veins. "He's a cop?"

Maura ignored my question. "Asher—"

Before she could get out the order, I stormed toward Dean. Asher stepped between us, blocking me from reaching Maura's precious goon.

"Jamie!" Maura yelled.

"Christ, Maura, don't rip out your IV," Louie said.

I faintly heard Maura's bare feet slap on the linoleum before she stood with Asher to block me.

Maura put her hands on my chest. "Look at me," she begged me. When I couldn't look away from the fucking threat to our family in the room—the threat that she'd known about—her voice turned firm and authoritative. "Look at me."

Obeying, I met her eyes. Without looking away from me, she ordered, "Asher, get Dean out of here, now."

"I'm not leaving you," Dean said to her as he glared at me. Through my rage, I respected that he'd risk me killing him to stand with her rather than run away like a coward.

Maura ignored him. "Asher."

Asher put his hand on Dean's shoulder. "You being here right now will only make things worse. Let her handle this," he said to Dean in a low voice.

Dean's jaw clenched as he looked from me to the back of Maura's head. I could see the battle between want and reason in his eyes. Reason seemed to win, because he stormed out of the room with Asher right behind him.

I stared down at Maura and it took effort not to roar at her. "You've known."

She dropped her hands from my chest and took a step back. Not out of intimidation, but to stare me down. "I've known for a while."

I took a few steps away from her before I lost it. I ran my hands through my hair and began to pace to calm myself.

I could feel Maura watching me as I did. "This right here is the biggest hurdle of our relationship, Jamie."

"Your precious goon?" I snapped.

"No, your lack of trust in me, in the decisions I make," she said. "You say that I am the right person to lead this family, yet you are losing it over the fact that I've known Dean was a cop without any more information than that. You can't know that I'm the right person to lead this family if you can so easily jump to the conclusion that I would put us at so much risk."

"She's right, Jameson," Louie said calmly. "Maura wouldn't allow a cop around us without reason."

They were right. "It's my job to protect this family," I said as if that would explain how I was feeling.

"No, Jamie." She shook her head. "Your job is to help *me* protect this family. You either trust me to do it or not."

I put my hands on my hips and exhaled my anger out. "Alright. What's the story behind Dean?"

"Dean is a cop who volunteered to go undercover to infiltrate our family. According to Dean, Brooks was in charge of the undercover mission—operation—whatever you fucking call it. The first year Dean was here working grounds security, he couldn't give Brooks much of anything."

"What about when he was assigned to you?" Louie asked her.

Maura shook her head. "I'll get to that," she said. "Apparently, my grumpy best friend has a little bit of a dark side. He didn't care for being a cop all that much and during his first year with us, he got to see how the other side lived and he began to care for those he worked with. I was the last push he needed to flip sides."

"Because he loves you." I voiced what I'd known for quite some time.

Maura didn't deny it.

"I fucking knew it," Louie growled, sounding more pissed about that than the fact that Dean was a cop.

Maura let out an annoyed sigh. "Don't mistake loving and caring for someone as the same thing as being in love with someone. There is zero sexual attraction between Dean and me. Dean is my family, my best friend, and someone I can count on a great deal, and I am all of that for him."

That seemed to calm Louie enough for her to continue. She went on to explain how she'd discovered that Dean was a cop and what she'd overheard Brooks say to him. "What I found odd was when Brooks learned Dean was my personal security, Brooks became obsessive over me rather than the family. He asked Dean to find out the type of underwear I like to wear, who I've had sex with, what shoe size I am."

Louie glanced at me with a murderous look in his eye. "It sounds like we need to kill Brooks."

Maura rolled her eyes. "When Dean wouldn't give him much on me, Brooks started focusing on the family again. Dean tried to ignore him and told him he was out. Brooks threatened that if he didn't give him something, he would tell the family he was a cop."

Maura went quiet for a moment, and I realized then why she had said the other day that not only would Dean's life be at risk, but so would hers. "You gave Brooks something."

She nodded. "I gave him information on Riona and evidence that she was responsible for Blake's murder."

Blake had been grounds security who Riona and her men had used to break into the manor to decorate Stefan's entire study with pictures of Maura throughout her life, which included the night Maura had been raped at seventeen. All the pictures had been taken from afar as if Riona had been clearly stalking and was obsessed with Maura. After Riona had finished her art project in Stefan's study, she and her men had left with Blake. They had killed him and left his body down the street from the manor.

"Your mother?" Louie said, eyes wide.

I exhaled heavily. "Ratting on enemies is really bad, Maura. There's an unspoken rule amongst criminals. If shit happens in our world, it's handled in our world. We never involve cops."

"Don't ask me if I regret it, because you won't like the answer," she said. "He didn't do anything with it anyway. I had Vincent hack his personal and work computers and the police database. There was nothing that showed he documented who Blake's killer is. His case is still marked as unsolved, which, again, is odd. After the detectives came to the house a few weeks ago, I had Vincent do some extensive digging on Brooks." Maura looked down and it was obvious that what she had to say was bothering her. "Detective Antony Brooks is Zack Mathews' older brother."

I was a little taken aback. "Zack as in...Zack and Tyson?"

Fuck.

Maura nodded. "Brooks and Zack have the same mother. Brooks was away at college studying marine biology when I killed Zack. After he learned of Zack's death, he dropped out of college to become a cop."

Louie let out a curse. "Does he know you killed his rapist of a brother?"

Maura's brow furrowed. "That or he knows the family is responsible."

I met Louie's eyes. "I guess we do need to kill him."

"The last thing we need to be doing is going out and killing a cop," Maura said, looking from me to Louie. "Brooks does have a vendetta against me or the family, but he hasn't tried to do anything that is outside of the law. We at least have that working for us."

"He hasn't done anything *yet*," Louie grumbled.

"We need to focus on keeping this family intact and finding Stefan," Maura said firmly.

"And finding Dylan," I added.

Maura glanced down. It was the only hint that she was still beating herself up over sparing his life. "The thing about us Quinns is that we're stubborn and vindictive. When word gets out that Stefan is missing, whether Dylan took him or not, Dylan will make an appearance, to either kill me or take the family from me."

"Why do you think that?' Louie asked.

"Because Dylan was afraid of Stefan. It's why he used the Aryans to try and kill her, instead of doing it himself," I explained. "But with Stefan gone, I wouldn't put it past him to try and gain allies to overthrow Maura."

"And because he is the next male Quinn related to Stefan, people will side with him," Maura added.

"Then we need to stop him before he does that," Louie said.

Maura headed back over to her hospital bed. "I'm already working on that."

"The alliance with the De Lucas," I said, understanding Maura's actions tonight a little bit more.

Maura climbed back into the hospital bed and lay down. "Yes. If Nicky agrees to it, I'm going to owe him a lot of favors."

Louie stared down at the floor. "I thought…"

"You thought I stopped caring about myself again," Maura finished for him. "I knew I was taking a risk going there alone, but in my gut, I knew I could trust Nicky. With Stefan being taken and not knowing who took him, it gave me doubt. That's why I had to test him."

"You could have gone about it a safer way," I said.

She shrugged. "It was a spur-of-the-moment thing." She let out a yawn. "How much longer do you think they'll keep me here?" Her voice came out sounding sleepy.

"I can go see," I said, taking a step toward the door.

"You're not going out there to hunt down my goon, are you?" she asked with a tone that warned me that she'd do everything she could to stop me, exhausted or not.

"Your goon is safe for now, Maura," I grumbled.

"Good," she mumbled tiredly as I opened the door. "I just want to go home and hold our baby."

I froze before leaving the room. Glancing back, I saw that her eyes were closed. Louie was staring at me, seeming just as surprised as I was. It was not only the first time she had admitted that Kieran was hers without Stefan forcing it from her, but the first time ever that she had referred to Kieran as mine and Louie's.

CHAPTER TWENTY

maura

"Are you ready?" Dean asked. I'd just finished stepping into gold Manolo Blahnik pumps. My suit was black, formfitting, and the jacket was very risqué. It was meant to be worn without anything underneath. The opening was a deep plunge and secured closed with one button. I had a lot of cleavage on display. My hair was curled, my eye makeup was dark, and my lips were red.

"I'm ready, Grumpy," I said as I stepped out of my bathroom, connected to my bedroom in the main house.

Brenna and Asher were waiting for me in my bedroom. I took in Brenna's suit. Her black slacks were high-waisted and wide-legged. Her top under her open, black suit jacket was a white bustier corset crop with thin white straps and a lot of push-up. It showed off a good section of skin from the bottom of the corset to the top of her pants.

"Don't bend over in that top," I said to her.

Her eyes dropped to my chest and smirked. "Don't sneeze in yours."

We both grinned at each other.

I reached into my pocket and pulled out a key attached to a clover key chain. I held it out to her. "Happy eighteenth birthday."

She took the key from me.

"Our gift is your lessons to ride it, which start next week," Asher said, pointing at Dean and himself.

Her eyes lit up. "You got me a motorcycle?"

I smiled. "Your matte black Kawasaki Ninja 650 is in the garage." It was the exact bike she wanted according to Dean, who I'd made talk to her about it so I would know which one to get. He hadn't been thrilled with my little mission I'd sent him on, but he hadn't let me down.

Brenna threw her arms around me tightly and thanked me.

I hugged her back. "Just don't die on that thing."

Brenna hugged Asher and Dean next. Asher gladly accepted the hug, but Dean looked so uncomfortable.

"Brody has something planned for you tonight to celebrate," I told her as we headed downstairs.

"Did he invite my mother?" she asked me with whatever she was feeling locked down tight.

"She's back in rehab," I answered.

She stared at the ground as she walked, appearing deep in thought. "Good."

As we approached the chamber, Asher took his post along the wall with the other enforcers. Brenna and Dean each grabbed a door, opening them both for me to walk through. The male voices in the chamber went quiet and the high-ranking members in the Quinn family who sat around the table stood as I entered the room.

The clacking from my heels echoed in the room as I made my way toward my father's chair. It felt foreign coming to this end of the table where Jamie and Conor would flank me instead of Louie and Sean. The weight of everyone's eyes as they watched me pull out my father's chair and sit in it added even more weight to the moment.

Dean and Brenna took their posts behind me as the men at the table took their seats. Everyone except for Sean showed respect as they stared at me. Sean held a smirk, as if he was the cat who'd caught the canary.

"Shall we begin?" I asked the table.

"I would like to be brought up to date on things," Sean said.

"If you'd cared to show up yesterday, you would know," Jamie said in a curt voice.

"I would have if I'd known I was supposed to be here." Sean's eyes flicked to me. "I lost my phone. I have a feeling it fell out of my pocket at the don's club during the exchange."

Brenna let out a single cough behind me. I wished I could have let myself react.

Sean looked back at Jamie. "I didn't hear the news of Stefan until later and tried to stop by, but everyone was gone from the manor. I also heard the rumor that the princess didn't waste any time claiming her father's throne. Given where she's sitting now, it seems that rumor was fact."

"She's Stefan's heir," Rourke said, glaring at Sean.

"Yes, but is she ready?" Sean argued. "She is still a baby in this world and some in the family would prefer someone that isn't still wet behind the ears."

"Her father has been preparing her to take his place since she was thirteen," Conor said.

"And in the twenty-four hours she has been in charge, she has put things in motion for an alliance with the De Lucas," Jamie said.

Pensive, Sean leaned back in his chair. "Has the alliance been made?"

"He's coming to the house today to give me his answer," I announced.

"He'll agree to it," Louie said with certainty.

The muscle in Sean's jaw twitched. "Not that I need to ask, but it sounds like everyone at this table is in favor of her taking her father's place."

"Who do you think should be sitting here?" I asked, refusing to look away from him. I studied him, taking in every movement, every flicker of emotion he couldn't hide.

"Your uncle," he suggested.

Conor shook his head. "Not only do I not want the position, but this family belongs in the hands of a Quinn."

"Rourke, then. His mother is a Quinn," Sean suggested next.

Rourke pointed in my direction. "That chair belongs to my cousin."

"What about Dylan?" Sean asked the table.

Jamie, who had his arm resting on the table, fisted his hand. "That traitor will never be the head of this family."

"If Maura is the next head of the family, who will succeed her, then?" Sean continued to push. "She can't have any children to—"

Jamie slammed his fist on the table. The loud sound echoed off the walls and the room fell silent. Tension built as Jamie stared at Sean like he would slit his throat if Sean said one more word. I was going to do some dirty things to him later while imagining that look he held.

"I didn't know being able to conceive children was a requirement." I looked to my uncle. "How was it determined for my father? Or my grandfather? Or my great-grandfather? Did someone at this table jerk them off so they could test to see if they had viable swimmers?"

The murder in Jamie's eyes faded.

Louie grinned.

Rourke snorted. "That's gross, cuz."

The corner of Conor's mouth twitched. "You can appoint anyone as your heir. Your child or someone else."

I knew that, but I'd had to break the tension somehow. "I think it's clear where the majority of this table stands on me taking over. For the sake of time, let's move this meeting along."

"We need to debut you before false rumors spread," Conor said.

Debut?

"The Underground is the best place to do it," Louie suggested.

"The Underground?" I repeated.

"It's under the pakhan's club," Rourke said.

"Sasha's club?" I frowned. "Anarchy?"

Rourke nodded. "It's a neutral place within our territory where those with any standing and enough money in the crime world go to fuck around, whether they are loyal to our family or not."

"Gambling, high-end prostitutes, drugs, alcohol, you name it," Louie said. "The only thing that's not allowed is fighting and weapons."

"Unless it's a sanctioned fight that can be gambled on," Jamie said.

Sounded like Disneyland for criminals. "Alright, we'll go there tomorrow night."

We discussed Stefan after that. There wasn't any new information and Vincent and Aiden had yet to find any leads.

After I dismissed everyone, Sean stayed seated. "May I speak with you?" he asked me.

Rourke and Conor went to leave, but Jamie and Louie didn't move.

"It's a private matter that I would like to discuss with the head of the family alone," Sean said.

I tilted my head toward the door, gesturing for Jamie and

Louie to leave. Reluctantly, they listened. Sean told his enforcer to leave, and he looked expectantly at Dean and Brenna to leave as well.

"Go," I told them, and they too seemed reluctant to leave but followed my order.

Sean tapped the top of the table with the tip of his finger. "I don't support you taking over for your father."

I let out a theatrical gasp. "I'm shocked." I stood from my chair and went over to the liquor trolley. "Who do you support, Sean? Other than yourself, that is."

As I filled a crystal tumbler nearly full of whiskey, he said, "Me and my men could go back to Boston as soon as tomorrow, leaving you vulnerable here in New Haven. In fact, I've been incentivized to do so."

There it was.

You work quick, Dylan.

I took a big gulp and relished the burn of the whiskey as it slid down my throat. "I thought it odd for you of all people to suggest a traitor." I turned around to face him. "Especially since you were originally passed over so he could have that chair your ass is currently occupying. He certainly didn't earn it." I took a sip. "He got a spot at this table simply because he was a Quinn."

"Like you did," he snapped.

I let a little bit of the darkness show as the corners of my mouth lifted. "One would think that all that useless dick-sucking you did for Samuel to get that chair would have smarted your pride for at least a lifetime." I headed back to the table and rested my arms on the top of Jamie's chair. "Or is the correct phrase 'ass-kissing'? I can never remember." I shrugged.

With how clenched his jaw was, I was surprised I couldn't hear his molars grinding. "Would you like to know what he offered me for my support?"

"Do I really need to ask? I can tell you're dying to tell me."

He grinned proudly, as if he was three steps ahead of me in the game we criminals love to play. "Dylan offered me Brenna, if I help him take over."

I didn't say anything because I knew the reason he was telling me was coming.

"Now, you are right about my feelings for the little prick. If I was offered something better..." He trailed off, leaving what was unsaid up to me.

I lifted my arms off Jamie's chair to stand straight. "What could be better than Brenna?"

"You could still offer me Brenna along with naming me your successor," he suggested.

"Is that all?" I quipped.

"Or...I can have you," he said. "You can still be the bitch queen of the Quinns, but you will fuck me whenever I want and if I don't like something, you will do what you can to please me."

I pretended to mull over what he said and took a drink.

As he watched me, he looked so damn smug. "I think I know which you will choose."

I arched a brow at him. "Oh, really?"

"You are clever and ruthless, I'll give you that, but your weakness is your love for your family. You'll sacrifice yourself before you'll ever hand over Brenna."

I moved back over to Stefan's—no—my chair, pushed it away from the table. Facing him, I took another sip from my glass before setting it near the corner of the table. Holding his eyes, I unfastened the button on my suit jacket and opened it enough for him to see my breasts. I watched as his disgusting, triumphant gaze dropped to take them in. Not letting him look for long, I turned around and hopped onto the edge of the table. I peeked over my shoulder at him. "Well?"

He stood quickly and came to stand in front of me, eyes

locked onto my breasts. The way he stared at me made me feel like I was nothing more than the spoils from a game he thought he'd won.

He grabbed the lapels of my jacket and shoved it off my shoulders to get a better view of me. My jacket got caught at the crease of my elbows. "Take this off," he ordered. So I did and tossed my jacket on the floor.

His hands gripped my breasts. "You're such a good girl when you want to be."

The way he groped me hurt and I could see that he was waiting for a reaction. I didn't give him one.

"Kiss me," he demanded as his fingers dug into the soft tissue of my breast and he pulled me toward him.

I leaned forward and his mouth slammed down onto mine hard enough to clank our teeth. His kiss was just like his touch. Sloppy and with the intent to hurt. His tongue explored my mouth and his teeth bit at my lips. He let go of one of my breasts to grab the back of my head so he could shove his tongue farther into my mouth as if to gag me with it.

Alright, I've let this go on long enough.

I reached to the small of my back, grabbed the grip of my gun, brought the barrel under the side of his jaw, and pulled the trigger.

Blood hit me from my cheek down to my belly button. Sean's body dropped to the ground like a sack of potatoes. I arched back a little with my hand on the table behind me and I set my gun down in front of Jamie's chair so I could scoop up my drink. As I took another sip, one of the doors behind Stefan's chair opened. Jamie poked his head in. His eyes went wide at the sight of me bloody and topless. He came into the room and shut the door behind him. As he got closer, his eyes dropped to the floor in front of me.

As he stared down at Sean's body, he sighed. He didn't ask

me for an explanation. Instead, he walked past me to the other end of the room where the other set of doors were. He opened a door, looked out into the hall, said something I couldn't hear, then stepped back with the door opened wide.

The two enforcers Sean had brought with him walked into the room. Their attention was immediately locked onto half-naked me. Meanwhile, Jamie shut the door, reached behind him, and pulled out his gun.

By the time they noticed their boss dead on the floor, Jamie aimed at the backs of their heads and pulled the trigger, one right after the other.

I looked Jamie up and down, admiring every delicious inch of him. He caught me checking him out.

"That's the second time today you've done something sexy," I said.

With a smirk, he walked toward me, taking his time as he did. "Did he hurt you?"

"No more than I allowed him to."

He set his gun down on the table. I watched as he bent at the waist, grabbed Sean by his arms, and pulled his body from the floor beneath me to the side of the room. The body may have been gone from my feet, but a pool of blood remained.

After dropping Sean's arms without a care, Jamie walked over and stood before me in the blood. He offered me his hands as if to help me down. I didn't take them. Instead, I wrapped my legs around his waist and pulled him closer. To catch himself from falling forward, his hands slammed down on the table by my hips. His face was now inches from mine.

I set my drink back down and leaned the small distance to kiss him. It was just a peck.

I pulled away enough to meet his eyes. "He tried to take what's yours. I can still feel his hands on me."

I kissed him again. This time, he kissed me back.

"Show me I'm yours, baby," I ordered against his mouth.

One of his hands went to the back of my neck and he took over our kiss. He devoured my mouth with his lips, tongue, and teeth until I was aching between my legs. I didn't want to stop at a kiss. I wanted to lose myself in desire—to take a brief break from reality. In order to do that, I'd have to let go of my darkness to give Jamie control.

"Where'd he touch you?" he asked.

I grabbed his hand at the back of my neck and dragged it over my shoulder and down my chest, through the blood until his palm covered my breast. I took his other hand and brought it to my other breast. "Here."

His eyes darkened with rage and lust. He cupped my breasts tenderly and ran his thumbs over my nipples.

"Can you take it away?" I asked him.

"What?"

"My control." My voice shook. "The need to think—to be in charge. Take it from me for just a little while." I reached up to wrap my arms behind his neck. "Just like this." I pulled him close enough to kiss again.

Understanding, Jamie's hands dropped to the waistband of my pants. I lifted my hips to help him as he pulled my pants and my underwear off. My heels and pants fell to the floor. I shoved Jamie's suit jacket off and it joined my clothes. I grabbed his black button-up shirt next and ripped it open, sending buttons flying. He took it the rest of the way off and tossed it behind him. I worked on undoing his belt as he took off his undershirt. The sound of the belt clinking reminded me of things best left forgotten and I couldn't help but wince as I moved on to unfasten his pants.

Before I could pull his pants down, he stopped me. "Turn over and get on your hands and knees." His voice was so authoritative, I almost had the knee-jerk reaction to rebel. He must have seen that, because he added, "Do it, Maura."

I turned away from him and got on my hands and knees on the table.

"Head to the table, baby."

I lowered my head, leaving my ass in the air—baring all of myself to him. His warm hands smoothed over my butt cheeks before he spread me open with his thumbs. My breath hitched as he licked me from my clit to my back entrance. He buried his face in me as his tongue explored every inch of my slit. He lapped, flicked, and prodded with that tongue until I was shaking and dripping.

I dug my nails into the table as I begged him to make me come. Rewarding me, his tongue focused on my clit and wouldn't leave it until I was screaming into the table as I reached the peak of release and exploded with rippling waves of pleasure.

As I rode those waves, Jamie climbed onto the table behind me, shoved down his pants to release his cock, and pushed into me. I moaned long and loud as I stretched around him. When he was about halfway in, he grabbed me by my hips and thrust the rest of the way in. He didn't give me time to adjust to him as he pulled back out and slammed back in. He did that over and over, fucking me hard and successfully making me lose my mind.

His hands went to my breasts, and he lifted my upper body up until my back was up against his chest. As he continued to pound into me, he moved one of his hands up, smearing more of Sean's blood over me, until his hand was around my neck. He squeezed just a little, not enough to cut off my air. "Is this what you want?" he asked as his other hand dropped between my legs.

His fingers rubbed circles around my clit, making me cry out, "Yes!"

"Are you mine?" he growled in my ear.

"Yes!"

"Tell me you love me and I'll let you come."

"I love—" Before I could finish saying it, he brought me to release, and I shattered in his arms.

Jamie continued to pound into me, making my orgasm last longer, until I felt him swell and pulse inside me as release hit him.

Breathing heavily, I reached behind his neck and turned my head to kiss him. "Thank you."

He huffed a laugh and kissed me back.

CHAPTER TWENTY-ONE

My panties were the only article of clothing that hadn't soaked up Sean's blood on the floor. Even though I was covered in drying blood, I didn't want to put on clothes dripping with it. Standing in just my black lace panties, I dropped my suit back to the floor.

Other than Jamie's suit jacket and the bottoms of his shoes, his clothes were blood-free. I couldn't say the same for his body. He had blood on one of his hands, on his inner arms, and the side of his neck. With a satisfied smirk, he held out his black button-up shirt to me. I took it and put it on. It covered me to mid-thigh, but it was missing most of its buttons. I found two below my sternum to fasten. The shirt was so big on me that it immediately fell off one of my shoulders. It didn't cover me much, but at least I wouldn't flash the whole house my nipples.

"I'll clean this up," Jamie said as he buckled his belt.

I winced at the sound of it clinking again before my darkness could slam down a wall between me and what I didn't want to feel.

Jamie paused. "That's the second time you've done that."

"Bad memories."

"I won't wear a belt after today," he said.

I shook my head. "Don't stop wearing one. If I get you out of your pants enough times, I'll start associating the sound with a good thing instead of bad."

Smiling at me lovingly, he replied, "I don't think you'll have an issue achieving that goal."

Just as Jamie finished putting on his black undershirt, the door at the other end of the room opened and Dean walked in. His eyes dropped to the dead enforcers at his feet and he slammed the door closed behind him. He took in the rest of the room. "I'm guessing your private meeting didn't go well."

I shook my head and began telling them what had happened with Sean.

By the time I was done, Jamie was pissed. "Help me with this, will ya?" he asked Dean, who nodded.

I scooped up my gun off the table and walked toward the door behind Dean. "Do you have a joint on you?" I asked Dean as I approached.

He reached into his pocket and pulled out a joint and a lighter. "Are you feeling alright?"

I took the joint with a tiny grin. "I just received multiple orgasms. Getting high will enhance this moment."

Dean blinked slowly as he stared at me. "You overshare sometimes."

Jamie snorted at his response.

"There's no such thing as oversharing with best friends," I said as I put the joint between my lips.

Dean sighed through his nose as he lit the end of it for me. I walked out after that, leaving them with the cleanup, and ran into Asher in the hall.

He whistled as he took my appearance in. "Did you kill someone or get laid, doll?"

"Both." I tilted my head toward the chamber as I passed him. "Jamie and Dean are going to need your help."

Behind me, I heard him open the chamber door and let out a curse, which made me smile.

As I turned into the foyer, I heard Brody say my name. Across the room near the front door, I found him staring at me wide-eyed. "I was just coming to find you," he said, and it was then that I saw Nicoli, Dario, Ivano, and two De Luca goons standing behind him.

Shit!

I blew smoke through pursed lips and plastered a polite smile on my face. Nicoli's and Dario's eyes drifted to the stairs on my right. Brenna was on her way down, but when she saw me, she froze, wide-eyed, and then her gaze traveled to our guests.

"I need clothes," I said to her.

She nodded and turned to head back upstairs.

I looked to Brody next. "Find Louie and send him to Stef—to the study." I walked across the foyer toward the hall that led there. "And I need you to call Conor and Rourke and tell them they need to come back to the manor."

"Should I send Jameson to the study?" Brody asked, seeming nervous to leave me with the De Lucas.

I stopped in front of him. "After he's done cleaning up the mess I just made."

Brody nodded, reaching into his pocket for his phone, and walked out of the foyer. I stared at the don. "I apologize for my appearance."

"What'd you do? Play around with your kill?" Dario asked.

"If that bloody handprint around her neck is anything to go by, I'd said someone played with her," Ivano said.

Nicoli grinned as his eyes bounced all over me.

Revealing nothing, I gestured for them to follow me, and I

led the way to Stefan's study. Once inside, I went to sit behind Stefan's desk, while Nicoli, Dario, and Ivano took in the room as they walked in.

"This was your father's office?" Nicoli asked as he sat in one of the chairs in front of Stefan's desk. Dario and Ivano went to sit on the couch in the seating area, while the two goons they'd brought with them stood up against the wall near the door.

"It is." I leaned back in my father's chair and brought my joint to my mouth.

"Is?" Nicoli repeated.

I blew out rings of smoke as I debated how much to reveal. "Yesterday, Stefan was taken. We don't know if he is dead or alive. My family wants to proceed as if he's already dead, which is why I am in the position I am in."

"You really are honest," Dario said.

I smirked at him. "Were you testing me?"

Dario didn't respond. He didn't have to. I could see it on his face that he had been expecting me to lie.

"What would happen to our alliance if you recover Stefan?" Nicoli asked.

Before I could answer, the door to the study opened and Brenna walked in with a new black suit and emerald-green heels for me. She made her way over and handed me my pants first.

I scooted my chair back and put my feet through the leg holes of the slacks. "Stefan would honor the alliance, but I know you probably won't take my word for it, so I'm open to suggestions on the best way to handle this," I said as I stood to pull up my pants.

"You asked us for the alliance. Shouldn't you be trying to convince us?" Ivano asked, frowning.

Brenna set my heels on the ground in front of me to step into. As if reading my mind, she held open my suit jacket.

"I may have asked for the alliance, Ivano, but I'm not the only one here who wants it." I held my joint between my lips while I unbuttoned Jamie's shirt. Without hesitation, I took off his shirt, revealing my breasts covered in dried blood.

Nicoli smirked as he stared unabashedly. Ivano's brows tried to touch his hairline. Dario also appeared slightly surprised.

I took the jacket from Brenna, slid my arms through it, and buttoned it closed. I pulled my hair out of the collar and took the joint from my mouth after taking another pull from it. "Close your mouths, boys, you'll catch flies," I said as I sat back down.

"Can't blame us for staring," Nicoli said.

Brenna went over and sat in one of the leather armchairs. Dario's eyes tracked her the entire time.

"I know you want an alliance, too, Nicky," I said, getting us back on track.

Nicoli turned serious. "I do, but I can't give you one if you're going to step down if Stefan returns."

Understandable. "What if I don't step down unless Stefan agrees to honor the alliance?"

"What if your father kills you if you refuse to step down? Or worse, it causes a war within your family?" Dario asked.

"Don't underestimate Stefan's love for his daughter," Brenna said, staring Dario down. "Stefan would kill every member of this family before he let any harm come to her. If you don't believe that, then know this...Stefan knows Maura used the cocaine as currency to buy your help. If it had been anyone other than Maura, she would have been branded a traitor because it lost the family millions. Or it would have, if Stefan hadn't paid all that money back to cover up what Maura had done."

Nicoli looked pensive. "Stefan did call me and thanked me for helping you."

Everyone seemed surprised by that information, including myself.

The door to the study opened again and Louie strolled in. "Don't mind me," he said with a charming grin as he took note of everyone, even Nicoli's goons. He walked all the way across the room to stand behind me up against the wall.

"Tell me why you asked for this alliance, Maura?" Nicoli asked, even though he knew the answer. He just wanted me to admit the vulnerability out loud.

I took another pull from my joint before I answered. "Because I could use your help. Not everyone is going to support me in power and others will underestimate me all because I am a woman. I would prefer to not have to kill a shit ton of people and having your support would help with that, but I will if I have to. Just by looking at me you can see that I've already started."

Nicoli was quiet as he pondered. "An alliance formed by trust and friendship."

"Normally, alliances are secured by marriage," Ivano said.

I understood his need for more reassurance when it came to this alliance, but baby De Luca was poking at a topic I did not care for. "I can't marry Nicky. For one, there isn't enough room in my bed. And two, I can't have children." I made my voice as nonchalant as possible. "Nicky wouldn't be able to have little heirs to take over for him one day, and if he stepped out on me... well, I do have the nickname The Castrator for a reason."

Ivano's eyes flicked to Brenna. She noticed and went completely still.

Before Ivano could even suggest it, I spoke. "No." With one word, I made myself very clear that I would not even consider it.

Ivano raised his hands up slightly in surrender.

"Out of friendship and because I trust you, I'll agree to the alliance," Nicoli finally said. "But under the condition that you won't step down if you find Stefan and he doesn't agree to honor the alliance."

That was a lot of faith he was granting me. As his friend, I wouldn't let him regret it. "I give you my word as a Quinn," I said, and thus, our alliance was formed.

"We should discuss terms," Ivano suggested.

I gave him a dry look. "You don't have any friends, huh?"

Brenna coughed to cover up her need to laugh.

I sighed and opened one of the desk's drawers. I found a pen and paper. "Rule number one," I said out loud as I wrote. "Don't be a dick. I feel like if this alliance is going to work, that's really important." I looked up at Nicoli, who was grinning. "Would you like to add anything?"

"No killing each other," he suggested.

"That sort of falls under the 'don't be a dick' clause, but I'll add it anyway," I said and wrote it down.

We spent a good hour discussing the terms. Some were serious and some were funny, especially when I had Brenna help me hand out drinks. About halfway through our discussion, Conor and Rourke showed up. Conor was tense at first, but after we poured him a drink, he relaxed a little.

"To make sure news of the alliance spreads quickly, Nicoli should join you when you visit the Underground," Conor suggested.

"I've heard of the Underground. It's run by the Bratva, isn't it?" Nicoli asked.

I nodded. "I was planning on going tomorrow night."

"I have business to attend to tomorrow night. Why don't we go tonight?" Nicoli suggested.

My eyes traveled to Brenna. She was already staring at me. "It's fine, Maura."

Nicoli looked from me to her and back. "Did you have something planned?"

"Today is my birthday," Brenna told him.

Nicoli's brows rose. "Happy birthday."

"The baby in the family isn't a baby anymore," Rourke said, teasing Brenna.

After we filled a whole page of terms, Nicoli and I signed it. "Would you like me to make you a laminated copy?" I asked him.

He smiled. "Sure," he replied as he, Dario, and Ivano stood to leave. We had made a plan to meet back here tonight before heading to the Underground together.

Nicoli walked over to where Brenna sat. "Because I messed up your birthday, you should let me make it up to you by getting you a gift. It can be as extravagant as you want."

"And why would you assume I'd want anything extravagant?" she asked, giving him a hard time.

Knowing Nicoli, he found that endearing. "I didn't assume. I just offered."

Brenna stared up at him and I could see that she was really debating how she wanted to respond. Before she could answer, her phone went off in her pocket. As she read over the message that was sent to her, she had difficulty keeping what she was feeling from showing on her face. For a split second, it was obvious she was upset, but by the next, she'd masked it. She got to her feet. "I don't think you'd be able to get what I really want."

"I'm a pretty resourceful man." Nicoli tried to smile at the challenge, but having seen that brief moment of upset on Brenna's face, his smile didn't hold.

"Okay, then." Brenna smirked up at him. "I'd like the bullets from the first men I killed made into jewelry." She turned to me.

"I'll be right back." She glanced at Nicoli one last time before walking out.

Nicoli looked to me. "Who were the first men she killed?"

I began opening Stefan's desk drawers looking for the newspaper I'd asked him to keep for me. I found it in the middle drawer and held it up so he could see the front page. Everyone, including Conor and Rourke, stared at the big picture of the bridge and read the headline.

"Brenna killed the men you hung from the bridge?" Conor asked, having just realized.

I placed the newspaper back in the drawer. "Three of the four. It was her initiation. She helped me kill them and then helped me hang them."

"Damn. Hers was better than mine," Ivano said, sounding jealous.

"It terms of notoriety, yes, hers was probably better than most of ours," I said.

After that, the De Lucas left and Jamie finally showed up. Conor and Rourke saw the dried blood on Jameson and then stared at the dried blood that was visible on my chest and neck.

"Why are you two covered in blood?" Rourke asked. "And more importantly, why does it look like the two of you fu—"

Conor smacked the back of his son's head before he could finish speaking.

"I killed Sean," I announced and went on to tell them what had happened, which led to me telling them the truth about Dylan. I had no choice.

As they listened, Rourke looked more and more angry. Conor was upset as well, but not as torn-up as Rourke appeared.

"I'm sorry, Rourke. I'm sorry to both of you," I finished.

"It's not easy to kill family, darlin'. Given how it's blown back on you, I think you deserve a pass on this one," Conor said.

Rourke ran his hands down his face. "I don't blame you, Maura. He's my cousin, too, and I wanted him to have the second chance just as much as you did."

"He's got too much of his father in him," Conor said.

The conversation got back on the topic of Sean and how to handle the fallout.

"We need to go to Boston to get ahead of this. We'll need to clean house and appoint a new person to oversee that area of our territory, preferably one that is alright with a woman being the head of the family," I said.

"You need to be here. I'll go with my men tonight," Conor offered as he stood.

I shook my head. "I think it would look best if more than one leader of this family went." My eyes drifted to Jamie. "You were Stefan's enforcer. Wherever Stefan couldn't be, you took over. It will be more of a show of power if the both of you go."

Jamie looked to Louie, and something passed between them. "I'll keep her safe," Louie told him.

"Both of them," Jamie corrected.

Louie smiled. "Yes, and our little dark one, too."

CHAPTER TWENTY-TWO

"Doing okay, beautiful?" Louie asked.

"Yeah," I said numbly as I rocked Kieran in his nursery, which Brody had decorated in blues and baby elephants. Jamie had left for Boston and with each minute he was gone, it got harder to ignore the things my darkness had been doing its best to hold back. I'd relieved the nanny, Caroline, who was a kind woman and very motherly like Jeana, Stefan's personal chef. I'd thought holding and rocking Kieran to sleep would help distract me. It didn't.

Louie came into the room and knelt in front of the rocker I was sitting in. "You're crying."

"I'm aware."

He put his hands on my knees. "You've been so strong through all of this, but you're allowed to take a moment to process."

A moment wouldn't be enough.

I closed my eyes and shook my head. "I can't. If I let go, everything I can't afford to feel right now will rush in and I will start screaming."

Louie swiped my cheek with his thumb. "It looks to me that what you don't want to feel is catching up to you anyway."

"I'm taking the edge off so I have a little more time to keep going," I said, opening my eyes. "I just need a few more minutes."

He nodded and left the room.

When I laid the baby in his crib a half hour later, I dried my face and headed to my bedroom. I ran into Dean on the way. He took one look at my face and I could see that he knew I had been crying. He didn't say anything, though.

As soon as we got to my room, I went to search my closet and Dean sat on my couch.

"What does someone wear to The Underground?" I shouted out to Dean.

"Clothes."

I poked my head out of my closet. "No shit, smartass. I'm asking if it would be overboard to wear a suit? Or should I wear a dress? I'm kind of hesitant to wear one of those, though. I feel like wearing a dress will really accentuate that I'm a woman and no one will be able to see past that."

"You could wear a cardboard box and everyone you come across tonight will still see that you're a woman," he grumbled. "So it doesn't matter what you wear."

"Are you trying to say that I'm too beautiful?" I teased. I knew what he meant, but it was nice to get the pep talk.

He pulled out his phone and began messing around on it, ignoring me. I supposed that meant he was out of nice things to say.

I went farther into my closet and picked out three different outfits: a black suit, a black jumpsuit with a deep plunging front and wide legs, and an emerald-colored dress that was short but had long sleeves. "Was Jamie nice to you while you helped him get rid of those bodies?" I asked as I walked over to him.

Dean just frowned at me as I approached.

"I'm going to take that as a yes." I held the suit along the front of my body. "Now help me pick what to wear."

His bitchy face didn't change as I showed him each outfit. "Don't you have Brenna for this?"

"This falls under best-friend duties."

He rolled his eyes. "The one-piece thing."

"The jumpsuit?" I asked as I held it up to me again.

He nodded.

I headed back to my closet. "I'm going to need your help picking shoes next," I said over my shoulder.

I heard him let out an annoyed sigh that made me grin evilly. I didn't need his help picking out an outfit, but I was in the mood to torture someone, and he was the only one around.

※

"The De Lucas are here," Louie said as he walked into my bedroom.

I was currently fastening the strap on my black, five-inch heeled Jimmy Choo sandals that showed off my dark red painted toenails. My hair was styled with loose curls, my eye makeup smoky, and my lips dark blood-red. I was wearing diamonds on my ears and around my wrist and my diamond clover necklace Stefan had given me around my neck.

As soon as I finished getting my shoe on, I stood from the couch and turned to face Louie. He raked his eyes over me from head to toe. "You look gorgeous."

I gave him a small smile and grabbed my black clutch before walking to him. He watched me as I approached, still admiring every inch of me. I took that moment to admire him as well. He was dressed in a dark blue, almost black suit, sans tie, and a black button-up shirt underneath.

He grabbed my hands. "You're going to turn heads tonight."

"The whole point of going to The Underground is to be noticed."

"They'll more than notice you."

I tilted my head slightly as I stared up at his unreadable face. "Feeling jealous?"

His thumb rubbed my ring finger on my left hand. "Maybe I'd feel better if you wore something that said you were claimed."

I couldn't stop my surprise from showing.

"I didn't like it when Ivano brought up marriage as a way of securing an alliance," he said.

"I would never—"

"I know." He took in a calming breath and exhaled it slowly. "I want to remove their audacity to ask. I don't want anyone looking at you like you're a prize available for the taking."

I smiled, enjoying his possessiveness. "Then you and Jamie better pick out something hard to miss." I didn't know how we would achieve what he was hinting at, but I knew the three of us would find a way to figure it out.

His smile matched mine and he gave me a small kiss so I wouldn't have to reapply my lipstick. Holding hands, he and I walked out of my room. Dean, Asher, and Finn were waiting in the hall and followed us as we made our way downstairs.

Rourke and his goons were waiting in the foyer with Nicoli, Dario, and some of their enforcers. They all watched me as I came down the stairs. "I apologize for the wait," I said as I walked up to Nicoli. He was wearing a black-on-black suit with the top few buttons of his shirt undone.

He took in my appearance with a grin. "Worth the wait, as always."

I glanced around the room. When I didn't see who I was looking for, I turned to my goons. "Where's Brenna?"

Finn took a step away from our group, intending to go look for her, when we heard Brenna say, "I'm here." Walking fast, she came into the foyer from the hallway that led to the backyard.

I was a little wowed by her appearance. Her hair was iron-straight; her makeup was dark and shimmery and made her look like she was a few years older than she was. She had on a white halter top with sparkly silver beading, black faux leather high-waisted shorts, and black, chunky-heeled, lace-up ankle boots. Over her halter she wore her dual shoulder holster that held two Glocks. As she walked farther into the room, she slipped into a leather jacket.

I peeked at Nicoli and Dario, and as I expected, both of them were staring at her as if they couldn't look away.

Louie squeezed my hand, requesting my attention. He was also watching Nicoli and Dario and when his eyes flicked to me, he gave me a look that said, *Do you see that?* He had seen what I had been picking up on for a while now.

"Are we ready?" I asked the room, and we headed out.

The cobblestone driveway was lined with black Escalades waiting to take us to Anarchy and beneath it, The Underground. As we walked down the steps to the cars, I leaned close to Brenna. "Where'd you disappear to this afternoon?"

"My mom sent me a message threatening that if I didn't call her back, she'd check herself out of rehab," she said sullenly. "I've been ignoring her calls for a while, and she resorted to blackmail to get me to call her back."

"What did she want?" I asked.

She hid emotion from her face and voice. "To wish me a happy birthday. I suppose I should feel happy she remembered."

We made it to the bottom of the steps, and I paused to tell her, "You're allowed to feel however you want."

Nicoli and our entourage walked around us as we made our way through the club. There were live bands performing tonight and I caught Brenna staring at the dance floor as we passed. Louie led the way to a single door with an Employees Only sign. Two Russian goons stood guard by that door and as soon as we approached, they opened it for us. We filed into a short hallway that led to four more Russian goons holding black leather boxes standing in front of an elevator.

One of the goons with a box asked us to disarm. Everyone began handing over their guns. Well, everyone except Brenna. One of the Russian goons eyed her expectantly and she let out a sigh. She shucked off her leather jacket and tossed it at Finn. He caught it with a glare. She slid off her shoulder holster with her two guns and handed it over. After she snatched her jacket back from Finn and went to put it back on, I saw the impression of another gun under her shirt behind her back.

Louie had told me in the car that they would disarm us before we could enter, but also that everyone who came here snuck in at least one weapon. As half of our group climbed into the elevator, I leaned toward Brenna. "Great performance."

She grinned like an evil little mastermind. "Thank you. I thought it was good, too."

Louie stood in front of the buttons to pick a floor. There were only two to choose from. One was labeled "1" and the other was labeled "2." I assumed that each button identified a floor, and we were currently on the first floor. Louie pressed the "1" and held it until the elevator began moving down. As soon as the doors opened, the smell of cigars filled my nose and low jazzy music filled my ears.

Louie and Dario got off the elevator first and stepped to the side so Nicoli and I could take point walking into the room. The carpet was dark red with gold swirls. It reminded me of something you'd see in a casino. As I took in the rest of the room, I realized the carpet was fitting. Poker and craps tables filled most of the large room and each one was occupied.

Some goons lined curtain-covered walls, others stood closer to their bosses, but none blocked walkways. Many young women in lingerie walked around with trays of drinks, poker chips, and cigars. A little blonde-haired and blue-eyed waitress with an empty tray noticed us and veered our way. She zeroed in on Nicoli right away.

"How can I help you, sir?" she asked him with a thick Russian accent.

"Where is Sasha?" I asked.

She frowned as she stared at me, almost as if she was confused that I was even talking. I stared back expectantly. She glanced back at Nicoli and when he didn't speak to her, she regarded me with a little more respect. "I'll go get him," she said and quickly went off to find Sasha.

"I'm trying very hard not to be judgmental right now," I said as I took in the rest of the waitresses, who obviously served more than just drinks here.

"I'm not," Brenna grumbled behind us.

I noticed Nicoli's smile as I went to look over my shoulder at her. Brenna was frowning at Dario, who was smirking back at her.

She leaned close to him. "It seems you have a type," she said in a low voice I could barely hear.

"And what's that?" he asked her.

I couldn't hear what she whispered, but I was able to read her lips. "Young and blonde," she whispered, and his smirk fell off his face instantly.

"Sasha's coming," Louie said to me.

I faced forward just in time to see Sasha's surprise at seeing me and then Nicoli.

"I never thought I'd see a day where Quinns and De Lucas walked through my door together," he said as he approached. His beautiful gray eyes locked with mine. "Good evening, Maura. I was very sorry to hear about Stefan."

I had the knee-jerk reaction to correct him—Stefan wasn't dead—but I managed to refrain. "If you've heard about Stefan, then you probably know why I'm here."

He nodded. "Rumors are already spreading of your takeover."

"And how does the pakhan of the Bratva feel about me being the head of the Quinn family?" I asked.

"We are as loyal to the Quinn family as we have always been," was his response.

"I'm glad." I gestured to Nicoli. "Did you also hear of the alliance I formed with the De Lucas?"

Sasha's brows rose slightly. "I did not." He held his hand out to Nicoli. "Sasha."

Nicoli shook his hand firmly. "Nicoli."

"Welcome to The Underground." Sasha's eyes roamed over us, and they paused on Brenna for a moment.

"Maura is going to need a few million in chips," Louie said.

Sasha nodded and looked to Nicoli. "Would you also like some chips?"

"I'll take the same," Nicoli said.

Sasha turned and gave the room a quick glance. When he saw whatever he was looking for, he leaned close to me and said in a low voice, "I recommend you start at the table in the far back and all the way to the left. They're big players in this city and they were loyal to Stefan."

I nodded my thanks.

"I will have your chips brought to you," Sasha said before he walked away.

Nicoli walked with me as we made our way through the large space. Heads turned, some did a double take, and people whispered as we walked by.

Louie leaned close and explained who each man was at the table we were heading to. "Rourke is going to mingle at other tables to try and spread the news faster," he said after he was done going over everyone.

I nodded and Rourke along with his goons broke off from our group.

As we approached our intended table, the men at it were laughing. My and Nicoli's goons went to stand by the wall, while Dario, Louie, and Brenna remained with us. Nicoli allowed me to take point in greeting the table.

"Hello, gentlemen. Do you mind if my friend and I join you?"

Their laughter stopped at the sound of my voice. Almost instantly, I could see them forming assumptions about me that were absolutely wrong.

"And who might you be?" said Conrad Johnson, the president of a local MC that had sister chapters all throughout the New England area. He was a bear of a man, clad in jeans and a black leather vest. He had a long blonde beard with streaks of white in it.

The other two men sitting at the table were a rich businessman named Erik Teller and...well, I supposed the other was a pimp. Hector Sullivan ran a high-end escort service, and I didn't mean the kind of escort service where the ladies stood in as dates to events for rich men. His style gave off an old-time gangster vibe, with his gelled, slicked-back brown hair and the emerald-green suit he wore.

"My name is Maura Quinn." I enjoyed the recognition that

graced all of their faces. I also noticed the table behind us and the table to the right go quiet.

"Stefan Quinn's daughter?" Erik asked.

"Heard you took out all the Aryans," Conrad said, winking. "Nice job."

"I also heard you were the head of the Quinn family now," Hector added.

"That's right," I said, and I watched as their eyes shifted to Nicoli.

"Did you say he was your friend?" Hector asked.

"Yes," I answered.

"Last time I checked, Quinns and De Lucas didn't get along so well," Conrad said as he looked back and forth between Nicoli and me.

I smiled politely. "Sounds to me like you're a little behind on current events. If you let us join you, I'd be happy to catch you gentlemen up."

Erik gave me a charming smile. "Have a seat, then."

Nicoli and I sat at the table while Dario, Brenna, and Louie stood behind us. Two practically naked waitresses showed up with my and Nicoli's chips. As I was stacking them, I heard a feminine voice say, "Will you be needing chips this evening, Mr. Dupont?"

I turned in my seat slowly and gave Louie a look that screamed, *What the fuck?*

He let out a nervous laugh and shook his head at her. "No. I won't be needing any chips to—"

"Go mingle, Louie," I ordered as I spun back around.

"I guess I'll be needing those chips after all," I heard Louie say behind me.

Nicoli huffed a laugh as he finished organizing his chips.

I leaned close so only he would hear me. "What?"

"I've never seen you jealous before," he said, keeping his voice low.

I smirked. "If I truly had been jealous, I would have killed her."

"So you make your men sweat for fun?"

My smirk turned into a sly grin. "I've been in a torturing mood today and I can't seem to help myself."

As the dealer began dealing out cards, the men at the table couldn't wait to inquire about things. They asked about Nicoli's and my alliance, which they seemed impressed by. Then they started asking questions about the Aryans.

"A lady doesn't kiss and tell. Or is that not how the saying goes?" I said, making them chuckle, and thankfully two wait-resses-slash-prostitutes came by to take drink orders and flirt.

After playing a few rounds of Texas Hold'em, I picked up on everyone's tells fairly quickly. Conrad's fingers twitched on the table when he was bluffing and were completely still when he wasn't. Erik inhaled before he bluffed, and Hector always touched his face. Nicoli took me a while to figure out, but every time he got a shitty hand, he'd tap his finger on the backside of his cards as he looked at them.

"You have a stone-cold poker face like your father," Conrad said as he folded his hand.

I smiled as I took a quick sip of the whiskey I had ordered. "Well, he was the one who taught me how to play." The only reason he had was to teach me to read people. It hadn't ever been for fun. Just another lesson. A year ago, I would have felt bitter about that, but now I understood. As hard and messed-up as my childhood had been, all of the games, tests, and lessons had been necessary.

Erik had to leave after that hand. "I would like to set up a meeting to discuss business and how the future is going to look now that you're the head of the Quinn empire. Can I still schedule through Brody, or do you have someone else handling your schedule?"

"You can reach me through Brody," I told him.

He nodded and left. As the four of us were halfway through another hand, someone pulled out the chair Erik had been sitting in. "Mind if I join you?" an Italian man in a gray suit asked as he sat down, which defeated the purpose of even asking. The man was very familiar to me, but I couldn't place him. With how Nicoli straightened in his seat and stared coldly at the new addition to the table, I'd say he wasn't a comrade to the De Lucas.

The new guy smirked and tipped his head at Nicoli. "De Luca."

"Romano," Nicoli greeted back.

Hearing that name triggered my memory. Sitting across from us was Vito Romano, the consigliere for the Romano family, who happened to be a rival family to the De Lucas and possibly the Quinns as well. Many generations back, the Romanos had ruled over my and Nicoli's territories until the Quinns and De Lucas had formed an alliance to remove the Romano family from power. Our families had succeeded and split the Romano territory in two. Of course, the alliance between the Quinns and De Lucas hadn't lasted long, and we'd been fighting with each other ever since.

"You're in the wrong territory, aren't you?" Vito asked Nicoli.

Nicoli folded his hand in the game. "I was invited."

Vito's attention moved to me, and his eyes dragged over what he could see of my upper body. "When did they start allowing girlfriends in here?"

I put chips in the pot, calling Conrad's current bluff, and smiled at Vito. "Why? Does my presence threaten you?"

Vito chuckled. "You got a mouthy one there, De Luca."

Brenna walked slowly out from behind me and around the table. Anyone else wouldn't perceive her as a threat. I knew otherwise.

Nicoli relaxed back in his chair with a smirk. "She's not mine."

Vito glanced at Conrad and Hector and they both looked away, shaking their heads.

"Then who does she belong to?" Vito asked the table.

"You might want to shut up, Vito," Conrad warned.

Vito frowned at him. "And why is that?"

Brenna came up behind him and pressed something into his back, making him go stiff. "Because you're insulting the head of the Quinn family," Brenna said in a low voice.

Vito didn't even look surprised, which told me he had been purposely insulting me under the guise of ignorance. "This is a neutral club," he growled.

The table's dealer backed away slowly and then took off, undoubtedly to go get Sasha or security.

"Yes, it is," I agreed. "But don't forget that no matter how neutral this club may be, it's still within Quinn territory. My territory. It is merely out of respect for Sasha that I honor the rules of his club. However, there isn't a rule that says I can't drag your ass out the fucking door."

"If you do anything to me, you'll be starting a war," Vito threatened.

Nicoli let out a dark chuckle full of malice. "Dominik won't start a war with the Quinns for you."

Dominik Romano was the don of the Romano family.

"Are you sure about that?" Vito asked. "Stefan is gone and a bitch—"

Brenna grabbed the back of Vito's head and slammed it down onto the table. "Oh! I'm sorry, sir! I must have tripped!" Brenna said loudly.

Vito sat up straight, cupping the side of his face as he did.

I tsked. "Brenna, what did I tell you about wearing those shoes?"

She let out a dramatic sigh. "I know. I hope it doesn't happen again. It would be unfortunate if I ended up *pulling* something."

"Yes, that would be unfortunate." I locked eyes with Vito. "Don't you agree, Mr. Romano?"

He glared at me defiantly, as if he knew with certainty that he was untouchable.

"I'm about to squelch that confidence you have." I leaned forward and rested my arms on the table. "I could draw a clover on your chest and drop your body on Dominik's front lawn and he still wouldn't go to war with me. Do you want to know why?"

Vito didn't ask, but Nicoli answered anyway. "Because if he did, he would be taking on the De Lucas as well. And that didn't end so well last time for your family."

It was very satisfying to watch the surety in his eyes disappear. Vito looked from Nicoli to me. "When did the De Lucas and Quinns become allies?"

We didn't get a chance to answer, not that we had any intention of answering to begin with, because Sasha, four of his goons, and the table's dealer rushed over.

"What's going on here?" Sasha demanded.

"Whatever do you mean, Sasha?" I asked.

Sasha approached Brenna. "I was told that the girl you brought with you was threatening another guest with a weapon."

Smirking, Brenna took a step back from Vito and held out an empty beer bottle to Sasha. "If this is considered a weapon, then I might suggest you start serving cans instead."

He took the bottle from her and watched as she strutted back over to me.

"Beautiful, isn't she?" Nicoli said, calling out the fact that Sasha not only had been staring, but it was obvious he liked what he saw.

Sasha ignored the don and looked directly at me. "She is also young. Why did you bring someone underage to a place like this?"

"Do you really want to argue what is legal?" I asked.

He nodded. "Point made. There isn't any fighting allowed here, Maura."

"We weren't fighting. We were just having a conversation about ignorance, which Vito here was just about to apologize for. Weren't you, Vito?" It hadn't escaped my notice that the entire room had gone quiet and there were many eyes watching us—waiting to see how Vito would respond. I tilted my head slightly as I took in the sweat that beaded across his brow. "Or would you prefer to give me that apology in private? Outside by your car, perhaps?"

If looks could kill, I'd have been dead ten times over with the glare he was giving me. "I apologize," he forced out in a low voice.

I was tempted to drag out his humiliation, but I refrained out of respect for Sasha. "To answer your earlier question, Vito, no, you may not join us."

Stiffly and angrily, Vito stood. Even though his jacket didn't need to be straightened, he pulled on the lapels anyway before storming through a quiet room of criminals, heading straight toward the elevator.

Sasha and his goons left after that and our table's dealer returned to his post. I looked at Hector and Conrad, who were staring at me with a little more respect than they had when I'd first sat down. "Would you like to play another round, gentlemen?"

They both agreed.

As the dealer began passing out cards, Nicoli chuckled. This time it was genuine. "And here I thought tonight would be full of boring posturing."

I scooped up my drink. "It has."

"Yes, but I should have known that you would find a way to make it fun," he said and glanced around the room. "I think you achieved what we came here to do."

"*We* did, Nicky," I said in a low voice. "Alone, I would've had to kill him to set an example, which would have started a war between the Quinns and Romanos."

Nicoli picked up his own drink and took a sip. "Taking out the Romano family would be child's play for you, Maura."

Maybe, but I'd rather focus on finding Stefan than killing Romanos.

CHAPTER TWENTY-THREE

W e visited a few more tables in The Underground before we left. News of who I was and the alliance of the Quinns and the De Lucas spread through the room rapidly. Because we had achieved our goal a lot faster than intended, I suggested we go upstairs.

"You want to visit the club?" Nicoli asked as he pressed the button to call the elevator.

I put my arm around Brenna. "I know a certain birthday girl who loves to dance."

A happy smile took over Brenna's face.

With the help of Sasha, our group was given a VIP section in the club that overlooked the dance floor. Brenna was currently on the dance floor, with Finn and Asher watching over her from the edge of it. I was sitting in a large round booth with Nicoli to my left, Louie to my right, and Rourke sitting on the other side of Louie. Dean, Dario, and one of Rourke's goons stood along the railing that kept them from falling to the dance floor below and stared out at the rest of the club. Well, Rourke's guy and Dean were. Dario was paying extra attention to the dance floor.

The four of us in the booth were talking about unimportant,

normal shit like sports, which was nice. Well, I didn't talk about sports, the guys did. Nicoli actually seemed to get along with Rourke and he made an effort to get to know Louie. I think what made it easier for Louie to be receptive was that he knew Nicoli wasn't truly interested in me anymore. Sure, he'd probably bump uglies with me if I showed an interest, not that I ever would, but it was clear that Nicoli, like Dario, was a lot more interested in Brenna. I didn't know how I felt about that. I could tell Brenna enjoyed flirting with the danger of Dario, but I wasn't entirely sure how she felt about him. At the end of the day, she was a smart girl who I knew wanted to focus on discovering who she was free from the control of men. I think that granted me some time before I had to worry about her heart getting broken. That, and the fact that Nicoli wouldn't allow anything to risk our alliance.

The four of us all had drinks sitting in front of us, plus Brenna's empty glass, which she'd gotten using the fake ID Vincent had given her. When she had asked if she could have a drink, it hadn't felt right to say no. I allowed her to kill people—it seemed dumb not to allow her to have a drink. When a cocktail waitress stopped by again, I pushed my whiskey toward Rourke to drink and I ordered Patrón. I felt Louie's and Nicoli's surprise when they heard me order tequila.

I wanted to be in a good mood. Most days it seemed like I would never feel good again. The closest I got was when I was intimate with Jamie or Louie, or if it was late at night and I woke up between them, or when I spent time with Kieran. Ordering tequila was me trying to manifest good feelings, I supposed.

When another band was setting up to perform, Brenna along with Finn and Asher returned to our VIP section. I had just swallowed down my third shot of tequila and I was feeling good in the sense that I was buzzed. With the way Brenna was holding Finn's hand, trying to get him to dance with her as they walked this way, and the champagne bottle in her other hand, I'd say Brenna was just as buzzed, if not more.

"Finny, stop being such a stick in the mud. I swear you're worse than Dean sometimes," Brenna whined, making Asher and me laugh.

Dean didn't turn around, but he did shake his head as he continued to stare out at the club.

Brenna came up to the booth and set her champagne bottle down on the table in front of Rourke before she wrapped her arms around his neck, hugging him.

Rourke patted her arm. "At least you're loving when you're drunk instead of crazy like Maura."

My mouth dropped open and I flipped him off, which just made him and Louie laugh.

"Maura, it's time to come dance with me," Brenna said.

"I'm not buzzed enough yet. Two more shots," I said as I threw another one back.

She sighed as her gaze wandered. When she spotted Dario, she released Rourke and walked over to him.

I put my elbow on the table and rested my chin on my fist. "This should be entertaining."

The men at the table, especially Nicoli, watched Brenna approach Dario, who was leaning against the railing with his arms folded over his chest. As she got close to him, she purposely tripped and fell toward him. I didn't think Dario noticed, because he reached out and caught her before she could hit the ground. She smiled up at him, said something we couldn't hear over the music that began playing. Whatever she was saying was clearly to distract him. Little did Dario know was that Brenna was taking the rosary off his wrist. When she successfully got it completely off, she pushed away from him, holding the beads up in the air to show him that she had them as she walked backward. He stormed toward her, making her giggle, and before he could catch her, she wrapped the rosary around her neck. Dario grabbed Brenna by her throat.

Rourke looked like he was about to stand, but I grabbed his sleeve. He glanced at me and I shook my head. Rourke looked back at Brenna, finding her smiling up at Dario and holding a gun to his stomach.

"Tell me I'm beautiful," she said to him.

Dario looked like it was taking everything in him to hold back from hurting her. He leaned close and whispered something in her ear that made her eyes go wide. As he did, he pulled his rosary from her neck, and then he stormed away. Brenna stood there stunned for a moment as if in a daze, with pink cheeks. When she was able to pull herself out of it, she spun around to stare at him as he left. The temptation to go after him showed in her eyes.

I had a feeling drunken hormones were overwhelming her, so I threw back my last shot. "Let's go dance, Brenna."

"Maura," a grumbly voice said, and the smell of coffee filled my nose.

I rolled over onto my stomach, groaning.

"It's time to wake up, doll."

I groaned again and pushed up off the bed to sit on my knees. "Why do I feel like death?" I rubbed my tired eyes to help open them.

"Because you drank a shit ton of tequila last night." Dean's voice came from the left.

Memories from last night flooded my mind. Brenna and I had danced until our feet hurt. I'd come up with the dumb idea of drinking more to help with the pain. After that, stuff got fuzzy. I vaguely remembered Louie carrying me into the house bridal-style, while Finn had carried Brenna over his shoulder with her arms dangling behind him limply. "Oh, yeah."

I opened my eyes and saw that I didn't have any clothes on. That triggered my memories of when Louie had brought me up to his room. I had stripped out of my jumpsuit and panties. I hadn't worn a bra last night. For some reason, I hadn't had shoes to take off. Once I had been naked, I'd dropped down on my knees in front of Louie. He had let me suck his cock until he'd been at the edge of coming, then scooped me up, bent me over the bed, and fucked me until I'd come screaming.

"I'm naked," I said.

"We're aware," Dean grumbled.

I looked to the left and found Dean standing there with a cup of coffee in his hand.

"I have clothes for you," Asher said, drawing my attention to the right. He was holding sweatpants and a T-shirt in his hands.

I held my hand out for the coffee because...well, priorities. "I'll be out in a min."

Asher laid my clothes on the bed and the two of them left the room. After a few sips of coffee, I got dressed, washed my face, and put my hair in a bun. Dean and Asher were waiting in the hall and followed me to Kieran's room. Last night had been the first night he had slept in his nursery, with Caroline being the one to get up with him through the night.

"Caroline took him for a walk," Dean said, stopping me before I went in.

"When did she leave?" I asked.

"About ten minutes ago," Asher answered.

I nodded, not at all happy that he was gone. I hadn't seen him since yesterday and I didn't like that.

"Want me to call her and tell her to come back?" Dean asked, making me realize that I was being transparent.

"No. Let him finish his walk," I said and headed for the stairs.

Louie and Rourke were sitting next to each other at the breakfast table when I entered. Dean and Asher didn't follow me in. They had headed to the kitchen instead. I tried not to look at Stefan's empty seat at the table as I made my way to mine.

"Morning, beautiful," Louie said in between taking bites of his pancakes.

The swinging door that led to the kitchen opened and Brenna came shuffling in. She was still in her pajamas, which were loose, navy silk shorts with drawstrings, a matching top with thin straps, and fluffy black slippers. "I'm never drinking again," she groaned as she sat in the chair beside me.

Rourke laughed, which made Brenna glare tiredly across the table at him.

Noah came in from the kitchen with a carafe of coffee, refilled my mug I had brought downstairs with me, and filled a new mug for Brenna. "Can I get you something for breakfast?" he asked us.

"No," Brenna and I grumbled at the same time.

Noah nodded and set down a little pitcher of creamer on the table before he returned to the kitchen. As Brenna and I were fixing our coffees the way we liked to drink them, Brody walked into the dining room, with Nicoli and Dario right behind him.

"The De Lucas are here," Brody announced.

"I can see that," I said as I stirred my coffee lazily.

Brody nodded and left us. Nicoli and Dario appeared rested and pristine in their tailored suits.

"I'm not apologizing for my appearance. It's too fucking early to look pretty," I grumbled.

Brenna grunted in agreement as she rubbed her temples.

Nicoli just smiled, his eyes traveling to Brenna.

"Have you eaten breakfast?" I asked them. "You're welcome to join us."

"I'd love to join you, but we must get back to New York," Nicoli said.

If I had known he was going to stay overnight in New Haven, I would have invited him to stay here at the manor. "What brings you by?"

He pulled a little box from his pocket. "I have Brenna's birthday present."

Brenna stilled next to me for a brief moment, until she pulled herself from her shock and got up. Nicoli and Dario tracked her with their eyes as she rounded the table, and when she was just a handful of feet from them, their gazes roamed over her pajamas and slippers.

Nicoli opened the small, black velvet box for her to see what was inside. "It wasn't easy getting these from police evidence."

She clearly loved what she saw, because a bright smile graced her face. She reached into the box and pulled out earrings. Right away she put them in her ears.

"I had them melted down and reformed," Nicoli explained.

After Brenna finished putting the earrings on, she pushed her hair back from her ears. "How do they look?"

Nicoli admired his gift on her. "Beautiful."

"I love them," she said, her words genuine. "Thank you."

Nicoli's eyes bounced all over her gorgeous, smiling face as if greedily wanting to absorb every inch of it. "You're welcome."

"We need to get going," Dario said, his voice bordering the edge of angry.

Nicoli politely said goodbye and the two of them left.

As soon as Brenna sat down, she showed off her new

jewelry. Nicoli had melted down the lead bullets into Celtic shamrock-shaped studs. They were stunning and suited her.

Later that afternoon, while I was doing tummy time with Kieran in the nursery, Brody showed up holding a package. The stricken expression on his face made me sit up quickly. "What is it?"

"This was delivered for you today," he said, staring down at the package. "I'm sorry, Maura, but I had to open it."

I got to my feet and took it from him. "Go be with Kieran," I ordered, knowing the distraction would be good for him.

Brody didn't argue. He scooped Kieran off the floor and hugged him close.

I set the package on Kieran's dresser and took a deep breath before I opened it. The entire box was full of photos of Stefan. Or at least that was what I thought at first. Hidden beneath the photos was a burner phone.

I laid out all the photos on top of the dresser. There were so many of them taken from afar over the years. Some were with me. Some with Brody. Most were of Stefan getting in and out of an Escalade or going in and out of the manor. The last of the photos were up close. They were of him tied up, gagged, and beaten. His clothes were dirty and ripped. Seeing that pissed me all the way the fuck off, but it could mean that he was alive. Reassuring myself of that kept me from losing it.

Staring down at the photos, I now knew who had taken Stefan. I picked up the cell phone and powered it on. There was only one number programmed on it.

"Stay or go, Brody?"

He was currently rocking Kieran. "I need to know, Maura." His voice wobbled as he spoke.

I hit call on the phone and brought it to my ear. It rang four times before the line was picked up.

"Hello, daughter," a feminine voice with a thick Irish accent said.

"Riona."

"Is that how you're going to address your mother?" she asked.

"It is your name, is it not?" I responded with an unbothered voice. "I received your message. I'm assuming you want something."

She scoffed. "You really are just like your father, aren't you? Always straight to the point. All you do is search and search, absorbing as much information as you can so you can use it to strike at your enemies. We won't be playing such games."

"And what game would you like to play?" I asked her.

She paused and I could hear the smile in her voice as soon as she resumed speaking. "A game of truth."

"And money," I added.

She chuckled. "If you want your father back, then yes. It will cost the Quinn family. But I wonder, when all of this is said and done, will the new Banrion want him back?"

Banrion was Gaelic for queen.

"Twenty million. In five days, I'll let you know how to get it to me. Until then, daughter," she said and hung up.

CHAPTER TWENTY-FOUR

It had been forty-eight hours since my phone call with Riona. Since then, I'd had meetings with Rourke, Louie, Brody, Vincent, and Aiden on what to do and how to come up with the money. I'd done my best to get advice from Jamie and Conor, but mostly I had wanted them to focus on what they needed to get done in Boston. Things had been successful on their end, and they were coming home tonight.

According to Brody, Stefan had enough money to cover the twenty million, but we couldn't access it without Stefan. So that was where Vincent came in. The whole reason the kid had gotten hired by Stefan in the first place was because Vincent had stolen money out of Stefan's account. We'd had him do it again, only this time he'd put the money in my account.

Aiden's help had come in the form of jewelry. Because we didn't know when, where, or how I was going to give the money to Riona, we needed to plan for multiple outcomes. Seeing how she'd said this was a game of truth and she had yet to reveal anything to me, I was pretty certain she was going to attempt to take me.

Aiden had given me a Return to Tiffany heart tag chain-link

necklace. It wasn't really a Tiffany's necklace, but made to look like one. Within the heart tag pendant was a tiny GPS device. The thick chain wouldn't unlatch unless there was a special pin key used, which Louie was given a copy of.

When Aiden had given Louie the key, Louie had gotten this glint of mirth in his eye. He had yanked on the chain around my neck with a finger. "I can think of some interesting roleplaying games we can do with this, my little pet."

I'd arched a brow at him. "I have never been drier." No shame to anyone's kinks, but that one wasn't mine.

Louie's hand had dropped from my necklace. "That's the rudest thing you have ever said to me."

Aiden had laughed at us.

Speaking of Aiden, I was pretty sure he and my father had slept together, not that it was any of my business. My father's past lovers weren't something I needed or wanted to know about, but I didn't like how Aiden interacted with Brody. The way he winked at him or smirked at him all seemed to be a tactic to get under Brody's skin.

When I had been able to get a moment alone with Aiden after he had given me the necklace, earlier this afternoon, I'd confronted him.

I had sat behind my father's desk in his study. "I don't know the extent of the relationship you had with my father, be it that you bumped uglies for a short time or that things were serious between you two. It is none of my business. What is my business and what I will not tolerate is you coming into my home and antagonizing my other parent."

Aiden had gone very still in the chair he'd sat in across from me. "How..." he had trailed off.

"I was taught to be perceptive, and I pay close attention to those who interact with the ones I love. You're not as discreet as you claimed to be," I had told him.

When the shock of me calling him out had worn off, he had agreed to leave Brody alone.

Now it was evening and Louie had left an hour ago to go pick up Jamie. Brenna was currently hanging out with me in Jamie's room while I waited for him to come home. I planned on pouncing on him the moment he walked through the door, which was why Kieran was spending tonight in his nursery with Caroline taking care of him.

"I moved into the main house today," Brenna announced from where she was lying across the foot of the bed.

"I thought I saw you bringing your stuff over from the guest house today," I said as I looked at my phone for the tenth time in the past five minutes. Jamie and Louie would be back any minute now "What made you decide to move out of the guest house?"

"Too lonely. I picked a room near yours, but not so close that I would hear anything in case you decide to do the nasty with one or both of your guys."

I snorted and tossed a pillow at her.

She caught it, giggling, which was cut off by a big yawn. "Okay, I'm going to call it a night." She threw the pillow back at me and climbed off the bed.

"Get some rest."

"Night," she said as she walked out.

As the minutes ticked by, my eyes kept threatening to close. I pulled back the covers on Jamie's bed, placed my gun under my pillow, and lay down with my phone. I tried calling Jamie and when I didn't get an answer, I called Louie next. He didn't answer, either.

The plane is probably running late.

I sent a text to both of them asking them to wake me when they got home, and I reached toward the nightstand to turn off the light.

I was woken by the sound of the bedroom door opening. Lying with my back to the door, I couldn't tell if someone was coming or going. Slowly, I searched the bed with my hand to feel for Jamie, but the rest of the bed was empty. The floor creaked, confirming that someone was in the room. It could have been Jamie, but my instincts were yelling at me that it wasn't. I slipped my hand under my pillow and just as I grasped my pistol, the blankets were thrown off of me and I was yanked out of the bed by my legs.

I kicked and screamed as loud as I could to alert the rest of the house. I was pulled until I fell to the floor. I did my best to catch myself with my hand, but I still slammed down onto my stomach. I tried to roll over toward my attacker with my gun aimed. A boot rammed into my lower back before I could and pinned me on my stomach. I thrashed and wriggled, trying to roll out from under him to no avail. He shifted and pushed both his knees into my back, making sure I stayed put. Unable to move, I did the only thing I could think of to get help and that was to be as loud as possible. I pointed my gun behind me and started firing, hoping to hit him, hoping the grounds security would hear it in this big house.

I fired as many rounds as possible until my attacker wrestled the gun out of my hand and tossed it out of reach. He then got a hold of my hands and wrangled them behind my back, forcing from me an angry growl.

"What the fuck is going on in here?!" I heard a familiar voice demand as my hands were zip-tied behind my back.

The lights flipped on and I turned my head to see my traitor of a cousin storm in. Dylan stared down at me with a triumphant, sinister smirk.

"Sorry, Boss. I didn't know she had a gun in bed with her," my attacker said.

"Of course she would," Dylan said to him, annoyed. "Do you think you can get her downstairs or can you not handle one woman?"

"We're right behind you," my attacker assured him, and Dylan stalked out.

The guy holding me down tangled his hand in my hair and yanked on it until my head lifted off the carpet. "You're going to behave, unless you want to get hurt."

I let out a strangled laugh that made me sound rabid. "You obviously don't know me."

Ignoring me, he yanked me to my feet by my hair.

"Pull harder. It's a turn-on," I demanded with a crazy smile as I tried to get a look at him. Right away, I recognized him as one of Dylan's goons.

"Stupid bitch." He pulled on one of my arms to force me to walk toward the door.

"Fucking traitor," I snapped as we left Jamie's room. "You won't make it out of this house alive."

The goon pulled my hair harder to try to shut me up.

"That's it, baby, harder," I goaded.

The goon stopped pushing me forward. "You're one crazy bitch." He sounded disgusted and his hold on my hair loosened.

I took advantage of that and dropped to the floor. I lost a few hairs in the process as he tried to catch my hair and arm. On my knees, I yanked myself out of his hold and I fell onto my side. Knowing he was going to grab for me, I rolled onto my back and kicked at him. He struggled to grab my legs as I kept kicking and kicking. With my hands bound behind my back, I didn't have a lot of options. The moment he captured both my ankles, I saw Brenna come up behind him, gun in hand. She aimed at the back of the goon's head and a shot echoed in the hall.

The goon crumpled to the ground and Brenna quickly helped me to my feet.

"The nursery," I whispered, and she ran ahead of me to open Kieran's door. As soon as we were inside, Brenna cut the zip ties from around my wrists with baby nail clippers that were on Kieran's dresser. Immediately, I went to Kieran's crib, but it was empty. The panic that burst through my darkness nearly crippled me. "They took him. They took my baby."

Hearing the hysteria in my voice, Brenna grabbed me by my arms. "We'll find him."

A noise came from the closet, making us freeze.

"Maura?" a voice said from inside.

I rushed over and ripped open the door. Inside, curled up in the back corner hiding was Caroline. Because it was the middle of the night, she was wearing a floral robe over her nightgown and had rollers in her white hair. Then I saw that Kieran was asleep in her arms.

The relief I felt almost made my knees give out. "Stay here until I come back for you," I ordered. She nodded and I closed the door.

"We need to move," Brenna said as she peeked out into the hall. "We have to assume that they took over the control room. Which means they'll know where we are in the house."

"There are guns in Jamie's room."

Brenna poked her head out to check if the hall was clear. "Let's go."

We both ran down the hall back to Jamie's room. Brenna locked the door as soon as we were inside. I went to Jamie's walk-in closet and started pulling gun cases and boxes of bullets off the top shelf. We both armed ourselves with AR-15 rifles and a pistol each.

We were both barefoot and dressed in short pajama sets. Hers were cotton and deep purple and mine were black silk. We didn't have time to change.

When we had what we needed, we left the closet, and I went to the nightstand to get my phone. As I picked it up, I saw that there wasn't any service.

"They have something jamming the signal. I already tried calling for help on my phone. The house line is dead, too," Brenna said as she watched me.

"How'd you not get caught?"

"I was peeing when I heard you screaming, followed by the gunshots. So when someone came into my room, I was ready."

At least I'd been able to warn her.

Where are Jamie and Louie? I wondered as Brenna and I headed for the door. We crept into the empty hall and, doing our best to avoid the cameras, we started heading for the stairs. I walked in front with my rifle aimed forward. Brenna walked backward, covering the rear.

I saw shadows on the carpet coming from the hall we had to turn down to get to the stairs. I stopped walking, making Brenna back into me. Before I could warn her, armed men who did not work for me flooded the hall.

I started firing, shooting one after the other. Brenna quickly joined me. The sound of gunfire filled the hall as we took out at least four of Dylan's men before the rest retreated back down the hall they'd come from. Brenna and I also retreated back toward Jamie's room, shooting off rounds as we did.

"Shit!" Brenna shouted and turned to fire at the other end of the hall. We walked with our backs to each other until we were able to dash back into Jamie's room. We both dropped our nearly empty rifles to the ground and worked quickly to push Jamie's dresser in front of the door. The moment we got it there, there was banging on the door.

"We can climb out the window down to the kitchen," I whispered.

Brenna rushed to one of the large transom windows and got it open as I grabbed my phone off the nightstand and put it in my pocket. Using a lot of upper-arm strength, we each took turns climbing out of the window and lowering ourselves to the steep roof over the kitchen. The shingles were freezing under my feet and then my legs as we slid to the ledge.

Moving quickly but carefully, we lowered ourselves over the edge of the roof. As I did, my pistol that I'd stored in the back waistband of my sleep shorts slipped inside, slid past my butt cheek, and fell out the bottom of my shorts. It landed on the grass below with a little thud. I released the breath I had been holding and dropped the rest of the way down to the ground. My feet hit the ground first and my ass broke my fall. Brenna hit the ground just as gracefully as I had.

I scooped up my gun and we both crawled behind the bushes under the kitchen window that sort of hid us from the view of a camera. I looked out onto the property. It was dark, but I didn't see anyone. Not even our grounds security.

I pulled my phone from my pocket and handed it to Brenna. "Cell-phone jammers only reach so far. I want you to run until you can get a signal and then call whoever you can for help."

Brenna shook her head. "I can't leave you, Maura."

"You have to. We need help."

"Then come with me," she begged.

I shook my head. "You are less likely to be spotted if you go alone, and I can't leave. Kieran is still inside."

She looked like she wanted to argue.

"Go," I ordered.

She did as I said and took off. She moved quickly as she kept to the shadows and stayed low to the ground. I watched from behind the bushes until I couldn't see her anymore. Sighing, I debated what to do.

I wasn't really given the time to think. The sound of footsteps came from the side of the house. I peeked into the kitchen through the window. Finding it empty, I crept over to the door and slipped inside. I got down on the floor and hid in front of the kitchen sink as Dylan's goons walked by outside.

"Find them, damnit!" I heard Dylan roar from the hall outside the kitchen.

The sound of two men speaking in Italian to each other approached the kitchen. I crawled around the kitchen island and hid out of view as they entered the room. They were talking shit about Dylan, saying that he was pathetic and as soon as he handed Brenna over to Dominik, he was as good as dead.

Fucking Dylan had formed an alliance with the Romanos.

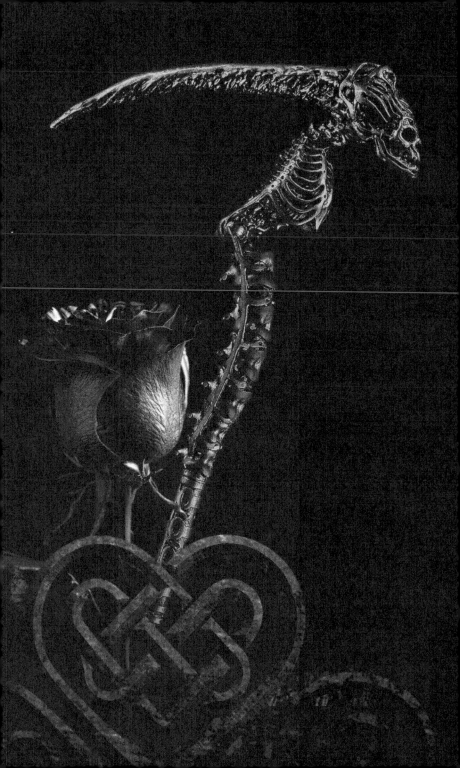

CHAPTER TWENTY-FIVE

I held still as I listened to them gossip in the kitchen. The moment one of them said something about the cameras, my heart skipped a beat, and I looked up. Sure enough, there was a camera in the corner of the room pointed right at me. Then the Italian men went quiet and I knew I had no time to lose. I shot up to my feet, gun at the ready. I used their shock at seeing me to my advantage and aimed.

Pop! Pop!

I took them down with a bullet to each of their heads. Of course, the loud sound would alert anyone who was nearby. I rushed for the swinging door that led to the dining room. Just as I entered, three of Dylan's goons walked in from the hall. I lunged behind the table, landing on my stomach as they fired at me.

"I want her alive!" I heard Dylan yell, and they ceased fire. When the room was quiet, Dylan spoke. "I have Jameson and Louie, Maura. And I have Brody."

I sat up with my back to a chair.

"I will kill them right now if I have to," Dylan pushed.

Shit! Shit! Shit!

Not having any other choice, I got to my knees and raised my hands above my head in surrender as I stood. I locked eyes with Dylan as his men rounded the table with their guns aimed at me. The first goon to reach me took my pistol from my hand and grabbed my arm.

With a bruising grip, the goon brought me to Dylan. When I was within his reach, his hand shot out and he smacked me across my face so hard, I would have fallen if the goon hadn't been holding on to me. Pain spread like a lightning bolt across my cheek bone and behind my eye.

I laughed. "What a pathetic excuse of a man. You couldn't land a hit when we were kids, and you still can't do it as an adult without someone holding me for you."

He smacked me again just as hard. "You've always been a mouthy bitch, cousin." He was so worked up, he was breathing heavily. "Bring her," he told the goon holding me, then looked at the others standing around us. "The rest of you keep looking for my sister." After giving his orders, he walked off.

We followed Dylan to Stefan's study. My heart skipped a beat when we walked in. Jamie, Louie, and Brody were on their knees, mouths taped and hands restrained behind their backs. There was an armed Italian goon standing behind each of them. All three of them looked bloody and beaten-up—Jamie and Louie more than Brody.

As soon as Jamie and Louie saw me, they tried to get to their feet. The goons behind them forced them back to their knees. The goon that held onto me dragged me farther into the room and forced me to drop to the floor a few feet in front of them. Right away, I tried to crawl over, but the goon grabbed me by my hair and yanked me back. He didn't let go of my hair and I let out a pissed-off growl.

Dylan went over to the liquor trolley like he was king of the fucking castle and poured himself some whiskey in a glass tumbler.

"I should have let you die right alongside your fucking father," I seethed.

Stop letting your rage in, Maura.

You'll end up chasing the rabbit if you don't.

Listening to my darker self, I made myself relax.

With his drink in hand, Dylan turned with a cruel smirk on his face. "For a smart woman, that was a really dumb move."

"Clearly," I said, my voice calm. "You went to the Aryans that night."

He looked so proud of himself. "I did. I needed allies and I knew they wanted our guns. Thanks to our family meetings, I knew when Rourke was going to do an exchange. It was like the planets were aligned when I heard that you were invited to tag along. The Aryans were already prepared to take the guns and all I had to do was add your death to the plan."

I needed him to keep talking to buy whoever Brenna called time to get here. "How did you learn that I was going to be with Rourke?"

Dylan seemed so happy I'd asked that. "From Rourke, of course. That day, he said it in passing when he stopped by to check on me before heading to pick you up."

"And when they didn't succeed in killing me?" I asked.

Dylan huffed a laugh. "I didn't have to convince them to go after you because you went and pissed Buck off when you killed a few of his buddies at his bar. They tried to blow up your car and failed because the damn bomb triggered before it was supposed to. Honestly, those racist fucks were dumb as shit. I had to come up with a better plan for them and walk them through it step by step."

"You mean when you gave Buck the security blueprints to my house," I added.

"Yeah. A lot of good it did them, because they still managed to fuck up killing you again," Dylan said irritably and took a gulp of whiskey.

I smirked at him. "Maybe I'm just too tough a bitch to kill."

Dylan glared. "Like a fucking cockroach." He shrugged. "Got your kid, though. Saved me from having to smother it in its crib."

Jamie began breathing heavily through flared nostrils as he stared at Dylan with dark eyes. Louie was also seething, but not at the same level as Jamie.

Dylan grinned down at Jamie. "I guess that means you were the father. Not gonna lie, I was curious which one of you knocked up my whore of a cousin."

I chuckled. "Man, you are such a pussy."

Dylan's triumphant glee dimmed a little as he stared back at me.

"You couldn't just come after me yourself, could you? First you asked the Aryans and now you're relying on the Romanos. Wow!" I shook my head. "I knew you were stupid and weak. Hell, we all did, but I didn't know how much your father raised a little bitch."

Snapping, Dylan's fist collided with my cheek, and I hit the floor. I pushed up off the floor as blood leaked from the corner of my mouth. I smiled back up at him. "You hit like a little bitch, too."

He punched me again and when I fell to the ground again, he followed it with a kick to my stomach. I grunted into the carpet as all the air left my lungs.

Jamie and Louie started shouting behind the tape on their mouths. The sound of a gun being cocked silenced them.

I turned my head to rest my cheek on the carpet and glanced up to see that Dylan was pointing a gun at me as he stared at Jamie and Louie.

"I heard you promised Brenna to Dominik Romano," I said, and my attention flicked to the Italian goons, standing behind Brody, Jamie, and Louie. "Dominik is going to be pretty upset when he finds out that she's already married to Nicoli De Luca."

Dylan's head whipped to face me. "What?"

"In order to secure an alliance with the De Lucas, I had to give him Brenna," I lied.

The Italians glanced at each other.

"They signed their marriage certificate on her eighteenth birthday, three days ago," I lied some more.

"You wouldn't have done that," Dylan insisted.

I sat up without looking away from the Italians. "I had no choice. Stefan was kidnapped and you disappeared. No one was going to support me, a woman, leading the family. Nicoli's family wouldn't agree to the alliance unless it was through marriage and Nicoli wouldn't take me because I can't have children anymore."

"You're lying," Dylan seethed.

"You're backing a man who can't deliver," I told the Italians.

Dylan pressed the barrel of his gun to my temple. "You are lying!"

"If you don't believe me, then call him!" I yelled back. "I'll give you his number."

One of the Italians spoke into a two-way radio that they all carried, asking someone to turn off the jammer.

Dylan gaped at them, with a little bit of panic etched around his eyes. "She's lying. Why would Brenna be here if she was married to De Luca?"

"Because we made the agreement that she wouldn't move to New York until this coming weekend," I lied again, and the Italian was buying all of it.

Someone on the other end of the two-way radio responded, saying the jammer was turned off. Ignoring Dylan, the Italian pulled a cell phone from his pocket and dialed a number before putting the phone up to his ear. He spoke in Italian to whoever picked up, passing on what I had just revealed. I had a feeling it was Dominik, and he didn't sound happy. The Italian hung up with his boss and came out from behind the guys. He held out his phone to me. "Call."

"She doesn't need to call. She's lying," Dylan insisted.

The Italian stared Dylan down. "Dominik says she calls."

I took the phone and dialed Nicoli's number.

"Put it on speaker," the Italian ordered. "And don't tell him shit or I'll kill this one." He pointed his gun at Louie's head.

I did as he asked. Because it was the middle of the night, the line rang for quite a bit. When I thought it was going to go to voicemail, Nicoli picked up. "Hello." Thankfully he didn't sound like I'd just woken him.

"Hello, Nicoli," I said. Not Nicky, and I was betting everything that he would pick up on that.

There was a moment of silence. "Maura?"

"I'm sorry it's late, Nicoli, but I wanted to make sure everything was all set for Brenna to move in with you this weekend now that the two of you are married."

There was another moment of silence. "Yes. Everything is all set," he said, playing along.

I wanted to let out a relief-filled exhale, but kept my breathing normal.

"How is my little bride? Has she been wearing the earrings I gave her?"

"Yes. She absolutely adores the diamond earrings you gave her," I said, purposely saying the wrong type of earrings.

"I'm glad," he said, continuing to play along. "I'm sending my people to you to collect Brenna's things this weekend. I'm sorry, I have to cut our call short. I'm driving with Dario and Ivano right now. We just left my club in Bridgeport."

I mulled over the information he'd given me as quickly as I could. If I understood him correctly, he was on his way with Dario and Ivano, but they were in Bridgeport. So it would be about twenty-five minutes before they could get here. "I understand and I appreciate you coming to the house to help with the move. Brenna has *a lot* of things," I said, forcing out a little laugh.

The Italian hung up before I could hear Nicoli's reply and called his boss back. Whatever Dominik said wasn't good for Dylan. The Italian pointed his weapon at Dylan as he hung up. The other Italians followed suit. Dylan and the goon behind me pointed their weapons at the Italians.

"You promised Dominik Brenna Quinn. You lied," the Italian right in front of me said to Dylan.

"I didn't know," Dylan said.

While they were distracted arguing amongst themselves, I tried to figure out what to do.

Suddenly, nonstop shots began firing from somewhere inside the house.

"Maura!" I heard Dean yell as the door to the study busted open, making Dylan and his goons turn.

I knocked Dylan's feet out from under him as something was tossed into the room. The moment Dylan hit the floor, the thing that had been tossed in exploded with a big flash and bang. My hearing and my sight blanked out for a little bit. Shots fired in the room and the Italians and Dylan's goon went down quickly. When I had most of my sight back, I crawled on top of Dylan and grabbed his gun hand before he could aim at me. With my free hand I tried to punch him in the face. He caught my wrist before I could. So I slammed my forehead down into his face hard, hitting him right in the nose. He let out a satisfying grunt and blood gushed out of his nostrils.

"I'm going to kill you," I growled as I struggled to keep him from aiming his gun at me. "And you will suffer."

My arm shook as I fought against his strength. Very slowly, the barrel of the gun shifted closer and closer until it was almost pointed right at me. Just before it did, a hand grabbed Dylan's wrist and slammed his hand to the ground. I looked up and met gorgeous hazel eyes. Jamie was crouched above Dylan's head. Together we wrangled the gun from Dylan. Jamie let me take it and I scooted down Dylan's body until I could press the barrel of the gun to his lower stomach. I pulled the trigger. Dylan jerked.

It's not enough.

"I need a knife!" I roared.

I didn't know who got me one. All I knew was that one was held out in front of me, and I took it. "Hold him down," I ordered. Jamie held Dylan down by his arms while I cut open his button-up shirt. When I started carving a clover into Dylan's bared chest, making sure it was big, he screamed pain-riddled screams and struggled beneath Jamie and me.

When I was done carving the clover, I stabbed him right in the center of it. Dylan's mouth was wide open as if to scream, but nothing came out.

It's not enough.

I stabbed him again.

And again.

I couldn't stop.

I didn't know how many times I stabbed him, but blood filled the center of the clover. Blood covered me. My hands, my arms, from my face down to the tops of my thighs, all of it covered or splattered with blood.

Jamie let go of Dylan's arms as I started to lose strength and my stabs became shallow. As I slammed the knife down into

Dylan's chest one more time, Jamie grabbed my wrist, stopping me from pulling the knife out.

"He's dead, baby," Jamie said in a gentle voice.

I looked up at him slowly, my eyes going blurry as I did. It was then that I realized that I had been crying.

CHAPTER TWENTY-SIX

louie

Dean, Asher, Brenna, Finn, Rourke, Conor, Brody, and I stood and watched as Jameson held Dylan down while Maura stabbed him over and over again. It was like she had snapped. There was so much pain and rage on her face, none of us could move to stop her. I hadn't seen her reveal so much emotion since we had lost our baby.

Tears began pouring from her eyes, but I didn't think she noticed as she kept burying the knife Dean had given her into Dylan.

Brenna let out a sniffle, making most of us glance her way. She was crying silently as she watched and Rourke wrapped an arm around her, looking sullen himself.

It took a while for Maura to tire out. Rourke's and Conor's enforcers and security were filling the hall just outside the study. Then there was a small commotion and Nicoli, Dario, and Ivano made their way through the crowd in the hall and walked into the study.

They took in the room. Nicoli and Dario seemed to both find Brenna at the same time and I saw different tells of relief on them. Nicoli's shoulders sank, and Dario's relief could only be seen in his eyes. Then they noticed Maura and didn't seem to be able to move to stop her, either.

Maura had covered herself in blood and gotten quite a bit on Jameson's hands and the sleeves of his suit, not that he looked like he cared. This was the closure they both needed.

When it was clear Maura's arm was becoming weak, Jameson let go of Dylan. He watched Maura stab him again, but before she could pull the knife free, Jameson grabbed her wrist. "He's dead, baby." My best friend's words were gentle.

She finally looked away from Dylan to stare at Jameson. Tears rolled down her blood-splattered cheeks. All the pain and rage she had been showing was quickly shut down. She let go of the knife and she numbly stood. She wobbled a little as she stepped over Dylan and turned for the door. I didn't think she saw any of us, or if she could, she just didn't care. She made it two steps before her legs gave out on her. Everyone in the room seemed to move to help. Dean was the quickest to react and caught her. With an arm around her back, he helped her get her footing.

"Let me carry you," Dean said to her in a low voice.

"I'm fine, Dean," she said, her voice numb.

We all watched silently as Maura walked toward and out the study's door, with Dean right behind her.

I stared at Jameson and saw that he hadn't moved from where he had been kneeling by Dylan's head.

"Go with Maura, Jameson," I said, knowing that one of us should be with her right now and it needed to be him. I would take care of things here.

Surprisingly, Jameson didn't argue and stood to leave.

"What happened?" Nicoli asked.

"Dylan offered to marry Brenna to Dominik if he helped him overthrow Maura," I answered.

"What?" Brenna blurted, clearly taken aback.

"Having figured that out, to turn Romano's men against Dylan, Maura said that she had already married Brenna to you in order to form our alliance," I added.

With an unreadable expression, Nicoli glanced at Brenna, who was frowning at the floor. "I picked up on that during our call," he said. "I'm guessing it worked?"

"It bought us enough time for the cavalry to arrive," I said as I looked to Rourke, Conor, Asher, and Finn. "How did you know to come?"

Brenna explained what she and Maura had gone through upstairs and how Maura had ordered her to go to the edge of the property to call for help. "I didn't want to leave her."

Conor put his hand on Brenna's shoulder. "It was good that you did."

"Maura really did a number on this guy," Ivano said as he stared down at Dylan. "It's hard enough to shoot family who betray us, but to do this..."

The room went quiet.

"Dylan wasn't just a traitor," Brenna said sullenly as she stared at the floor.

"Brenna," Rourke snapped at her, his voice laced with warning.

Understanding why Brenna felt the need to explain and despite Rourke's worry about sharing family business, I said, "Dylan was the one who enlisted the Aryans to kill Maura and why Maura can't carry children anymore." It wasn't easy sharing that, but like Brenna, I knew it was best they understood that Maura hadn't lost her mind. She could be crazy, but it was calculated crazy. It served a purpose. What had happened with Dylan was her releasing grief she had been carrying for far too long.

I thanked the De Lucas for coming and they left shortly after that. Dean returned and reported that Jameson was taking care of Maura. Conor and Rourke helped me with directing everyone in cleaning up the manor.

Dylan had killed all of our nighttime grounds security and he had brought with him twenty men to do it. Eight of which were Romanos, and we had every intention of dumping their bodies on Dominik's front lawn. What the fuck was he going to do about it? With how small his family was, it'd take him years to refill his ranks. I called Aiden to help find security coverage. We'd need his guys until I was able to get word to the whole family across our territory that we were in need of muscle willing to relocate to New Haven, or vet and hire guys who had zero association with the family, like how I'd recruited Dean.

Even with the help of everyone, it took all fucking night to remove all of the bodies and clean up bullets, shell casings, and blood from the entire property. Brody was going to call a discreet company to come out and make repairs to the house when they opened.

"How did Dylan get you?" Rourke asked as the sun started to come up.

"We were on our way home when I ran over a spike strip. It flattened all of my tires, forcing us off the road. Then Dylan rolled up with his new friends."

My feet were dragging when I was finally able to go upstairs to take a short nap before I had to get up and tackle more shit this attack had caused.

I found Jameson, Maura, and Kieran sleeping in my room. I entered quietly and headed straight for the bathroom. Maura's and Jameson's bloody clothes were in a pile on the floor. I'd have to get rid of them after I woke up. I dropped my clothes right next to theirs before taking a hot, quick shower. Once I had washed away the night, I returned to my bedroom. Kieran was awake in his bassinet, making little cooing noises. I scooped him up. "Hey, little man," I whispered as I cradled him in my arms. His blue eyes locked onto me with recognition.

"I was about to get up with him," Jameson said.

I turned toward the bed and saw that he was sitting up, watching me. "Let me hold him for a minute."

He nodded, understanding. After the night we had just had and what we could have lost...I had the strong urge to lock the four of us—my family—in this room and never fucking leave.

"Is she sleeping?" I asked as I tried to peek past him to see Maura.

"She's out," Jameson assured. "It took most of the night for her to fall asleep."

"Was she dealing?" I asked. So much had happened in less than a week—Stefan being taken, her mother being the one who had taken him, becoming the head of the family, and Dylan. Jameson and I had been waiting, watching for when she might need some time to process everything so we could be there for her. She'd had small moments. One with Jameson after she had killed Sean and the other when I'd found her crying silently as she had rocked Kieran before we had gone to The Underground. Other than that, she'd had everything locked down so tight so that she could take charge and be what the family needed her to be.

Jameson shook his head. "I don't think she'll allow herself until we get Stefan back."

I stared down at Kieran and gave him my finger for his little hand to grab. Right away he tried to pull my finger to his mouth. "I don't want to think about what would happen if we don't get him back, but I know we need to prepare for it. Not when it comes to the family, but for her and what it will do to her."

"She's strong."

I wasn't doubting her ability to overcome the loss of Stefan. "I miss the crazy, theatrical side of her. We only get glimpses of it now. I'm afraid if we lose Stefan, we will lose more of her, too."

Jameson let out a long and heavy sigh. "This way of life changes us. It chisels away the good to make room for the bad. You know that."

I did. "I just wish we could have protected her from it."

"We couldn't even protect ourselves from it," Jameson said bitterly. "I understand your worry, because it's mine, too. All we can do is have some faith that as time moves on and wounds heal, we will see more of the old Maura again, but we have to accept that it won't be the same."

Kieran began to get fussy and I bounced my arms a little to soothe him. "Because I love her, I'll accept it, but it still makes me angry."

Jameson locked eyes with me. "For as long as we love her, we will probably never stop being angry about it."

Well, it looked like I was going to be pissed for the rest of my life, because I didn't think I'd ever stop loving her. Speaking of the rest of my life... "Want to finish our conversation from last night?" I asked him. Last night on the way back to the manor, I had brought up the topic of marriage. Dylan had fucking interrupted us before I'd gotten a response.

Realizing what I was talking about, he asked, "How would we make that work?"

"She would be legally married to you, and I will legally be named as Kieran's father," I suggested. "Of course, Maura will still be my wife, as Kieran will still be your son."

Jameson mulled it over for a moment. "Are you sure?"

I nodded. "Yeah. I've been thinking on it for a while."

Jameson went quiet as he thought again. "Alright."

The corner of my mouth lifted. "Maura hinted at wanting a big rock."

Jameson smiled a little as he stared down at her adoringly, because hearing that gave him a glimpse of the old Maura and moments like those were something to be cherished.

CHAPTER TWENTY-SEVEN

maura

It had been five days since I'd spoken to Riona. All morning I was unable to sit still as we waited for her to get into contact with me. Conor, Rourke, Aiden, Vincent, and my goons were at the house. We, along with Brenna, Jamie, Louie, and Brody, had all congregated in the lounge that was near the front door and just to the side of the foyer. We were all either sitting or standing around the coffee table where I'd placed the burner cell Riona had sent me. Stefan's study, along with a bunch of other areas in the house, were still being repaired thanks to Dylan.

After lunch time, Jamie's phone went off. He answered it on the second ring. "Yeah?" As he listened to whoever was speaking to him, he locked eyes with me. Without responding, he hung up. "Brody, call Adam."

"Our lawyer? Why?" I questioned.

"Because the police are pulling up and they have a warrant for your arrest, Maura," Jamie said, and I could feel the shock of everyone in the room.

"I don't have time to be arrested today" was my response. Not "What for?" or "Why?" All that mattered to me was that I was here when Riona called me—my only chance to save Stefan.

"Why is she being arrested?" Louie was the one to ask.

Jamie put his hands on his hips and took in a calming breath. "We're about to find out."

There was a knock on the door and Jamie left the lounge to answer it. We watched as he opened the door. Detectives Cameron and Brooks walked in with two cops in uniform right behind them.

As soon as Detective Cameron saw me, he reached behind him and pulled out cuffs from his back pocket. "Maura Quinn, you are under arrest for the murders of Tom Morris and Christina Barker," he said and forced me to turn around so he could cuff me. "You have the right to remain silent..."

"What proof do you have that she killed them?" Jamie demanded, because he knew for a fact that there was none.

"We found an email sent from Maura to Miss Barker threatening to kill her and Tom Morris if Miss Barker didn't stop the affair they were having," Detective Brooks said.

"That's bullshit," Louie growled.

I huffed a laugh, drawing everyone's attention. I only had eyes for Brooks. When the corner of his mouth lifted, I knew he could see in my eyes that I had pieced it together.

Detective Cameron started ushering me out of the lounge. I spared one last glance at Louie. "Your little pet loves you." His eyes narrowed in confusion and as I was walked out of my house into the backseat of the detectives' gold sedan, all I could do was trust that he would eventually understand.

"I don't think we need an escort back to the station," I heard Brooks tell the two cops they had brought with them as he rounded the car. "We got it from here, guys."

Taking Brooks' word for it, the two cops got into their squad car and drove off before us. As Cameron climbed into the driver's seat and Brooks into the passenger's, Cameron frowned at Brooks, but didn't say anything.

We were about five minutes from my house when I let out a dramatic sigh. "Tell me, Antony—you don't mind me calling you Antony, do you?" I didn't wait for an answer. "How long have you been working with my mother?" It was too much of a coincidence that he had done nothing with the file on my mother I had given Dean and that my mother had left photos from the night I'd been raped in Stefan's study the day she had broken into the manor.

Through the cage that separated the front seats from the backseat, I watched Cameron give Brooks a confused look. "What?"

Brooks didn't respond. Instead, he pulled out his gun and pointed it at Cameron.

"What the fuck, Brooks?" Cameron growled, completely shocked.

"I'm going to need you to turn left up here," Brooks said to him.

"You know, she could have just told me where to meet her instead of writing a fake email and framing me for murder," I said.

"And risk your family following you?" Brooks said as he stared at me through the cage. "And the email may be a fake, but we both know you killed your ex and his side piece."

I didn't bother denying it. "You didn't answer my question. How long have you been working with Riona? Since before or after you sent Dean to infiltrate us?"

"Did Stefan kill my brother?" he snapped.

I didn't react. I kept my face schooled. "You mean after he raped me."

Brooks seethed, "Lies!"

Cameron let out a curse.

"I know the truth," Brooks insisted. "I know you lied. You lured my brother into a bathroom to have sex, and when he turned you down, you got mad like a spoiled little bitch and went to Daddy crying rape."

I threw my head back laughing. "Oh, you poor thing," I said with a condescending smile. "Riona has twisted the story in a nice little bow for you to accept, hasn't she? Would you like to know what really happened? Hmm? Your brother and his friend cornered me in a bathroom at a party. His friend held me down while your brother shoved my legs open and raped me on the bathroom floor. He left bruises and bite marks on my body. I was seventeen and a virgin and your brother ripped away my innocence like it was his to fucking take."

Brooks stared forward, refusing to look at me.

"If you don't believe me, ask Riona for the pictures. She was there that night," I said. "Honestly, I wouldn't be shocked if she was the one who put your brother up to it."

"Shut up," he said, still refusing to face me, but I knew I had planted the seed of doubt in his mind.

For the rest of the ride, Brooks told Cameron where to drive until we were pulling up to the warehouse owned by my family on Stone Street.

"Recognize this place?" Brooks asked me.

I didn't respond.

"This is where your father killed my brother," he said.

No, this is where I killed your brother, you fucking fool.

Men dressed in black opened the chain-link fence that surrounded the warehouse and I wondered how they hadn't triggered the security system. Brooks instructed Cameron to pull up close to the warehouse's front entrance, where many armed men clad in black were waiting for us.

My door was ripped open and one of the armed men yanked me out of the car. "Easy, Rambo. Do I look like I'm resisting?" I yanked my arm from his grasp. "Just point where I need to go and I'll walk."

As he glared down at me, I took in his sandy hair and hazel eyes. He eventually pointed toward the front door. "That way." He had a thick Irish accent.

With my hands still cuffed behind my back, I started walking.

"Get your hands off me," I heard Cameron yell. I glanced back at the car to see him being dragged away by two of Riona's lackeys. I could only assume that the men who were helping her were associated with her family in Ireland or they were her family, and by extension, my family. Riona had been born into a family of arms suppliers, who we'd used to get our guns from before we'd switched to my uncle Conor's extended family.

I was escorted to a large room where there was nothing but two chairs in the center of it. Stefan was occupying one of them and the other was empty. As we got closer, I realized "occupying" wasn't correct. Stefan was tied to the chair by his wrists and ankles. He looked like hell. The bruising and cuts on his face showed that he had taken quite a beating. His clothes were even more ripped and filthy than in the pictures Riona had sent me.

Stefan's eyes locked with mine when he heard my heels clacking on the concrete floor. He didn't react or show any emotion and neither did I.

"Sit," Rambo ordered, gesturing to the empty chair.

I sat. Brooks and the guards stood off to the side quietly. When Riona didn't make an appearance right away, I looked at Stefan. "I'm really angry with you."

He turned his head slowly to stare back at me. "I had a feeling you would be."

"I can get kidnapped, but not you," I said, keeping my voice calm because despite how relieved I was to see him, I wanted to roar at him. "This week has been hell."

A small smile lifted the corners of his mouth and a brief glimpse of emotion showed in his eyes as we continued to stare at each other.

The sound of a door opening echoed in the large room, followed by the sound of heels hitting the floor. Stefan and I faced forward and watched as a redheaded woman in an all-white pantsuit strutted her way over to us. Riona approached us with the confidence of a queen. But she was in the wrong kingdom to be doing that.

One of Riona's lackeys set another chair down in front of Stefan and me. Riona sat in that chair gracefully and crossed one leg over the other as she stared at me. "Hello, Maura."

"Birth-giver," I greeted her back.

She smiled. "Do you like how I got you here?"

I shrugged. "You mean how you manipulated a cop into helping you, when really, you're the reason his brother is dead. I'm a tad bit impressed, actually. So kudos to you."

When Riona didn't deny it, Brooks stepped forward. "Riona, what—"

Pop!

Blood hit the floor before Brooks did and when his body fell, a lackey with a gun was revealed, standing behind him.

"He was a good pawn," Riona said as she stared at Brooks' lifeless body with zero remorse. "Are you going to ask me why I've done all of this?"

I wasn't in the mood to feed her ego or listen to her monologue. So I just waited.

She stared at me, her eyes bouncing all over my face. "He really raised you in his image, didn't he?" Her voice held a hint of disgust. "Tell me, are you as cruel as your father is?"

I didn't answer her, which seemed to frustrate her.

"I didn't want you," she said, and when she didn't get a reaction out of me, she went in a different direction. "You see, your grandfather—"

"I don't care," I cut her off.

Anger hardened her face and she narrowed her storm-gray eyes. "Stefan let your grandfather and uncle rape me—"

"I don't care," I said again.

She released a frustrated noise.

I smirked. "What did you think you'd accomplish? That I'd turn against my father after you told me your *oh woe is me* life story?" I looked her up and down. "I'll admit that you have been clever and your dedication to revenge is impressive, but you do not know how to play the game."

"Oh, really?" she said with attitude.

"To answer your first question, I do know why. So let's just get to the point, shall we?"

She arched a brow. "And why have I done all of this?"

"Because of your obsession with me. Everything you have done has been to get back at me. Not Stefan. He was just a happy bonus because you thought you could torture him to get to me. You didn't want to have me and because of that you think I ruined your life."

"You did ruin my life," she snarled.

"Did I, though? Or is it just too hard to look in the fucking mirror?"

"Shut up," she snapped as she uncrossed her legs and slammed her foot down on the ground. "Because of you, I lost everything. My husband. My home."

"It wasn't my fault you got addicted to cocaine," I pushed.

"The only reason I got hooked on cocaine was because your grandfather used it to drug me so he could rape me!"

"And how is that my fault?!" I yelled back at her.

She stood from her chair and reached behind her back as

she stormed toward me. Riona pulled out a gun and pressed it to my forehead.

"Riona!" Stefan roared.

She looked at him. "You chose her over me, Stefan. You promised to take care of me, and you tossed me aside for her." She talked about me like I was his other woman.

Stefan looked from me to her, his eyes filled with true fear. "She's my daughter—our daughter. Please."

Hearing Stefan beg made me grind my teeth. My father was the strongest person in the world to me and I hated that Riona was using me to gain power over him.

"You loved her more than me," Riona said in a broken voice.

"Shoot me, Riona," he begged her. "If you want Maura to pay, then shoot me."

"Shut up, Stefan," I snarled.

Stefan shot me a stern look, warning me to stay out of this.

"Admit it!" Riona screamed at him.

"Don't do it," I begged him.

Stefan's eyes went wide as Riona's finger curled around the trigger.

"Yes, Riona! I do!" he yelled, his voice riddled with fear. "I love my daughter more than anything. So please shoot me."

Riona glared down at me with absolute loathing. "Daddy's little girl."

She moved the gun from my head to aim it at Stefan and my worst fear overtook me.

Before she could shoot him, her gun was shot from her hand, making her drop it. There was no doubt in my mind that it was thanks to Brenna's amazing aim, which meant help was here. I took that as my chance to act, and I leaped out of my chair. I threw my body into Riona's and took her down to the floor.

The warehouse filled with gunfire, taking out the lackeys

around us. I got my cuffed hands under my butt and out from under my legs so that my hands were in front of me. By the time I was able to get to my feet, all of Riona's men were down and Jamie, Louie, Dean, and Asher were rushing toward us.

Movement on the ground caught my attention. Riona was crawling toward her gun. I quickly grabbed her by her hair, stopping her. She let out a yelp as I dragged her backward and flung her to the side.

I held my hand out to Dean as he approached. "Gun."

Without question, he handed over his Glock. I aimed it at my mother as she rolled over on the ground to stare up at me with tear-soaked cheeks. For a split second, I felt like I was nine again, standing in Stefan's study and being made to choose. My father or my mother? It had been a cruel thing to ask a nine-year-old girl who had been desperate for her father's love and up until that point had wished her mother had been alive. Then that second passed and I realized that I wasn't nine anymore. I had my father's love, and as I stared down at my mother, I was disappointed that she had not died the first time I'd been faced with this choice. "You asked me if I was as cruel as my father," I said to her with a voice I knew was cold and detached.

"Maura, wait!" she begged, holding up a hand.

"Here's your answer." Without hesitation, I pulled the trigger three times, putting two bullets in her chest and one in her head.

For a moment, I couldn't look away from her lifeless storm-gray eyes. One day, I might mourn her. She had been my mother after all. But right now, when I stared at her, I only saw a threat to what I loved, and I couldn't find it in me to regret killing her.

I gave Dean his Glock back and I turned to face Stefan. Jamie had just gotten done untying him from his chair and was helping him stand.

"I am very angry with you," I told him again.

Holding his ribs, he let go of Jamie to walk toward me. "I know."

"Good, because we'll be addressing my anger later."

As he approached, I felt like I could breathe, and when he put his arms around me, my darkness loosened its tight hold. Because my hands were still cuffed, all I could do was sag against his chest. I closed my eyes to keep myself from crying.

"I love you, too, Daddy," I said just loud enough for him to hear.

His response was to hug me tighter and kiss the top of my head.

Once Stefan and I pulled away from each other, Jamie and Louie yanked me into their arms. Louie curled his finger around the fake Tiffany's necklace around my neck. "*Your little pet loves you.* Really, Maura?"

I gave him a small smile. "It worked, didn't it?"

"Hey!" Rourke yelled as he escorted Detective Cameron over. "What do we do with him?"

Detective Cameron glared at him.

"We let him take things from here," I said, surprising the detective. "Would you like a phone, Detective?" Dean handed me his.

Cameron stared at me, confused. "You're just going to let me go?"

"I'm not the one who took you and my people haven't done anything illegal here but defend themselves from a group of criminals who kidnapped my father, me, and you," I said, holding the phone out to him, but before he took it, I pulled it out of reach. "And because Detective Brooks admitted that the email you have that incriminates me is indeed forged, I'm no longer under arrest, correct?"

He exhaled through flared nostrils. "That is correct."

I handed the phone to him with a smile. "Good."

CHAPTER TWENTY-EIGHT

O*ne week later.*

I was woken when my hand was grabbed. I didn't open my eyes. I could feel Jamie and Louie on either side of me, so I knew I was safe. When I felt something slip onto my ring finger on my left hand, I couldn't stop myself from smiling.

"You can stop pretending you're asleep now," Jamie said.

"Is the suspense killing you?" I teased.

"Just open your eyes, beautiful," Louie said.

I brought my hand to my face before I opened one eye. When I saw a huge, princess cut yellow diamond, my other eye shot open, and I scrambled to sit up so I could get a better look at the jaw-dropping ring on my finger.

Louie chuckled. "I think she likes it."

"She likes it," I said and kissed him, then Jamie. "Thanks for the ring," I teased as I started to climb out of the bed.

Both of them just lay there on the bed. They were in nothing but their boxer briefs, which made them look like confused, sexy statues.

Louie was the one to snap out of it first. "What?"

I stood from the bed and began to head to the bathroom. "It's a wonderful gift," I shot over my shoulder.

An arm wrapped around my middle and I was flung back onto the bed before Jamie climbed on top of me. "We're waiting on an answer."

I gave him an innocent look. "I wasn't asked a question."

A slow smile stretched his mouth. "Will you marry us?"

"Hmm." I tapped my chin with the tip of my finger as my eyes flicked from Jamie to Louie. "Yes."

Jamie grasped my chin and slammed his mouth onto mine, kissing me to the point I became breathless. He pushed off of me and scooted down my body. His fingers grabbed the waistband of my sleep shorts and he removed them from me. Louie helped me out of my shirt and brought his mouth to mine at the same time as Jamie buried his face between my legs.

"We're going to be late to breakfast," I said between kisses.

Louie pulled away a little, grinning. "You don't eat breakfast."

Jamie's tongue licked me from ass to clit, making my whole body shudder. "Good point," I said with a breathy voice as I grabbed the back of Louie's head, making him kiss me again.

We were very late to breakfast, and strangely, my goons didn't show up to get me out of bed. I had a feeling Jamie and Louie had asked them not to bother waking me this morning. Stefan, Conor, Aunt Kiara, Rourke, and Brenna were all in the dining room and were just sitting there silent as we walked in.

"Good morning, Daddy," I said as I passed him to sit in my chair.

Stefan studied me with his perceptive eyes. "You're in a good mood this morning."

I supposed I was, because I truly felt good—happy even—and it was wonderful. Smiling, I reached for the coffee carafe.

Stefan grabbed my hand and inspected the ring on my finger. "Is it because you have a very pretty ring on a special finger?"

Aunt Kiara let out a loud squeal and came rushing over. She snatched my hand from Stefan's. "Oh, it's beautiful, sweetie," she gushed and started rambling on about a wedding I had yet to think about.

Brody came rushing in carrying Kieran. "What happened? I heard a scream."

Brody was back to helping me watch the baby. Caroline had quit after what had happened with Dylan. Not that I could blame her. That night had traumatized the poor lady. The person we'd hired to replace her wouldn't start until tomorrow. I got up from the table and took Kieran from him before showing him my ring.

He smiled down at it, unsurprised, and gave me a hug. "Congratulations."

A hand touched my back as I pulled away from Brody. It was Stefan. Standing close to us, he placed a kiss on top of my head. "Yes, congratulations." He rubbed Kieran's head gently. "Family meeting today."

I nodded. "I know."

As I stood in front of the bathroom mirror, I smoothed away the nonexistent wrinkles on my skintight suit. Today, I would return to being the Banphrionsa and my father's heir. Stefan had already spoken to Nicoli, assuring him that he would honor the alliance and all its terms. Stefan had asked me why I was so eager to hand the kingdom back to him, so to speak.

"I'm not ready, Stefan. Don't get me wrong, I can do the job. I know I can. Being you for a week proved that to me," I had said. "But when it's time to take your place, I don't want to have to kill a bunch of people or hide behind alliances. I want to step into your role with everyone knowing I deserve to be there or fearing me enough not to question it."

"There will always be someone who won't support you in power," Stefan had said.

"I know, but if you give me the time that I need, most will."

Stefan had respected my answer.

Of course, in the past week I had forgiven him for being taken. It would have been hypocritical of me not to. If I thought about it, Stefan and I were guilty of the same mistake. I had let Dylan live and paid for it. Stefan had let my mother live and he had paid for it. We would both carry scars from our mistakes, emotionally and physically. Now that we were past it all, we were at a point where we could breathe deeply and work to move on.

"We're going to be late," Dean said as he poked his head into the bathroom.

"I need heels."

He just blinked at me with his resting bitch face. Then he went back into the bedroom. "Brenna?"

"Which ones should I get?" I heard Brenna ask him.

"Do I look like I know the answer to that question?" I heard Dean reply, making me smile in the mirror.

"You're her best friend," Brenna shot back, and I knew she was messing with him.

I went into the bedroom—one that I was temporarily storing my stuff in until my old bedroom was done being remodeled to be my, Jamie's, and Louie's new room. "I just need heels that will make me look fierce."

Understanding, Brenna went into my closet and returned with a pair of yellow pumps, studded with black spikes.

"How do shoes that look like bumblebees make you look fierce?" Dean asked from where he stood next to Asher near the door.

"Grumpy, I let a lot of shit go, but never insult my shoes," I said as seriously as I could.

Brenna snorted as she set my heels in front of me to step into.

Dean rolled his eyes.

"Are we ready?" I asked, and we headed downstairs.

Goons were already in the hall outside the chamber as we approached. Asher took his position and Dean walked ahead of me to open the door. As I entered, the room went quiet. "Sorry I'm late," I told the men in the room as I walked to my chair, my heels clacking on the floor.

Brenna and Dean took their positions standing behind me as I sat in my chair, the heir's chair. Leaning back, I stared across the table at my father. It felt good to see him there. It felt right. And where I was, both sitting and in life, was where I was supposed to be.

For now.

"Shall we begin?" I asked.

The end.

Want to read more by Ashley N. Rostek?
Check out her WITSEC series.

Turn to the next page to read the first few chapters of Find Me
(Book 1)

FIND ME

My feet felt cemented to the floor as I stood frozen by fear.

"Shi, run!" Shayla cried out just before Mr. X slid his knife across her throat, silencing her forever.

Blood poured like a crimson waterfall from her neck. Her gray eyes were wide, filled with terror as they bored into mine.

I couldn't move.

I couldn't look away.

With each passing second, I had to watch the spark of life within her eyes dim.

Mr. X unhooked his strong arm from around Shayla's middle and shoved her forward. Without resistance she fell, crumpling to the floor in the hallway right in front of my bedroom. Blood pooled around her, seeping into the beige carpet, and staining the ends of her cotton candy pink hair a bright red.

My heart raced at a painful rate, booming in my ears with a rapid **thump! thump! thump!**

Internally, I begged myself, **Move! Run! Do something because he's coming!**

My gaze tore away from Shayla—my sister, my twin—to Mr. X. His booted foot took an ominous, slow step over her body while his *monstrous coal eyes held mine. There was blood splattered across his face, clashing against his alabaster skin. An evil smile pulled at the corners of his mouth as he took another step, then another, closing the distance between us.*

*"**Shiloh**," he sung my name. His voice was light yet haunting and made my entire body tremble. I'd never forget his voice, no matter how much I'd wish I could.*

*My soul screamed, **Run! Run! Run!***

But my body wouldn't listen.

Mr. X finished his walk down the long hall to stand before me. As if stuck in a trance, I watched him lift his bloody knife.

Closing my eyes, I screamed.

"Shiloh!" Firm hands grasped me by my upper arms and shook me. "Shiloh, wake up!"

My uncle Logan's gruff voice broke through my chains of fear. Forcing my eyes open, the first thing I saw was his face. I sat up panting, drenched in sweat. If it hadn't been for Logan sitting next to me, I would have panicked because I didn't immediately recognize my surroundings. Blinking away the fog that still lingered from sleep, I took in the dark, bare room, from the few boxes stacked in the corner to the very uncomfortable air mattress I was lying on. Slowly, my memories came back to me. This was my new house. It was our first night sleeping here. I was safe. Mr. X didn't know where I was.

"Christ, Shi," Logan cursed, running his tattooed fingers through his coffee-brown hair. "It's been a while since you've had a dream like that. I'd be surprised if you didn't wake the neighbors."

I clenched my jaw. How did I respond to that? *I'm sorry?*

Why? I couldn't control what I dreamt or how messed up my past was.

Logan sighed. He was kneeling on the floor next to my air mattress, looking tired, in nothing but black boxer briefs. The rest of his body, from his shoulders to his toes, was covered in colorful and beautiful tattoos. The ex-Navy SEAL turned U.S. Marshal was an ink addict. I had no idea how he got away with being so heavily tattooed working for the feds. But what did I know? I just wished he'd invest in some PJs.

"What time is it?" I asked, my voice sounding coarse. I pushed a strand of sweaty lilac hair away from my face. Seeing the bright color still took me by surprise. I'd dyed it the wild shade for my eighteenth birthday a few days ago as a way to honor my sister, Shayla. She'd dyed her light brown hair all kinds of crazy colors to set herself apart from me—her identical twin. She'd been the lively and edgy twin, who gave our parents hell, where I was the shy and obedient daughter who was too timid to disappoint anyone. I wished I'd been more like Shayla. Maybe she would still be alive today.

Logan stared at me for a moment, like he was debating how he should answer. Not that it'd do him any good. "A little before five." He got to his feet. "Wear your tracker," he ordered over his shoulder as he stalked out of my room.

I crawled off my air mattress and went inside my closet. Flipping on the light, I opened one of the boxes on the floor full of my clothes that needed to be hung. I dug around until I found a pair of leggings and matching tank.

Even though it was summer, and we were now living in the desert, I still put on an athletic zip-up jacket with thumb holes in the cuffs. I had scars on my arms. They were hard to look at and I hated the attention they drew. I pulled my hair up in a messy bun, grabbed my tennis shoes, and put on my GPS anklet tracker before making my way toward the front door of my new house I'd received the keys for yesterday.

I'd bought this three-bedroom Craftsman without even seeing it first. I had been relieved and happy it had looked just like the pictures the realtor had sent me. Because Logan and I had been hidden away in the Alaskan mountains for the past year, I'd had to do the entire house-buying process online and through email. *Why?* Well, because of WITSEC—a.k.a. the witness security program or witness protection.

My life in WITSEC had started the summer before my senior year. Because I'd been weeks away from turning seventeen at the time and Logan was my only living relative, he had been assigned to watch over me, thus resulting in him taking a break from his job. Logan's position as a U.S. Marshal and my guardian had given him a little pull in deciding where we would be sequestered. Alaska had been beautiful but cold and isolated. The nearest neighbor had been miles away and it had been an hour drive to town, which had a population of no more than five hundred people. It was the perfect place to hide, temporarily. I'd needed time to recover, rehabilitate, and get a crash course in intense survival skills from Logan. Just in case. The past year had been the hardest of my life both emotionally and physically. But now that I was eighteen, Logan wanted to return to work and I needed to move on and finish high school.

Sitting on the wood floor by the front door, I was slipping on my shoes when Logan came back out of his room. He was dressed in jeans this time. My eyes were grateful. He held a small handgun in a shoulder holster. "Put this under your jacket. It's small and lightweight."

I unzipped my jacket and slipped it off, revealing the long scar on my inner right arm. It started at the crease of my elbow and ended at my wrist. Even a year later, I could feel the phantom sensation of Mr. X's blade tearing open my skin.

Around both of my wrists and ankles were inch-wide scars. I supposed I'd given those to myself. For hours, I'd rubbed my skin raw and bloody in order to escape from the tight rope bindings Mr. X had put me in.

Just by looking at my wrists, one could guess how I had gotten them. They always guessed wrong, though. Back in Alaska, each time we'd driven to the closest town for supplies, I would receive lewd stares from men, and one time in line at the grocery store, an old lady had called me a sexual deviant. Everyone around us, even the cashier, had frozen and glued their gazes on me. Mortified, I'd dropped my basket of groceries and practically ran out of the store. I regretted how cowardly I had acted. I wished I could have been more like Shayla in that moment. She would have flicked her colorful hair, looked that old lady in the eye, grinned, and said, "Jealous?" But I wasn't as strong as my sister had been. At least not yet. I was working on it. Until I found that strength, I refused to leave the house without wearing clothes that covered my scars, no matter the temperature outside. Just thinking about the heat, I started to second guess my move to Arizona. Only a tiny bit, though. It was beautiful here, with its breathtaking mountain views and vast deserts.

I dropped my jacket on the ground and took the leather gun holster from my uncle before slipping my arms through the holes. The straps rested over my shoulders and across my back, allowing the small holstered gun to hide between my left arm and ribs. Logan glanced down to make sure my slim black GPS anklet tracker was around my right ankle, then back up to the holster before I covered it with my jacket. I caught him taking me in from head to toe. I twirled around for him because I knew he was memorizing my appearance and exactly what I was wearing in case I didn't come back.

"Don't forget your phone," he said.

I opened my mouth to argue, then snapped it closed. *Crap!* I'd left it in my room. I would've noticed I didn't have it eventually. It was my source of music and who ran without music? I dashed back into my room to grab it and my Bluetooth earbuds. When I walked back into the living room, Logan wasn't there. I didn't search him out to say goodbye. Instead, I walked out the front door, put my earbuds in, selected my running playlist, and stuffed my phone into the snug side pocket of my leggings.

It was gray out. Standing on the front lawn, I could see the rays from the sun shining from behind the mountains as I did a few stretches. After I was warmed up, I headed north through the neighborhood.

Three and a half hours later, I slowed to a jog on my way back to the house. I was soaked with sweat and my breathing was labored and raspy. Logan was sitting on the top step of the porch waiting for me while texting on his phone and sipping coffee from a Styrofoam cup.

Note to self, pick up coffee mugs today.

He looked up at me as I paced the front lawn with my hands on my hips, trying to cool down. He shook his head. "If you quit smoking you wouldn't sound like shit."

"I'm down to one cigarette a day," I wheezed before bending over with my hands on my knees. "I think I'm going to puke."

Three and half hours was a new record for me. I knew all the ins and outs of my new neighborhood now. It was a big one and my new house was smack dab in the middle. I had ventured down all the streets, passing my house a few times, and when I'd started to feel like I was going to throw up I'd known it was time to stop.

"You pushed yourself too far," my uncle admonished.

I didn't argue. I did, however, ignore the disapproving look he was giving me as I focused on breathing. He didn't approve of my "therapeutic methods" but wasn't the type to dissuade me either.

"Your furniture should be here in a few hours," he added.

Apart from a few boxes already here that held personal things like clothes, toiletries, and memorabilia from before I went into WITSEC, I'd had to order furniture to fill the rest of the house. It was scheduled to arrive later this morning.

I'd been able to purchase all of it and this house with some of the life insurance money I had received from both of my parents and my sister after they'd been killed. It wasn't the only money that had been left to me, but I liked to pretend that money didn't exist. It was blood money to me, and I didn't like having it. I didn't like having the life insurance money either, but Logan had convinced me to use it. He explained that my family had gotten life insurance for a reason and that was to make sure I was taken care of. So I compromised. I'd live off the life insurance money until I finished college and got a job. If I budgeted properly it'd last me until then and I could continue on pretending the rest of my family's money didn't exist.

"Why don't you go shower and then we'll get breakfast?" Logan suggested. "Yesterday, you said you were craving crepes. Want to go somewhere that makes them?"

I frowned. Logan was a bona fide drill sergeant. If he wasn't ordering me about, something was up. Acting apprehensive was his tell. "If you got something to say, just say it."

His eyes locked with mine and I instantly became nervous. I knew whatever he had to tell me wasn't good.

"Ian called." Ian was his superior and the only other soul who knew my whereabouts. "They got a lead. Highway patrol pulled a man over matching X's description in North Carolina a few days ago. The cop radioed in for backup, but they didn't get there in time. X fled. The cop was DOA. Ian's calling me in to help."

DOA meant *dead on arrival.* My stomach churned, making the urge to throw up even stronger. North Carolina was on the other side of the country, yet it still felt like I was within his reach. As long as he was out there, I didn't think anywhere in the world would feel safe.

I tried to appear calm. On the inside I was freaking out. "When do you leave?"

He stared at me intently, as if he could see past my fake bravado to my terrified soul. "Friday."

That was four days from now. The following Monday was my first day at my new school. I was going to complete my senior year and if everything went as planned, I was going to try and get into a university nearby. Even though my life had been forever changed and my parents were gone, I was still determined to complete my goals and make them proud.

"I know Friday is a lot sooner than we planned, but we prepared for this," he said.

I couldn't tell if he was trying to reassure me or himself.

FIND ME

My furniture delivery was late. The truck didn't get here until noon and it took them a few hours to unload everything. Logan shook his head at the purple couch I'd ordered as it was carried inside. The color reminded me of the suit the Joker wore in Batman. I might have been a closeted superhero nerd and the Joker was my favorite villain, but that was beside the point. The couch had been a bold choice—for me. I'd lived my whole life in bland colors and played it safe because I'd been too afraid to stand out. Look at what it had gotten me.

WITSEC had given me a new life. I couldn't take it for granted. It was time to move forward and I was going to do that bravely and adventurously. Like Shayla. So if I wanted a purple couch, then I'd get the purple couch and the bright yellow armchair to go with it.

For the dining room, I might have gone a little overboard and splurged on a six-seater, turquoise-painted wood table. My mom had used to say the kitchen table was the heart of the home. Some of my best memories from growing up were of dinner time, with my parents and sister sitting around the table laughing while talking about anything and everything. Staring at my new table with its six empty chairs made my chest tighten. My mom had been wrong. It wasn't the table that was the heart. It was the people who sat at it.

The rest of what I'd ordered filled my bedroom and the spare bedroom that Logan was using. I hadn't ordered anything for the third bedroom. Logan was converting it into a panic room of sorts, with a rolling metal shutter on the window and a steel-reinforced door. It wouldn't be a completely impenetrable panic room, but it would hopefully hold up until the police arrived. He was also setting up an impressive security system with panic buttons and cameras, which he was currently drilling into the walls outside the house. To anyone else, a panic room, cameras, and security system might have been excessive. After what I'd been through, it still didn't feel like enough. Not with Mr. X still out there looking for me.

Now that my furniture was here, I needed to go shopping for everything else I would need, like linens and coffee mugs. Not to mention there wasn't any food in the house.

Dressed in ripped, light blue jeans, a long-sleeved white shirt, and boots that had a knife tucked into the left one, I grabbed my purse and headed toward the front door. The delivery men were about to leave, and I was following them out. I had my long lilac hair pulled up into a high ponytail because it was hotter than Hades out. Sweat was already sliding down the back of my neck.

Outside, I could smell grills cooking, hear cicadas buzzing and rock music playing from my neighbor's house to the right. I glanced in that direction. A few cars were parked in the street in front of their house and a group of guys were working on an old classic car in the driveway. I briefly scanned over them, counting six, some just standing around drinking beer and talking while a few actually hovered over the engine of the old car. They all appeared to be friends hanging out, carefree and having fun. *Must be nice.*

"Miss Pierce, I need you to sign here, confirming that everything was delivered." One of the delivery guys held out a clipboard and pen.

Hearing my new last name instead of my real last name, McConnell, was going to take some getting used to. Standing in the middle of my lawn on the stone pathway leading to my car in the driveway, I read over the receipt, verifying I had indeed received everything I'd ordered. After I signed, I was handed a copy of the receipt and the delivery guys drove their truck away from my curb.

The sound of a drill made me glance back at the house. Logan was standing on a ladder in front of my bedroom window, drilling holes to install a camera.

"Logan, I'm running to the store!" I shouted as I made my way over to my car. The group of guys hanging out at my neighbor's stopped talking and I got that feeling of being watched. My car and a short wall made up of oleander bushes that separated their property from mine was all that was standing between us.

Logan stopped drilling and looked over at me. "What'd you say, Shi?"

"I'm going to the store," I said, opening my car door.

"Do you have your phone and...everything?" His gaze flicked to my neighbors behind me before pointedly looking back at me. He'd noticed we had an audience and didn't want to ask if I was armed in front of them.

"Yup. Do you want me to pick anything up for you?"

He glanced at his watch on his wrist, taking note of the time. "No, I'm good. Check in every hour," he ordered and returned to his drilling. I rolled my eyes as I climbed behind the wheel. How was he going to handle leaving me here to fly to

North Carolina if he couldn't handle me going to flipping Target ten minutes away?

I put my black Toyota 4Runner in reverse and when I went to look out the rearview window to back out, I caught two of the guys next door watching me. They both had the same shade of pale golden blond hair. One of them had it styled in a faux hawk where the other had that messy, I-just-rolled-out-of-bed style. Their eyes were the same color of light blue or aquamarine. I couldn't tell from how far away I was.

They were both really attractive. If my life wasn't messed up, I'd be crushing hard. But my life was an actual nightmare and that was why I didn't just see two gorgeous guys when I stared at them. I only saw twins.

I looked away with a clenched jaw and backed out of the driveway.

By the time I returned home it was dark outside. Whoever said retail therapy could make you feel better was a liar. After hours of shopping and filling my car to the max, I still felt a heavy sense of dread. Friday would be here before I knew it and then I'd be alone.

Turning off the car, I sat in the darkness, staring at my new house. This wasn't where I was supposed to be. I should have been moving into a tiny dorm room and scrambling to find my classes on a big college campus. A tear escaped my eye and I quickly wiped it away.

"So much for being brave, Shi," I grumbled to myself. Who was I kidding? Buying brightly colored furniture didn't make me brave. At the end of the day, I was still me.

I sighed heavily. I needed to stop beating myself up. Change and moving on took time.

But how did I move on when *he* was still out there?

I opened one of the bags I had on the passenger's seat and pulled out a new pack of cigarettes and a bottle of Jack. I'd been using Shayla's fake ID to buy booze to drown my sorrows. It was a perk of being a twin that I'd been definitely taking advantage of over the past year.

I stared at the bottle of Jack as temptation to open it gnawed at me. Sitting there, I thought back to a time I'd used to look down my nose at Shayla when she'd first told me that one of her bad-influence friends had made her the ID. She'd laugh at me now if she could see the hypocrite I'd become with how I had smoked like a chimney and drunk like a fish this past year.

I made no excuses for how I'd chosen to cope. I knew it had been bad. At the time I hadn't cared. Therapy hadn't been working as fast as I'd wanted it to, and I'd been desperate to numb the pain. At first Logan hadn't said anything when he'd caught me smoking or smelled liquor on my breath. As long as I'd continued my therapy and hadn't slacked off in self-defense training, he'd turned a blind eye. That was, until he'd found fourteen empty liquor bottles hidden under my bed. Logan had dished out some tough love then. He'd told me that my vices were just a band-aid and if I ever wanted to move on, I needed to do it the right way. He was right. I was working on quitting smoking and it'd been a while since I'd had a drink. Running helped the urge. It was a healthier outlet when things become too much to handle. Nicotine, however, was a tough drug to kick. I was slowly winning the battle, though. I was down to one cigarette a day.

I was very proud at how far I had come since I'd lost my family. But then days like today happened. With the news of Logan leaving in less than a week...I was struggling.

I broke my unblinking gaze from the bottle of Jack and set it on the passenger's seat. It wasn't that I had an addiction. I just needed to stop using it as a crutch.

Pulling my lighter from my purse, I got out of the car. In a lazy attempt to hide from Logan, I walked around to the back of my 4Runner and perched my butt on the bumper. I put a cigarette between my lips, set the new pack on the bumper next to me, and cupped my hand around the end of my white cancer stick as I lit it. That first drag of nicotine had me closing my eyes, dropping my head back against the rear window of my vehicle before blowing it out slowly through my lips. Without opening my eyes, I took another drag, basking in the euphoric feeling.

"Smoking kills, you know," a masculine voice said, startling me. My eyes snapped open and I whipped my head in the direction of the source. Standing on the other side of the oleander bush was one of the twins I'd seen earlier today— the one with the messy bed-head hairstyle. I watched as his eyes roamed over me from my lilac ponytail to my boots.

"So can sneaking up on a girl at night," I said.

His lips curled up on one side. He looked right around my age or maybe a little older. He had nice skin. It was smooth and tan, proof he lived in the desert. I probably looked like a ghost and stood out like a sore thumb here with how pale I was.

He stuffed his hands into the pockets of his dark jeans. His t-shirt was black and form fitting, which showed off how lean and fit he was. "I wasn't exactly quiet when I approached. Then again, you seemed lost in your head for a moment there."

I smirked. "You're saying it's my fault you startled me?"

He rubbed the back of his head with a shy smile. "Wow, this friendly introduction isn't as easy as I thought it was going to be."

I decided to cut him some slack and held out my hand over

the oleander bush. "I'm Shiloh Pierce. Are you one of my neighbors?"

He stared down at my hand before engulfing it with his larger one. "Colt Stone. And yeah, I live here with my brothers." It took a lot of effort not to react when he said brothers.

"Shi, you out here?" I heard Logan call out from the front porch. I gave Colt a small smile before stepping back to look over at Logan.

I purposely took another drag to show him I was smoking. "Yeah. I'll be inside in a minute." Logan noticed Colt standing behind me and crossed his arms over his chest. When I saw the evil glint spark to life in his eyes, I inwardly groaned.

"You're not peer pressuring one of the neighbor boys into smoking, are you?" he drawled as if really serious.

"Well, you know me. My life of debauchery wouldn't be as satisfying if I didn't add the corruption of others," I said, my tone sounding caustic.

Logan's eyes went vacant for a moment before his expression turned sad. I knew that look. He got that way when I did something that reminded him of my mom. "Yeah, that sounds about right. Carry on," he replied in a deflated tone, then turned to go back into the house.

I stared at where he'd retreated into the house for a moment, biting my bottom lip with worry until I remembered Colt standing behind me. I turned back around on my heels and found him staring at my house with a puzzled frown.

"Sorry about that," I said, bending down to put out my cigarette on the ground and walking over to the trash bins sitting by the curb to throw out the butt. "My uncle thinks it's funny when he tries to embarrass me."

"Your uncle?" he said, tone riddled with surprise.

He wasn't the first to assume that Logan wasn't my uncle. In fact, it had happened all the time back in that small town in

Alaska. Logan and I were only sixteen years apart in age and because he took extremely good care of himself, he looked a lot younger than he actually was. Everyone had mistaken him for my boyfriend and rumors had spread like wildfire because that was what happened in a small town. I'd overheard two girls whisper behind me once that Logan and I were into BDSM and that was how I'd gotten my scars, which was freaking disgusting. "Yeah, he's my mom's baby brother."

Colt opened his mouth to say something but was cut off when someone yelled, "Colt!" A guy stepped out the front door of Colt's house and glanced around. When his eyes landed on us, a look of intrigue took over his face and he walked over. "What's going on?"

As he got closer, I got the feeling this was one of the plural brothers Colt had mentioned. They looked very similar, but he was clearly older and taller than Colt by a few inches and his eyes were brown. They had the same pale golden hair. His was shaved on the sides and styled messily on top.

"I was just introducing myself to our new neighbor. This is Shiloh. Shiloh, this is my brother Keelan."

I reached over the oleander bush again. Keelan gave me a charming smile in return before he shook my hand. "Shiloh, huh? That's a pretty name." His voice was smooth and oozed flirtation.

A year ago, I would have swooned. Now, all I felt was caution. It was astonishing how something traumatic could leave you changed to certain things and boys were one of them. "Thank you."

"Colt! Keelan! The movie is about to start!" a really deep and growly voice shouted from inside their house.

I took that as my cue to leave. "I better get inside. It was nice meeting you."

"We better go too before Knox hunts us down," Colt said to Keelan and took a step back. "See you around, Shiloh."

They both gave me gorgeous parting smiles before walking back into their house. I scooped up my pack of cigarettes from the bumper and opened my trunk to start unloading my purchases.

FIND ME

Friday got here faster than I wanted. The rest of the week had been crazy busy with Logan finishing up on the panic room and fortifying the rest of the house. He'd even strategically hidden guns in multiple places throughout the house. Under the coffee table, behind the TV, inside the fridge. I wished I was kidding about the fridge. He'd tucked a small pistol between a carton of eggs and the sidewall. I'd positioned a gallon of milk in front of it so I wouldn't have to see it every time I opened the fridge. Those were just a few examples of where Logan had gotten *creative*. If you counted the rifles in the gun safe in the panic room, there were ten guns in my house. Again, it might have seemed excessive, but if Logan thought it was necessary, then it was necessary.

While he'd been busy with all that, I'd finished unpacking and getting the house put together. I'd also joined a gym and I'd finished registering for school. I was officially a senior at Copper Mountain High School. My classes were pretty standard, apart from the two AP classes I was taking. The only class I was nervous about was gym class. I wasn't afraid of the class itself. It was the changing in front of others. High school girls were the worst. My sister had been popular and downright awful. As her sister I'd gotten a free pass despite being quiet and nerdy, which had been who her group of *friends* would bully. I wouldn't have her as a buffer at this new school. I had more than just the scars on my arm, wrists, and ankles. I had two really bad ones on my stomach and one on my back shoulder. The ones on my stomach were from stab wounds that had almost killed me. If gym class hadn't been a requirement to graduate, I would've tried to drop it in exchange for another class.

"I could have driven you," I said as I followed Logan out to the curb where a car service was waiting to drive him to the airport.

Rolling his suitcases behind him, he said, "It's easier this way. Airports are a nightmare."

I chewed on my bottom lip nervously as the driver of the car got out and helped Logan load his bags into the trunk. This was it. I was going to be on my own for who knew how long. Logan hadn't left my side since I'd woken up in the hospital a little over a year ago. He'd helped me heal, stood with me through my pain, and held my hand after I'd had nightmares. He'd helped me become stronger, a fighter, a survivor. I told myself I wasn't going to cry, but my eyes were beginning to burn.

Once his last bag was loaded, he turned to face me. His shoulders slumped. "Shi." He sighed and pulled me into his arms for a hug. "I'm going to catch him."

My tears fell and my body shook with silent sobs. What if he did find him and Mr. X killed him? What if Mr. X found me and Logan wasn't here?

I squeezed my arms tightly around Logan's back, trying to absorb his strength because no matter how much I wanted him to stay, he had to go.

His hand stroked my hair. "You are to check in by text two

times a day on the burner phone. Never try to reach me on your regular phone. It's too easy to track the signal back to here. Make sure you find a range to practice your shooting and keep practicing your escape drills in the house. You can do this, Shi. You are the strongest person I know."

I took in a deep, shaky breath before stepping back. With the sleeves of my shirt, I wiped away the tear tracks and nodded. "Okay. I've got this."

"I'll try calling you Monday night after you're out of school."

I gave him a forced parting smile, then watched him climb into the car and be driven away. After he was long gone, I turned to look back at my house and tried to remind myself that this was the plan. This was where I needed to be. I had my goals to achieve and my new life to start. Everything was going to be okay. I could do this.

Feeling a little more determined, I went back inside. It was just after seven in the morning and I had the whole day to do... absolutely nothing. For my sanity, I had to keep busy. Silence and boredom were a recipe for flashbacks and panic attacks. Speaking of recipes, I guessed I could bake something. I'd used to love baking. Maybe I could run by the store, but after I went to the gym first. It was the perfect plan to stay busy.

Desert Stone Fitness was a highly reviewed gym in town. It had all the bells and whistles. An indoor pool and an indoor track on the second floor. It even had a boxing ring smack dab in the center of the large room with all the workout equipment surrounding it. It also provided many classes such as yoga, spin, self-defense, karate, boxing, judo, jiu-jitsu, Pilates, and Zumba. The gym literally had everything. And because of that, it was crazy busy.

With my gym bag hanging off my shoulder, I made my way to the women's locker room to lock up my stuff. I'd chosen to wear long purple athletic leggings and a matching racerback top covered by a black, slim fit, zip-up athletic jacket with thumb holes. I pulled my hair up into a high ponytail, put my earbuds in, grabbed my water bottle and phone, then headed out. There was a designated area for stretching on the first floor by the boxing ring. I got stretched and warmed up there first, then went upstairs to the track. It was a mile-long oval track that circled and overlooked the gym below.

I set my water bottle in one of the cubbies for personal items on the wall next to the stairs, selected my running playlist on my phone, and picked a lane on the track.

I'd started running four months ago, slowly building up my endurance. I had read somewhere once that exercise in general was therapeutic for the mind. It either gave your mind a break from the stress or allowed you time to really work through it. The former was true for me most of the time.

Running allowed me to free myself of the pain my memories caused. Nothing else existed as I pushed forward, my muscles burning, lungs expanding, endorphins soaring. If I were to have an addiction, it would be running, and it was one I was guilty of pushing past my limits with. Because some days were worse than others and an hour or two of freedom just wasn't enough.

I ran for three hours before I cooled down by walking the last quarter mile back to my water bottle. My workout clothes were drenched with sweat and there was nothing more I wanted than to take my jacket off. I was seriously considering shedding it for a minute. Then I looked around at all the people and my insecurities won. I settled for just unzipping it.

After the gym, I stopped by the grocery store to pick up ingredients. I might have gone a little overboard with how much I bought. But I convinced myself that it was okay. I did have the whole weekend of nothing to do.

As soon as I got home, I put my perishable ingredients away and took a long shower. I decided to put on a pair of jean shorts. I had no plans of leaving the house for the rest of the day. I chose to pair it with a black tank, then made my way to the kitchen, where I spent a good chunk of the afternoon.

My kitchen turned into a war zone, or at least it looked like a flour bomb had gone off. Patches of flour and sugar were scattered on the counters. Some had even sprinkled on the tile floor. Mixing bowls, whisks, measuring cups, cookie sheets, and pans filled my sink. Every surface of my kitchen was filled with cooling baked goodies. I'd made two dozen cookies, a pan of gooey brownies, a dozen blueberry muffins, lemon bars, and key lime bars. It looked like I was ready to have a bake sale.

What had I been thinking?

I hadn't. That was the point. With a heavy sigh, I started cleaning up.

I was washing the last dirty dish when my doorbell rang. My heart immediately started racing with fear. I quickly dried my hands with a dish towel as I exited the kitchen into the living room. Barefoot, I padded my way to the front door and peered through the peephole to find Colt, my neighbor, standing outside.

"One second!" I shouted and quickly grabbed a zip-up hoodie from the pile of laundry I'd placed on the couch. I had planned on folding it after dinner tonight while I settled down to watch TV.

Once my hoodie was on, I looked down at my ankles and cringed. I didn't have time to cover them up with pants. Praying that he wouldn't notice, I unlocked my front door. "Hey," I greeted him with a smile and saw that he was holding a stack of mail.

"Hi." He smiled back. I watched as his smile grew the longer he stared at me. "Were you baking?"

I narrowed my eyes at him. "How did you know?"

He chuckled. "You have flour on your face."

Heat scorched my cheeks. Using my sleeve, I wiped at my face. "Did I get it?"

He shook his head, and I could tell he was trying not to laugh at me, which made me flush even more. "Your forehead," he mumbled. I wiped there too, and he nodded.

"Thank you. What's up?"

"We got some of your mail," he said, holding it out to me. "Are you going to Copper Mountain?"

I took the mail from him and before I could question how he would know that, my eyes fell on the top envelope. It was from Copper Mountain High School addressed to Shiloh Pierce. "Yeah. I registered there for my senior year."

"My brother Creed and I go there," he said.

"Oh."

"If you want, I can show you around before class starts Monday morning."

That was sweet of him to offer. It would be the first time I'd be starting a new school without knowing anyone and without Shayla by my side. "I might take you up on that."

At my response he smiled brightly and my heartbeat picked up a beat. "So what were you baking?"

It took me a second to comprehend what he was asking. "Oh, uh." I felt my cheeks getting hot again. As I stared at Colt sheepishly, I got an idea. "Do you and your brothers like cookies, brownies, and such? Because I may have made enough to fill a bakery and there's no way I could eat it all."

His eyebrows rose. "We're growing boys. Of course we do."

I smiled and opened the front door wider. "You're welcome to come in while I pack up a container for you to take home."

He stepped inside.

"If you'll follow me," I said over my shoulder, catching him looking around as we walked through the living room. His eyes went wide when we entered the kitchen. At least it wasn't a mess anymore. "Yeah. One of my many faults is I sometimes get lost in what I'm doing. I've been known to go above and beyond. Especially if I'm having a bad day," I explained as I pulled out a bin filled to the brim with new Tupperware I'd bought the other day.

"You had a bad day?"

I looked away from him. "Yes and no." I didn't elaborate and he thankfully didn't push. "Are you or your brothers allergic to anything? I don't want someone going into anaphylactic shock because I put peanuts in some of the brownies."

He shook his head. "No known food allergies. Can I try one of these?" he asked, pointing to one of the peanut butter cookies.

"Help yourself." I smiled and began filling a plastic container with an assortment of goodies.

Colt took a bite of the cookie and groaned. "Wow, these are good."

I chuckled. "You sound surprised."

With his cheeks puffed out around the cookie, he shook his head. "There you go again. You're kind of a ball buster, you know that?"

I'd been called worse. Stuck up, snob, whore. Not that what he'd said was an insult. In fact, it sounded like he enjoyed that I gave him a hard time.

"I'm glad you like the cookie, but wait until you try the key lime bars. They're my mom's recipe." The moment the words left my mouth I regretted them. I turned away to hide the pain I was undoubtedly showing and busied myself with packing up two-thirds of everything I'd made. Once I had my face schooled and my emotions at bay, I turned back around and stacked two large plastic containers in front of him. "Okay, here you go."

"Are you trying to make me fat?" he teased, taking the containers from me.

"Aren't guys supposed to be bottomless pits? Besides, there's what, three of you—?"

"Four," he corrected.

"There are four of you and only one of me. I still won't be able to finish what I have left but it's nice to know most of everything I made won't go to waste. You taking all this off my hands is doing me a favor, really."

He tilted his head slightly, seeming confused. "What about your uncle?"

Oops.

"He left today," I replied honestly and tucked some of my lilac hair behind my ear. "He was only here to help me get situated."

Colt went quiet as he stared at me. I felt the urge to squirm or palm-smack my face, so I busied myself with packing up the rest of the baked goodies in my own container.

"Don't take this question the wrong way, but do you live here alone?" he asked.

I tensed up. It wasn't wise to advertise that you lived alone to a stranger. Logan would kick my butt if he knew. I forced myself to relax. I'd seen what a monster's eyes looked like. Colt's eyes didn't have a speck of evil in them and my gut told me he was a nice guy.

"Yes." I could tell he had more questions. They were dancing behind his aquamarine eyes.

"I should get back," he said, scooping up the containers off the counter. "Thank you for these."

Relief washed over me, and I followed him back to the front door. When he stepped out onto my porch, he turned back to look at me. "If you ever need anything you can come next door and get me."

I smiled at the kind offer. "Thank you, Colt. That's very sweet of you."

He nodded and took a step back. "I'll see you around."

I gave him a little wave and went to shut the door.

"Wait!" he said, and I paused. He balanced the containers in one hand and reached into his back pocket. "We should exchange numbers," he said as he pulled out his cell phone.

I hesitated.

"You know...for Monday," he quickly added.

"Okay," I said and gave him my number.

After Colt left, Monday didn't seem so nerve wracking.

Get your copy of Find Me on Amazon.

ABOUT THE AUTHOR

Ashley N. Rostek is a wife and mother by day and a writer by night. She survives on coffee, loves collecting offensive coffee mugs, and is an unashamed bibliophile.

To Ashley, there isn't a better pastime than letting your mind escape in a good book. Her favorite genre is romance and has the overflowing bookshelf to prove it. She is a lover of love. Be it a sweet YA or a dark and lusty novel, she must read it!

Ashley's passion is writing. She picked up the pen at seventeen and hasn't put it down. Her debut novel is Embrace the Darkness, the first book in the Maura Quinn series.

SOCIAL MEDIA

You can find out more about Ashley and her upcoming works on social media!

The Inner Circle ~ Ashley N. Rostek's Book Group
https://www.facebook.com/groups/arostektheinnercircle/
(THE BEST PLACE TO STAY UPDATED)

FACEBOOK

INSTAGRAM

NEWSLETTER

Printed in Great Britain
by Amazon